EARTH'S VEIL

J.F. BLOOMFIELD

Many thanks to my supportive mother, and Lucy, my love. They believed wholeheartedly that I could do it and helped me proofread this wild project.

CHAPTER 1

WILLIAM RITTER PREPARED himself in the waiting room of the therapy office lobby. There was an abundance of green plants, meant to instill a sense of peace and patience as one waited. He would love to have more patience. He would love to have more sleep, too. But it was too late for that. The dreams were too important. Posters were tacked to the walls advertising the benefits of daily exercise, a complete diet and not using electronics before bedtime. It was a small lobby with only six chairs in it and Will was the only one waiting. He was originally recommended this place by a work friend of his, Alex, after mentioning his lack of sleep over three weeks ago. He was bracing himself for the uphill battle of trying to convince his therapist that the world was going to end.

"William Ritter?" the receptionist called out. "The doctor will see you now."

He got up, breathed in, and strode confidently into the small, cozy office. It was again adorned with plants just past the door. There were pictures of people smiling calmly on the neatly organized shelves flanking both sides of the room. There were no pictures of the doctor's family. Behind her desk and off to the left of the room were various degrees, awards and all the things necessary to prove why she was on that side of the desk, and the patient was on the other.

Dr. Miriam sometimes felt like a cold, calculating, existential threat to your identity. Therapy isn't an easy thing to go through. Will thought it was one part identifying the problem and two parts identifying your role in it. Will was defensive to her tactics. He felt like he was being warned about the end of the world in his dreams. She felt like he had anxiety. It was a little war, fighting to be understood clearly, not just clinically.

She was middle aged, short but lean, and had the cool blue eyes of analysis and experience windowed behind bold black frames that dwarfed the narrow bridge of her nose. With thin lips and a pointed chin, she could disarm everything you thought was going on and make you see it in a different light.

"So, you've been having more of the dreams again?" Dr. Miriam started in a raspy voice that was far too used to asking questions like this. She always had the same mannerism of asking the question that brought him here and then leaning forward on the dark oak desk to assure him that she was listening.

"I came back because I finally realized that they aren't dreams. They're warnings," Will said. The last time he came to see her was two weeks ago, when the dreams started. This was the earliest follow-up appointment he could get.

Dr. Miriam leaned back in her chair, curled her slim hand under her narrow chin and seriously contemplated what she was just told. He sensed that an unexpected surprise came from his words. She deeply considered a number of things, then leaned back in.

In a voice that was critical and yet inviting, she asked, "A warning from whom?"

"I don't know," he said, feeling pressed. "It's not really a person telling me. I'm just being told."

"And what are you being told?" She looked down to reference his file on her desk. "You said, in your last visit, that it was a warning of the end of the world as we know it. That all of physics and chemistry would change because of nuclear war and that it would start very shortly after an earthquake, which would also be happening very soon. Has any of that changed?"

Will didn't like how crazy that made him sound. He realized that was now in his file forever and cringed slightly before getting back to the topic at hand. "No, nothing has changed in terms of details."

"And yet you still feel as though these dreams are worthy of being labeled warnings? Why is that?" She crossed her legs and leaned back once more, as if certain already of what was going on.

"It's a feeling that has gotten stronger over the last couple of weeks. Everything seems clearer. It's like the image has finally resolved... and... you're in it. Something about this has to do with you and that's why I'm here." Will was clearly in distress. He came to warn her about impending doom. He didn't expect to be questioned so logically.

"Will."

Dr. Miriam paused, unsure of how to go about this. She saw that he was even more distressed than last time and that he was second guessing his sanity. He was confusing the feeling of urgency with truth, and she thought he felt particularly alone in this regard, given his constant reference to himself. She knew that people sometimes recover better when they know they are not alone in their thoughts and feelings, so, taking a calculated risk, she told him some additional information.

"Will, I'm telling you this as a professional courtesy so that you don't feel so alone in your thoughts." She lowered her eyes briefly before centering them on him again. "Every single patient I've had for the last two weeks has told me about similar dreams."

Will sat up straight. "Others have them? How many? I need to speak with them!"

She held her hands up as if to stop him. She regretted that this had become a bad move. In her attempt to help him feel like he wasn't alone in his thoughts, she had potentially opened up her other patients to targeted harassment. A rookie mistake, some might say. But sometimes you must take a chance for intervention.

She needed to play this very carefully. First, by disarming expectations. "Mr. Ritter, there are a few things you need to understand. Dreams like yours are vague enough that multiple people can report something similar without there necessarily being a connection. I think that you are all experiencing a similar cause. Lack of sleep. The truth is, I see a lot of people who work rotating shifts."

"Well, the reason I lose sleep is because of these warnings," he quipped.

She paused for a moment, seeing that he was convinced of the cause and effect only going one way. She decided to discredit the foundation of the idea that had him so convinced.

"You call them warnings, yes? A warning is usually for something that will happen at a specific time, in a specific way, or imminently. Does this 'warning' give you any evidence of a specific time?"

"No, just soon."

"A specific way?"

"Well, no. Just that things will begin with an earthquake…"

"Do you have any actual reason to believe this will happen within the next few days?"

"Aside from the feeling getting stronger, I guess not." Will was annoyed at her persistence.

"Mr. Ritter, I have looked up the history of earthquakes where we are in southern Ontario over the last two hundred and fifty years. There were only three earthquakes above magnitude five. One in 1929, the second in 1986 and the last in 1998. All three were located below the US/Canada border and we have never had a strong earthquake capable of doing serious damage whose epicenter is here in this region. There are professionals who speculate that it cannot happen because of our position on the tectonic plate. We're too stable."

That was pretty much the nail in the coffin for Will's argument, but the feeling of urgency was not totally gone. "Maybe the earthquake doesn't happen here. Maybe…" He trailed off. He knew now that he was simply making stuff up, trying to justify his feeling, and that she would take him to pieces over it.

"Will." Dr. Miriam's voice became warmer and much more compassionate than it had been. "You're a smart young man. Tell me which you think is more likely: That these dreams of yours are simply caused by a sleep disorder, or that southern Ontario will have its first ever major earthquake at your insistence."

"Please," he began. He didn't know what he was even asking for, but being taken seriously would be nice. If not by her, then by someone with similar experiences. "I just need to ask them about the images in my dream. You have to tell me who else has these dreams."

This wasn't working, she had to cut her losses with him to protect the identity of her other patients. "I'm sorry, Will, I'm going to have to ask you to leave for now until you decide that you want to be more constructive with this."

Will boiled over. "The names of the others…"

"…will be kept secret following the principles of patient confidentiality!" she boomed and finished the sentence for him. Her voice had turned cold as ice. She stood up. Her small body was considerably more imposing given that Will's tall, athletic frame was sitting down. She leaned her palms flat on the desk and, authoritatively, she continued, "Will, look. I can tell that you're just trying to warn people. But I'm here to help you realize that the care you place into these dreams is unwarranted, and worse, is actively harmful to your mental health. If you insist on harassing my other patients, I can't allow you to. They've entrusted me with their care, not you."

Both of them paused right there. There was a feeling of uneasiness and then an unsettled look that the two of them shared before glancing around the room. Dr. Miriam looked down at the glass of water she had on the desk, which was rippling in delicate concentric circles. Will looked over at it too and the ripples increased in size. The small jittering of items in the room which came next was quickly overtaken by the loud buckling of everything else.

Realizing what was happening, she made a futile effort to hold everything steady on her desk. Will was paralyzed with disbelief as he listened to that sickening groan coming from the ground and the car alarms going off outside. He clasped the chair. Nobody actually knew what to do in an earthquake, they never had one. It completely tore through the books on the shelf and clumsily dropped them on the floor. Pictures fell, lights went out, and Will could hear the receptionist wailing in fear. Then, in the next moment, it was over.

"So," Will said, "now do you believe me?"

Dr. Miriam had to think about this for a few moments. On the one hand, freak coincidence. On the other hand, the probability that they would have an earthquake of that strength at all, let alone while talking about it… she decided to meet him halfway.

"I cannot disclose a patient because it's in violation of the law and ethics. But you yourself said you were recommended here by another patient of mine…"

"Alex, yes! I can ask Alex!" He jumped up from the seat.

"I didn't say that you could." She gave him a cold stare of warning.

Will took that and respected her barrier of plausible deniability. "You should get out while you can," he warned.

"My husband and I were planning to go up north this summer to our cottage. I can convince him to move up our plans. I'll cancel my upcoming appointments and send Sandra, the receptionist, on vacation. We'll meet back here in two weeks. I still don't believe your dreams are real, but I'm not stupid enough to chance it."

This was a Friday afternoon, so Will would have to wait until Monday to speak with Alex about the dreams. But he wouldn't get that chance. Will and Dr. Miriam parted ways and he ran to his home, fifteen minutes away, to call his wife, Rachel. Surprisingly, there wasn't much that was actually destroyed out there. A few signs knocked over and plenty of traffic pulled over, but nothing collapsed. He lived in a two-bedroom apartment on the edge of the city which was in an old building, five stories tall with a hefty brick and concrete structure and an underground parking space. Its residents were mostly elderly and had been living there for thirty years or more. Will had lived on the third floor for three years. He sprinted up the stairs, figuring that it was faster than waiting on the sluggish elevator, and tried to call Rachel with no answer. She wasn't quite done getting settled in Florida, it would seem.

Rachel's new job was in sales, primarily, and that meant representing the company's interest to prospective new clients. Her company decided to test her by sending her to Florida to meet with an existing buyer. It was merely a trip to renew an existing deal. The contract had been renewed for the last five years so it wasn't going to be a difficult sell. They wanted Rachel to gain some experience meeting with clients and traveling as it was important for her job. She was to be gone for two days. One to settle into her accommodations and another to get the deal done and come back. The compensation was good, and it seemed to offer her new experiences that the old factory job could never cover. When she left to catch the flight, Will told her how proud he was that she was going out of her comfort zone like this.

Fortunately for his sanity, she returned his calls a little while later.

"Hey, hon. Sorry I missed your call. I wasn't through airport security yet, and then I forgot to take my phone off airplane mode…"

He didn't let her finish. "You'll never believe what happened today. There was an earthquake; a big one! Just like in the dreams."

Rachel didn't react immediately. Eventually, in a worried tone, she said, "Will, that's not possible. I looked at the seismology."

His face furrowed a bit. He knew that she never believed him all this time. She was the one who told him to get help for the obvious distress this was causing him. He just didn't expect to get fact checked by his own wife over it. It stung him a little as it was the very same thing that cold, distant therapist did to him. A cross-examination of sorts.

"What? When did you look at the seismology?"

She scrambled around a bit to find the remote to the television so she could flick through the news to find the report. "Back when you first mentioned this. You were worrying me, so I looked. Southern Ontario hasn't had…"

"A strong earthquake capable of doing serious damage in two hundred and fifty years," he concluded for her.

"Wait, you knew?" she puzzled. She saw the report on national news. It was being reported officially as a 5.1 magnitude. The rental house was on the outskirts of Daytona Beach and had been arranged for her by the company. It was small, but for one person it would do just fine. Better than a noisy motel room, at least.

"Yeah, I knew about the statistics. The therapist threw it in my face right before it happened."

"Yeah, well, I'm not throwing it in your face, I just care about you. I'm seeing it on the news, now. They're calling it historic," she said in a state of disbelief.

"Yeah, right at the *end* of history. The look on her face was priceless, by the way. She was trying to hold everything on the desk!" Will smirked. It felt good to have his supposed madness justified finally. That feeling would not last long. "Look, you have to hunker down for a bit…"

A bizarre, loud alarm sounded from Will's phone that made him stop mid-sentence. It wasn't a ringtone he thought his phone could make. But when he saw what was on the screen, he froze solid.

BALLISTIC MISSILE THREAT
INBOUND TO ONTARIO.
SEEK IMMEDIATE SHELTER.
THIS IS NOT A DRILL.

He was immediately beset by denial and outrage. There was no way this was happening already. He simply paused, unable to consider the message truthfully and yet unable to look away from it. The emergency broadcast ringtone continued to sound obnoxiously from his phone.

"Will, what's that alarm?" Rachel said.

Will had no answers. Not yet. Then he heard a car crash outside his apartment window. He looked down to the street below and saw people panicking. They got out from their cars and moved about with urgency. Will knew now that it wasn't simply a glitch in his phone. He knew that others around him got that alarm and were taking it seriously. But it could still be a glitch in the national system. Despite this being in his dreams, he was still in denial. He figured any minute now, the signal would come through that it was a false alarm, a technical error of some kind due to the earthquake. Maybe it set off a sensor or something. Tripped a switch or a circuit.

But then he heard a different tone. A fainter one. It was in the background of the call on Rachel's end. It was a steady, shrill siren compared to the blaring alarm on his side.

"Ba-be. What is THAT alarm?" Will pleaded this precious sentence as his voice trembled. He never really panicked in general, but now he did. Will was able to hear different sirens in the background of her call. Old machines from the Cold War slumbering in the sweet dreams of outdated circuitry. Air-raid sirens that everyone hoped the populace never had to hear. But now it was certain. There couldn't be a glitch in both the US and Canada's early warning systems. This was really it. Rachel closed the blinds to the windows, stuck the phone between her shoulder and her ear and got busy preparing. Will was still frozen to his phone.

They both made moves in their desperate dance of confession. Will went first and suddenly started moving. "I love you, please go into whatever basement you have and take some food with you. I think it's three weeks you have to stay down there. I will see you again. Somehow."

"I know you will. Get down somewhere yourself, baby. That carport should work. I love you. Always remember that and please be careful. If your dreams are right, then we know how the world ends. But we don't know what it will become afterwards."

Will didn't get a chance to say anything else before the phone call dropped. They were among the lucky ones to be on a call when it happened. Everyone got the news at the same time. Everyone tried to call their loved ones at the same time. They seized up the network. He sent the same text to both of his parents:

"Seek shelter now I love you both and well be fine dont worry"

No punctuation, no grammar, no time. Every second he wasted on this message might be another second they'd never live to see. They were up north a way, but there was no telling where this ballistic missile threat was going exactly. He hoped that if the message wasn't carried out through cell towers, it might be wished there with a quick prayer. It lasted one second. The most important prayer of his life was printed in bold upon the begging front page of his mind.

"Please…"

It was a coarse whisper as he tried to cram his feet into shoes that he was always too lazy to untie. But that limp prayer served as the end of modern telecommunications. It was a good run over the past few decades but in five minutes, the world was excommunicated from everyone.

Cars on the road pulled over harshly, traffic ground to a halt all over the city. Some people ran to ditches, jumped in dumpsters, and dove into the back-yard swimming pools of strange families. Many broke the windows to buildings that looked secure. But there weren't that many people who took the threat seriously, in total. Most of the people who saw it thought, like Will, that it was more likely a technical glitch than the actual end of the world. They didn't know that sirens were going off all over the continent. How could the world end? It was simply an earthquake a small time ago.

Simply because one cannot understand something does not mean that the thing is unreasonable or impossible. Most people, because they were unprepared or because they thought everything in the world was going all right, decided that the end of it all was impossible. The truth was that their bewilderment didn't determine anything. Yet that was the very natural response of most who saw the warning. Most people in general didn't see it. Some were sleeping, others were busy and away from their phones.

Somehow, amongst the panic, Will's apartment building appeared invisible to these people seeking shelter. It was such an old building that it was more like a part of the scenery than a target. It was also at the edge of the city, so it avoided most of the panicked crowds. Will gathered his bag and some food. He had a duffle bag of high-calorie snack foods to last a couple of weeks just in case of times like this. He gathered his things and brought as many gallon jugs of water as he could carry. He had been stocking up. Loaded now with close to one hundred pounds of supplies, he made his way down the emergency stairwell slowly at first to get used to the weight of the bag, and then quickly, to save his life. He had no idea how much time was left before those missiles, those messengers of hate, delivered their package. As it was, he did not have enough time, as he would see through the windows in the northern wall of this very staircase.

He took just one second to glance outside. However, he was too late to soak in the sights of nature. In that second, the color drained out from the world. The sky turned white with unfathomable energy as the trees shriveled black with an instant decay. The contrast was immediate and harsh. The leaves lifted off in slow motion, crumbling and wrinkling up like burning paper and then were viciously shredded by an unknown force. Soon everything outside began to blur as the black ash lifted off and away from the direction of that nuclear detonation.

It was the last image he would see of the world for a while. The power of that light could not reach him in the stairwell just yet if he looked away. But from this instant onwards, nature would go to war against humanity. And everything else, for that matter. For this new war, she would become that legendary Medusa, cursing every glance at her with madness and death. The light of those bombs filled all of existence. Thousands of times brighter and hotter than the sun. Will shot down the stairs, but he only made it four steps down before the window which gave him his very last look at a peaceful world shattered under the swell of superheated air. Shards of glass chased him down the stairs as he rounded the corner of the railing. The steps only briefly touched Will's flustered feet.

He barely made it down to the underground carport before that terrible sound made reality stutter. Will heard its cataclysmic assault through the safety of the old metal door. It wasn't just loud. It was strange. Exactly like the kind of sound humans weren't designed to hear. Something that would normally burst your eardrums and crush your soft brain before you ever really had a chance to interpret any-thing about it. A sound not born for this Earth. It was in some ways like a cannon, yes. A boom that seemed larger than the sky that held it. It was in other ways like a nuclear chainsaw cutting down millions of trees in a single pass.

It was high-pitched as it rang through the corridors of the building, sounding eerily like a smoke detector going off. It was low-pitched in the sense that his feet felt the rumbling before it slithered up his legs to reassure him of just how bad this was. To confirm that it wasn't a dream.

His spine shot him up straight. Goosebumps covered his sweaty, panicked skin. He felt his heart skip a beat. He felt the air get pulled out of his lungs on a thousand cables of terrible pressure. The simple act of breathing became a tug of war between his will to live and whatever was trying to kill him. The heat was intense and heavy, like a scalding shower that he couldn't turn off. He had to step away from the door as it was heating up like the element on a stove.

The radiation would begin to dissipate immediately. But it would take many weeks before the surface would be safely traversable. It didn't look as though anyone else made it down to the carport or even thought to go there. How could they? Will counted five minutes from the emergency message to that bellowing, awful sound. But he really had no idea. How long did it take him to grab that old gas mask and filters? What about the extra set of clothes he stuffed in a freezer bag last year during one of his paranoid states? And the food bag? And the water? No one could have told him.

But he was panicking in a new way, now. He felt disgusting. It could have been the sweat, sure, he thought. And then it dawned on him. He ripped off absolutely every bit of pajamas he had on in a mad dash of nudism. He hastily produced the freezer bag of clothes from under the food in the duffle bag. He dumped the clothes from their sealed sanctum and then stuffed his used items in it as hard as he could without caring for their fold.

It was an odd time to be sorting laundry. But the fever of cleanliness didn't stop there. He grabbed one of the four gallons of water he managed to take with him and generously dumped it all over himself. He systematically washed his face, neck, chest, arms, pelvis and legs with one of a couple spare cloths he kept in the same large freezer bag. Once done with his crude bathing ritual, he tossed the cloth in the bag as well and sealed it shut. He hurled this bag across the empty carport as far as he could. And stayed well clear of it. He toweled himself off with the other dry cloth before putting on his new clothes.

He remembered reading about how radiation sticks to you. The small formations of dust can give off radiation directly into your skin for some time. He cleansed himself of this possibility before turning on his Geiger counter. It was one of those handheld ones no bigger than the calculators used in schools. Substantially heavier, though. It had a small needle that was useful to determine the radioactivity of water and food. He bought it, as well as most of the rest of this kit, in a fevered rush after the dreams started. The rest was leftover from camping trips.

He waved the apparatus over the rest of his belongings and himself and found only the outer layer of his backpack remained at significant, though not immediately dangerous, levels. Nothing a quick scrub couldn't fix. If he didn't cuddle it when he slept, he'd be alright. Disturbingly, Will wasn't immediately paralyzed by what had just happened. What had *really* just happened, that is. He was far too preoccupied with running through the reasonable safety measures he had seen in online videos. He checked over his equipment to see if he would have to make a short trip up again for anything important. As if that was even an option.

His pack was substantially full. Packed with do-dads too innumerable to list here. But most important was his kukri, a machete that he bought online from Nepal some months prior. He had several fire-starting materials and methods. He had his fold-up bow and a quiver of twenty arrows and twenty replacement heads for those arrows should need arise to hunt. He had small bolt cutters in case it was necessary to cut a lock or fence. All the rest were small implements like extra batteries, various ways to filter water, multitools of various function and form and some creature comforts.

This would form the basis of his expeditionary gear. Yes, he was actually thinking of going out there. He would try to find a car that worked and navigate his way to Florida. But, as it was, there happened to be an entire country full of invisible cancer-fire between himself and that objective. He wouldn't last even a few minutes out there right now. He had to wait. He didn't have a lot of water, though. If he had been preparing properly, he might have kept some down there, just in case. It's not like anyone looked around for stuff to steal down in the carport. Regardless, if he rationed it and didn't do much moving, he could probably make the rest of those three jugs last about a week, saving some extra to hydrate himself properly just before leaving and carrying a day's worth with him when he left.

And so, he decided to wait, just as his emotions had run out of patience.

CHAPTER 2

WAITING IN SOME concrete square was somehow the hardest part of all this. It wasn't just that Will was trapped inside the echoes of his own thoughts. Those echoes soon became real. He would talk to himself. Try to convince himself that the world might not really be over. Maybe there were only a few working bombs remaining and they hit Canada because of lackluster defenses? Perhaps it had a low radiation yield. He talked of other things too. Was it really his fault for letting Rachel go to Florida? She was a tough nut to crack. It was hard to read her emotions sometimes. She didn't seem that excited for the opportunity to fly. It was fairly alien to her, and she was considering offers from more local jobs before finally accepting this. He didn't listen to his intuition on this one.

He was in disbelief at the chances of this happening on the exact day that they would happen to be two thousand kilometers apart, but it had to happen to someone, he guessed. He wanted to object to her going because he was nervous about the flight, yet he didn't want to become overbearing. Another part of the problem was that he didn't want to treat his paranoid delusions of the apocalypse as real enough to disrupt the life of his dear love. He could allow them to disrupt himself, but not her. He wondered if that made him wise and responsible or simply a man of half measures. Certainly, if they had been living as though the apocalypse really would happen, that would mean ushering the apocalypse into their lives before it even took place. It would mean an acceptance of the end, which was, even in the moments when the warning sirens were blaring, unacceptable to think about.

They both had plans for a better life if society continued. He still couldn't believe it was ending, even with these sirens. But these were questions of his character that didn't matter as much as he thought they did. It didn't mean anything now that it was over, whether he made the right choices before he could have reasonably known. The end of the world could no longer be relegated to the background of human fear and fiction. It was no longer reasonable to believe that they should have acted differently. It merely created uncertainties. These uncertainties were settled shortly before by the sound of banshees bouncing through the halls, shrieking at their new life and whispering out their quick death. The feeling like the deep churning of a ground thoroughly sick with that intimidating, stalking resonance that crept up his legs. He didn't need a conference of research papers to tell him those questions of the likelihood of the war to end it all were answered scientifically. Irrefutably. Indeed, the last science article ever written was published crudely on the trunk of every remaining tree, and as the ghostly graffiti of shadows flashed onto any concrete still standing.

Will's challenge was in three parts. The first was not to blame himself for things he could never possibly control. That was very hard to do when he was alone now and never used to be. The second was to ease himself into the idea of getting out there. It was more difficult facing the unknown when he knew it was going to be the worst thing he could imagine. The third was the dreams. Those terrible dreams. Artifacts of a shattered psyche trying to hold itself together with glue, duct tape and faith. He only had one dream that he could remember once he woke up, two days after the bombs, and it started like so:

He was camping, like he sometimes did with Rachel, but this time in a place unknown to him. It was wide open, like a desert of grass and gravel. He could identify snow in the background. He couldn't see any civilization in any direction. No roads carefully carved into the hills. No lights on Earth as far as the eye could see. He was alone in this field of untold expanse, but not for long. Quickly, the sky surged, full of waves of an electrical color. Stretching from all horizons, this aurora of blues and greens with a hint of orange collected in the middle of the sky. Then it began what it had come to do. It twisted itself into fantastical shapes which were clear enough to understand, but still ambiguous enough to lead to questions. The images were muddled. The best he could make out was the image of several lines bending at various hard angles. Along several joints, these lines would all come back into themselves.

Elsewhere in this spectral collection were shapes of speckled mushroom clouds, tunnels, people, old stores, snakes, rats and spiders of huge proportions, a great tree with a light on top and two women of distinct shape elsewhere in the cosmic painting. The first he did not recognize, though her shape led him to puzzle over it for a second. The other was unmistakably Rachel. And then the lights moved on. That was it. He just sat there for a moment, filled with anxiety over the meaning of this projection constructed from atmospheric light. He paced back and forth for a while, hovering on what should have been solid ground but felt more like unsteady clouds. And then he felt it. Something watching him. Over in the treeline between the bushes. Will didn't remember a treeline or bushes there before. He was pretty sure this was a wide-open space and was disturbed deeply by the nature of his apparent misperception. He approached cautiously, even though he didn't want to get closer, and bundled his fists.

The darkness did not recede. As Will approached, he began to realize that it was a wall of darkness. It was a barrier. He stuck his hand in, and nothing happened. But after retracting his hand, the darkness took on a small, sly human smile. He looked at his hand and it was extended out from his arm an unrealistic distance. Then the darkness covered his body and stretched him to a ridiculous height, and he was startled awake from his sleep. He did not know anything about these images, though he found some renewed determination in seeing Rachel's form. And then there was the fact that he was forced to come closer to the darkness. It wasn't his choice that he came close to that thing.

He spent the next few days reflecting on everything. He thought considerably about that run home from his appointment; the hours just before the sky became white with rage. That fleeting time when he caught the last glimpse of green on the leaves. He held that image in his mind and thought about it deeply. The trees were healthy and confident, the sun was prominent, and the birds were back from the south. Everything was business as usual. The color of normalcy. He then realized what he was truly looking at. The confident trees held no consciousness of the end. That prominent sun was 93 million miles away and held not a care in the world for the fact that its children were playing with fire and were about to be scorched. The birds were clueless casualties of nature's desperation for progress through sexual selection. They were still building nests under the now defunct presumption of environmental stability.

But the environment wasn't in control. We were. Or at least, we were supposed to be. A responsibility we were already slowly failing. Now, with the end, that failure had become critical, irreversible and absolute. We pretended we could forever escape the consequences of our psychopathy by developing ever-advancing technology. And then, at the end of it all, we did it to ourselves.

Will was forlorn at the sight of that indifferent world before the end. The light from the sun outside was bright. Profuse, even. Careless. But then it all changed when that bright, atomic light washed over everything.

CHAPTER 3

WILL HAD BEEN down in this carport for seven days. He noticed a few things about the surface world even though he had not yet laid eyes on it. He listened, however. The wind was much stronger than before. This told him that in all likelihood the surface was barer than it used to be. There was not much to block the wind anymore. It was also hollow sounding. There wasn't much sound carried by that wind. Normally it would harbor the sounds of nature with it. The rustling leaves or the tweeting of birds or the road noise of traffic. But now it was empty. It was the expected result, but it was still a new thing. Society must've been so busy that the only thing yet unheard was silence. Will looked at his water supply across his mopey sleeping setup and counted that he had one day left after today.

That told him everything he needed to know about whether or not it was time to leave. He looked at his map of the area and put together a plan. Given that he was in southern Ontario, he had two options to begin his excursion down the United States coastline. He could take a straight shot through the border near Buffalo, New York. That could mean radiation as it was almost certainly hit, one would think. Given Will had waited about a week after the detonations silenced the world, the radiation from such events could be a small fraction of their level at the moment of detonation. It should be survivable with his mask and filters, but he didn't have that many. He had six forty-hour filters in his bag. And he had no idea how crucial they could be later. He didn't know the radiation level exactly. He didn't know how long he could traverse it and he couldn't change clothes at all to get it away from his skin. He simply had to rely on his dull, gray poncho, so it was still a concern.

The other option was to go through the other border crossing at Detroit, Michigan. This was going to be a misstep. It was actually moving away from his destination considerably. He would be going west, then have to cross another two states, coming back towards the more familiar layout of the east coast. It was decided then, Buffalo. He had to figure out transportation next. It was always unclear whether electronics would continue to function at all after the electromagnetic pulse of these nuclear weapons reached out. But Will's items all seemed to be in working order and he was out there when the detonation actually happened. Any EMP would have affected him if it worked like that.

But, as it stood, it seemed that small electronics were going to be fine. He would have to see about cars. He imagined that anything connected to the grid at the time had shorted out. He had his phone charged, but had it turned off to save power and he had a little power bank that could hold enough for all his electronics a couple times over. He had also planned for radiation protection. He had a poncho for the rain that went all the way down to below his knees. It was a nice gray-brown color instead of bright yellow. The idea was that in any scenario where he had to bug out, the protection of his primary clothes was the top priority. The protection from wet and cold, sure. But a secondary function was that he could come into contact with the irradiated world and the dust of it would stick to the poncho. The tough and weatherproof exterior of which could simply be washed off with water.

The plan of radiation protection centered around controlling his exposure as much as he could because he did not have a hazmat suit. But transportation would have to be opportunistic. If there were trains on unobstructed tracks, he could maybe find the operator's manual. If there were cars on an unobstructed road, then maybe someone left the keys in a mad dash. His need to go down there was almost neurotic. He didn't want to give himself the time for the thought to sink in that this world wasn't really worth living in anymore. There was simply no point to going on if he and Rachel were to be separated. There was no point hunting for food and camping out with no electricity and no future. There was no point being just another scavenging critter that would devolve into a caveman again as soon as his power bank gave up.

He might just be the only person left with working technology and he had to press the advantage while he still had it. It was decided then, tonight, he would sleep. Tomorrow, he would walk out there and see what planet he was on. But the time on his watch read one o'clock. Not quite bedtime yet. He supposed that he could sleep now and try to leave at night but ultimately decided against it as he didn't know what kind of predators would be out there. After a week of silence on humanity's part, the coyotes might have become brave. And he didn't have a gun. Only his bow and kukri. He decided instead he would spend the time double checking his thought process.

If he had powered gear, then he likely would have to hide it from others if he met them. He figured there would only be two kinds of people exposed where he was going. The first kind were the desperate ones. Those who were desperate for resources and yet clever enough to not get themselves killed fighting over the last scraps at the supermarket. Places like that would have been death zones. The other kind would be whoever was not desperate, but instead lacked any kind of self-preservation. Will also had to consider that all people would be in the throes of grieving. It would be very rare to find someone who hadn't lost, or become separated from, a loved one.

Given the time of day that the bombs hit, it was clear that whatever apparent enemy launched them wanted as much damage as possible. They waited for everyone to go to work in the cities. They waited for kids to go to school. They waited for Rachel to go on that trip. They wanted the discord of the roads being as unusable as possible at the height of traffic and travel. They wanted people to be awake so they could be blinded by the light. They wanted society to flex at the height of its congestion before they struck. That was the way to do it. So, it would be wise to avoid the unknown number of mourning parents, all of whom were convinced they were in a bad dream or some simulation or another. It would be wise to stay away from any collection of wailing individuals. Their psychology would be on the very precipice of madness.

Will thought in terms of his technology again and thought of the probability of others being as prepared as him. He needed to maintain the advantages he possessed so long as it served his main goal of getting to Florida. He needed to maintain distance. Most people wouldn't have guns that were very useful for targeting at range until he made his way down past New York, he thought. However, as a counterpoint, most of those who survived the initial waves of desperation from people would have been those with guns. Perhaps there would be a heavy survivorship bias towards those with guns, increasing his likelihood of running into them. In any event, he had very good binoculars, so keeping a distance from any structure was probably good. However, the thought did occur that he should get his hands on a firearm as soon as possible. That must end up being a priority along the way because it would increase his survivability later, especially in the south.

He knew that distance would be a priority going forward due to his equipment, but also because it allowed him to gather precious information and gauge the interactions of people before getting close. He also knew that stealth was preferable to overt travel. He would end up less of a target that way. He would have to consider that people would not only be desperate and reckless, but also curious. He would have to wait sometimes and see if he was being followed.

Will was thinking of these things partially as a means to run away from a certain uncomfortable thought. The thought that he might have to kill someone in very uncertain circumstances. Life was never black and white before the war. Self-defense was often a more difficult situation than the courtroom would like to believe. People's intentions are unknown by the defender. They can be proven in court later, but no one knows what someone really wants until they act in the moment. No one knows the danger someone presents or the weapon they're carrying. It was still possible, however, to take most people at their word and live normally. That was no longer possible now. What kind of people remained? The good natured and harmless?

Maybe it was enough to consider that there would be some people whose panicked instincts would have calmed down after some time. They would have found a group, a shelter and a reason. It was absolutely certain that whoever was without shelter this last week was dead or dying right now. So, there was another survivorship bias. Only those with shelter would remain alive enough to be mobile. It was also likely that only those with a group would dare to venture out and about. Those who were alone probably preferred the cloak of nighttime or at least weren't very eager to pose a threat and expose themselves. For certain it could be said that whoever was alone, and went out in the last week, was smart enough to not be trouble. Or was that true? It was so hard to tell. It had only been a week and Will was trying to filter out who would have made it as a guessing game to keep himself sane for one thing and prepare for the outside for another. Nothing could really be said for certain at this point.

He remembered that humans had been compared to cockroaches for their survivability. And would people really have the psychology of raiders at this point? One week? One week without food, maybe. But most people had a week of food in their cupboards and most of that wasn't burned or flashed with radiation due to being closed away behind the house walls. Anywhere that the cupboards had burned, the people likely burned with it. It was very puzzling to figure out the exact logic here. All of these conclusions seemed logical, but it would be absurd to accept them without the nearly equal probability that they might be wrong. This was a doozy. He decided to hold one idea. That the people he would meet on the surface were likely some combination of desperate, had a shelter and a group. And that was good enough for him to conclude that avoidance was the best policy.

He would have to wear the mask when he first went outside, until he could measure the background radiation level. That would be the priority, he thought. The second priority would be to deduce ground zero. That would require some height, as detecting that from the ground was likely fruitless. So, his first objective tomorrow was to gain some elevation and use that to scout his immediate area. He felt anxious. He knew that leaving the safety and quietness of this carport would put him at immediate risk. Going to the roof would invite a certain level of exposure. He would just have to buck himself up to do it tomorrow. And with that, he went to bed.

CHAPTER 4

WILL DECIDED IT would be daylight enough to see what he was looking for. He sat up and felt arrested by a sense of dread. He was so genuine in his wish that this was just some nuclear drill that he took way too seriously. He even entertained it for a minute and laughed at himself. But then swift were the flashbacks of the leaves burning black and disintegrating before his very eyes. Sudden was the memory of glass chasing him down the stairs. And horrible was that sluggish and weighty boom. No, it definitely happened.

He put on the poncho, boots and his gloves and the mask. He hoisted his pack and grabbed the Geiger counter. He pulled his belt through the loops of his kukri sheath so as to position it on the left hip for a right-hand draw. He screwed on the filter and went for the door. He noticed immediately the relative restriction that the mask placed on his breathing. It took some convincing, but that flat metal slab of a door moved reluctantly with a groan. The hinges must have expanded due to the heat. Will noticed the stairwell was not white with paint anymore. It was some combination of black and gray. He turned around to the door and noted that it had melted irregularly.

He scaled the dusty staircase, crunching glass underfoot until he reached the first-floor window. The same window he was looking through a week ago. He remembered the birds and the trees and the grass. He remembered the neighbor's fence too. All gone. Some of the trees were still standing but were disfigured terribly. Long sticks of black soot without their branches, leaning away from the epicenter at dramatic and almost performative angles. Most were broken right off from the ground. The sunlight was no longer oppressive as it was the very minute before the end. The outside realm was a gray one. This was the very early summer, and yet the feeling outside resembled a sulking day warning of Canadian winter frost. Dust and charcoal covered the ground like a sickly snow and even piled up like small sand dunes due to the hot wind.

It looked like the kind of gray hell that didn't take an active part in your torture. He didn't see anything still on fire. No magma pits. No chains or impaled prisoners. It really looked like a kind of old hell that had been around far too long to hate anything anymore. It was too lazy now. It would leave you free to suffer in your own way. It didn't need to have the overt intensity of an eternal Inferno, rather it simply knew that there were no more green pastures. No more days in the sunbathing ethos of late spring fever. It was a hell that didn't try to tell you so. It would just wait until you figured it out on your own. And even then, it didn't care.

The cars which were parked seemed to suffer the same fate as the stairwell. They were dust covered, with broken glass and burned paint revealing a scorched and disfigured metal. Finding a working car out there was going to be a lot more difficult than he thought. There were working cars in the carport, however, he just needed to find a key that was maybe still usable.

He climbed the stairs to the fifth floor. There was an old ladder that looked like it was made of rebar which led to a hatch in the roof. It was stuck right into the concrete floor and crudely welded together on the way up. He climbed the old ladder and breached the hatch to the roof. He had never been up here before and it was an odd feeling. He crouched down on the roof instinctively to avoid sticking out on the skyline. Retrieving the binoculars, he made his way to the edge of the building and peeped over the short ledge.

The view on the first floor really hadn't prepared him for what he was seeing now. It was conflicting. On the one hand, he could see the epicenter of the explosion clear as day. On the other hand, everything in the landscape was running away from it, but not by choice. An army of trees went to sprint away from it in a useless tandem of unnatural panic. The cars on the road tried to steer away at odd and inconsistent angles.

People must have escaped their cars in a hurry, he thought. But if that's true, where did they go? They probably went closer to downtown. It would be away from this bomb's direction anyway and would probably be the source of any emergency response. That's also where the hospital was. He looked around more to notice that all of the signs on the road that tried to advertise in that direction were now blacked out, as if censored by an all-seeing eye. Every bit of glass in visual range was completely shattered.

Will brought up the binoculars to take a better look. It

was a little difficult to line them up, pressed against the visor of his gas mask. The rubber pads on the eye sockets of the binoculars squeaked and rubbed against the hard clear material of the mask awkwardly. The binoculars didn't really tell him anything he didn't already know. It's just that more of the same had happened the farther you looked. But at the very edge of the burned trees, you could still see trees that weren't black. This was a comforting sign as not only was the bombs' destruction not total, but also it meant that there might be valid firewood out there for camps in the future. He thought he might have to be careful with the light of his campfires when he made them. That was something he forgot to consider last night. He definitely did not want to get noticed from miles away with a big flashy fire. He would have to cover the sides of it somehow.

There wasn't any sign of people, contrary to expectation. He thought people would be out here if they were alive at all. They'd be scavenging or raiding or pillaging or something. It could just be too early in the morning, he thought. Maybe hooligans like to sleep in.

Just as he was about to go, he decided to utilize his binoculars for one last thing. It would be easier to check multiple cars from here for any signs that they might work. He looked at a few cars and noted just how matte black they all were. It was a strange thing to happen because most of the stairwell wasn't actually burned that badly, just the paint was. He was confused as to why cars got it worse. Then again, they were outside. All of the seats in the cars were burned, as you would expect. It also seemed like they melted into strange shapes, which was odd to him. The fabric in those seats didn't really melt. It was mostly foam and cheap covering. It would burn up completely, not melt. He focused the binoculars on the driver's seat of the closest car. And that's when it rose from the background of the seat to meet Will's horror dead on. It started with the teeth and cheekbones and violently rounded its cranium into the seat. The ribcage grew out from it like warped prison bars. No, the seats didn't melt and burn into odd shapes. The people did.

It took everything in Will's power not to hock bodily fluids into his mask. He lurched forward, clutching the edge with a desperate, gasping, trembling grip. He began to breathe sporadically with the very same emergency. He recovered enough to open his eyes into the angry orange sunrise and tried to force his breathing into a controlled rhythm. He wanted to flee but his knees wouldn't let him. He was stuck for a moment, trying to forget about what he just saw. But now, Will knew the score. This wasn't like the popular media of post-apocalyptic scenarios. There weren't going to be any raiders. Nobody had the time to prepare for that much. Will had temporarily forgotten just how quickly it all happened. Whoever was likely enough to become a violent troublemaker in a world without laws was down there somewhere right now, melted to his seat.

After a while, he recovered from the sight. Will decided to gaze outward and away from his immediate vicinity. He saw that the bomb went off in a strange place. It was placed outside the city limits. It was unclear why. There were certainly not enough bombs in the world to hit every city. But the idea that his city would even be a target was strange. They didn't have anything strategic nearby. There were no missile bases or military depots or population hubs. Will thought that the bomb was maybe evading countermeasures and so it couldn't land exactly on target. Or maybe the enemy wanted to poison the landscape as well as hit the major cities. It was anybody's guess at this point.

Then Will thought about the actual number of bombs that must've hit. He knew from his own internet searches that Russia had around six thousand nuclear warheads with about one thousand six hundred ready to deploy. He also knew that China had some stockpiled as well. He thought China might've had six hundred. He didn't remember how many were deployed. So, of all the warheads ready to drop, some would go to Europe, some would go to the US and probably less than half would be shot down or intercepted somehow. He figured that he could count on about five hundred to seven hundred hitting the US and Canada and only about two hundred and fifty standing in the way between himself and Rachel throughout the east coast. Yeah, only, he thought. His guesswork did not bring him the comfort he thought it would.

He let that sink in for a minute. And then he decided to continue. He realized he was running his filter. He had only been up there for five or so minutes, but he only had these filters, and he was fairly confident that he would not be able to find more. The last bit of business was to bring out his portable radio and give a few tries to see if there was any noise. He tuned the dial to all stations on the AM and FM frequency bands. There was nothing but static.

It made sense as all radio stations were connected to the grid and that would have rather catastrophically ended due to the EMP effect of these high-energy detonations. It was time to go. He made his way to the ladder, still shaken by what he saw, and descended. He thought of checking his apartment on the third floor to see if there was anything useful that he missed.

He hadn't bothered to lock it on the way out in all his panic. Entering, he found his home ruined. The consequences of staying put would have been fatal, without a doubt. The wallpaper had burned quietly in his absence. The mattresses and cushions of his furniture were shriveled to a crisp. His Geiger counter started warning him whenever he got close to the fabrics of the sofa and chair in the living room, so he backed off. There were only two spots worth looking at. He opened the pantry door, which broke free from the hinges like cardboard. He set it aside to gaze upon the predictably useless mess of what used to be food. He then went to his closet. It was only one of the closets in the apartment, but it was a walk-in closet with lots of space and was designated storage for a lot of miscellaneous things. The closed door was burned nearly to a crisp, but it protected the things behind it fairly well. Waving the counter around before stepping in, it reported nothing back to him. So, he entered.

He scanned the scene and found not much had been flammable. He picked up a small measuring tape and put it up to the counter. It didn't bother clicking at such a boring item, but Will thought it might be useful. He also took the time to grab a small prybar from the toolbox so that he didn't have to use his kukri for such tasks, even though it was perfectly capable, with nearly a half an inch of steel making the spine of the blade. He opened up the plastic bin which was sealed in the back of the closet. In it he found something that he couldn't believe he forgot to pack. A small tarp. He couldn't camp without shelter very well in case it rained, so he took it and proceeded to strap it with a couple bungie cords to the outside of his pack. He found nothing else of use.

He did have a thought, however; there was a small pickup truck down in the carport with some of those after-market rails bolted to the front of it. Will could probably commandeer that from the owner. He happened to know her up on the fourth floor. She was middle-aged and had a real tomboy feeling when she talked about anything. Will thought about the funny euphemisms that she produced in conversation. Different country sayings like "a bat outta hell" or "thinks her shit don't stink" were common variables of her very strange character.

She wasn't one to fret about the details of things, wearing the same plaid long coat basically everywhere in the cooler months right into winter and even into late spring. She loved that coat. She was strong and definitely struck Will as being fearless. She even used to call him "hon" in that typical way that older women do. She just seemed so dominant over the world. Her husband left her for being just that way, as she told the story. "Too much woman," she adamantly maintained. She decided never to remarry. Will thought there was a glint of sadness that was being projected by that tough veneer. A certain emptiness that she was too proud to face. A dominance that she was too big and too old to lose now. Will didn't think it was his place to judge, of course. But the feeling was inescapable whenever she talked about the past. She seemed wary of this weakness, enough that she would suddenly jump out from that topic into the modern day. She was very fond of the power to dismiss the past with a hand wave and say, "Ah, well, that's old news. What's up with you guys?"

She was very fond of Rachel. She thought Will hit the jackpot with her and was very keen on telling him every time she was brought up. If Rachel was there when she said it, she would bunch up her shoulders and blush over the compliment. The lady's name was Rayne. He never knew her last name. They didn't talk all that often. They simply met in the common areas and the hallways occasionally.

Her talkative nature was profuse, but mostly welcome. Will decided he had better check on her, even though he thought he knew the answer. He went to her apartment. It was numbered 427. He knocked on the door, producing the only sound in that building since the day of disaster. It was a useless gesture of the old world to knock before entering someone's place. But Will felt that he owed her that respect. The other reason was because he was terrified of going in there. He didn't know what he would see. If the destruction of his own apartment was any indication, it might be the same here, but what if she had been home? He wasn't yet over that person that was stuck into their driver's seat on the road. Could he handle more? Especially when he knew this woman...

He decided that the truck was worth it, and Rachel was counting on him to be brave. This wasn't the worst thing he'd be seeing. He had to buck up now if he was going to make it to Florida through the burnt-out husk of the old world. He called out to whatever was beyond the door in a weak attempt to pull her back from the dead. "Rayne? You there?" He knocked again as a final gesture of old-world faith before committing himself to an act that would be considered a crime if that old hierarchy of law wasn't thrown upside down. He shouldered the door open. It really didn't take much. Those doors were solid, before they were burned. And then he looked at the place. It was quaint for a place the fire seemed to claim. The fire wasn't total here, though.

Will started in the living room. He was here for the keys and that was it. However, as he looked around, he noticed things he just couldn't ignore. A six pack of beer bottles was sitting neatly on one cushion of the sofa. The cushion beside it was depressed more than the other one. That one must've been her spot. There was a television of an older make that sat opposite that. The television was tucked into an old cabinet, now blackened by the apocalypse but still standing strong, to its credit. Those older televisions that had the backs sticking out were no laughing matter on weight.

There was a picture frame on the top of the stand that was knocked flat on its face. Lifting it up to his eyes, Will softened a little. It was a picture of Rayne and her husband on their wedding day. She was so beautifully made up. Cloaked in rich layers of white with a blue-ribbon sash, she was clearly the star of the show. Her rounded face was glowing with youth, even as her crows' feet and rarified gray streaks of hair gave it away that this wasn't more than ten years ago.

Her arms were around him, coming up from his right side to his tall left shoulder and holding on to her future with him strenuously. Her right leg was kicked up behind her like a giddy schoolgirl. Will supposed that she was probably more comfortable being vulnerable and girly back then. Either that or she was just so excited that it changed her for a day. Or maybe it was just for the picture, but Will sensed that this was as genuine as it gets. The husband was solidified in place with a grin as he looked down to his newlywed wife. He was bloody tall. Based on how tall he was to her, and the fact that she was wearing heels there, Will guessed the husband might have been a good three inches taller than him. Will didn't know his name. He never felt like prying.

He looked back at the beer bottles on the sofa. That was all of what kept her company now. Why? Will strained to think of how one thing could evolve into another. Such a beautiful picture of promise and a wealth of happiness evolved into a parasitic relationship, with alcohol sharing the space on a couch that was too big for just her. What the hell could have happened? Then Will noticed the outside. The glass to the sliding doors was shattered inward, as expected. And he saw the trees and things outside just as they were on the roof. And then he realized that things change sometimes for no good reason. Just like the world changed.

He saw something else, too. The keys were bundled up on the coffee table. He grabbed them solemnly. And one final thing struck him as he went for the door. She wasn't here. He decided to check quickly in the other rooms just for some closure. But she wasn't there either. Now he was truly puzzled. Rayne wouldn't have completely vaporized. If some of that poor person in their car remained to haunt him, she wouldn't have it any worse. But she wouldn't be anywhere else either or she would have taken the truck. Her keys were just sitting there, the beer bottles were just sitting there. As a matter of fact, the only thing not just sitting there was her. The only clue remaining was that depression in the couch cushion.

He came back out of the bathroom as his final check and went out to the living room area in bewilderment. He checked the kitchen with no luck either. But when he turned around, there it stood. A shadowy entity not unlike a dense cloud of smoke haunted that once empty living room. A short, overweight female silhouette staring longingly out the doors to the balcony. Will felt a very unique sense of powerless fear and sickening regret pass over him as he stared at her. He dared to beckon sheepishly. "Rayne?" The entity didn't respond. It just kept staring out there. Then, a few seconds later, it reacted violently. Not towards him, but towards the balcony, reeling backwards and rubbing itself frantically.

A dream-like scream echoed in the room. The thing then lunged toward the balcony and, with the athleticism of total panic, launched itself over the edge. Will chased after it, choking down the fear he had and looked down. There it was. The skeleton of a torment that met its resolution on her terms, he thought. He began shaking and convulsing the tears out of his body. The tragedy of what he just saw hit him like a bus. There was never anything more unfair than the glance into this woman's life that he just witnessed.

But there was something wrong with it.

Will gathered himself after five minutes and managed the thought that something just wasn't right. It didn't all make complete sense. It wasn't airtight, like a poorly framed murder with an unlikely motive. Will was very good with the small details of things, and he went to check the closet again out of one part denial and one part instinct. Many of her clothes were not burned and those that were still had some way to identify them. He couldn't find her coat. That favorite plaid long coat of her never-changing fashion sense. She wouldn't have been wearing it if she was just casually here in the beginning of summer.

It would have to be retired to the closet at this time. He zipped over to the kitchen, still tasting the tears of whatever cruel lie this was. He opened the cupboards and found that her shelves were well scorched, but organized and full, except for the canned foods part. That appeared to be cleared out with only one or two remaining and one was knocked on its side. Will was starting to gather that she might've bugged out, too. But where on Earth would she be? She couldn't have left the building; she'd be cooked in minutes even if she survived beyond the blast, and she likely knew that. She couldn't have stayed in the building anywhere on or above ground level or she would've met a similar fate to everyone else. She wasn't in the carport, or he would have been living with her for a week.

He would have to measure the skeleton outside to be sure, but now he was ready to make the accusation. He mumbled to himself confidently, "No. No, she didn't die. She didn't jump off that balcony. That tough old woman must've escaped somewhere."

He then froze upon hearing the shuffle of boots in the entrance behind him.

"Lucky guess, hon," Rayne congratulated him on his discovery. He whipped around and sprinted in for a hug. He had never been so happy to see the most basic of acquaintances. Her face was covered mostly by a thick rag. She was wearing the plaid coat as protection. They released from the hug and then Will had some questions.

"Where the hell were you this whole time?" He released her and moved back to look at her face.

"Oh, I was in the underground storage area. You know the one that got cleared out and locked up a couple years ago?" She waved dismissively.

"Ah, yes!" Will pressed his hand against his visor. He felt so dumb for forgetting about that old place. It would've been safe enough. It only had one entrance and was populated by nothing more than empty rooms with old padlocks on them.

"Yep, that's where I thought no one else would go. Where did you end up, hon?" She shifted her weight to one hip and leaned against the wall.

"Oh, I was in the carport. I just grabbed as much of my stuff as I could before running down there. I still almost got caught in the blast." He remembered those moments with grief and anxiety.

"Then, and you know I gotta ask, what in the hell are you doing in my living room?" Her muffled voice came in with a slight giggle and was more curious than accusatory.

"Well, you see. I needed your truck to get to Florida… Rachel is down there," he admitted with reluctance.

"Oh, sweet Jesus, hon, that's terrible." She covered her mouth despite having the rag over it already. "I'm so sorry. But you don't have your own car?"

"No," Will confessed, rubbing the back of his head. "I never got one because I was comfortable taking the bus to work every day. I have my license, but I just never took the plunge to get a car."

"Ah, I see. So why were you home? It was mid-afternoon…"

"Oh, I was supposed to be on night shift for this week and I just woke up about an hour before she landed in Florida. What were you doing home?" None of that was true. He skipped over the therapy visit on purpose.

"Hah, I got lucky. The boss texted us to let us know he had to close the office. Something came up. His daughter wanted to go to see the doctor. She said she was scared of these dreams she'd been having."

Will swallowed hard. "Wow, that's fortunate for you then," he said.

"Exactly. So, hon, you have to really think you'll find her out there if you're gonna go. I have enough supplies for both of us if you wanted to stay a while."

"Well, that's just it. I have to go and see for myself. I'm pretty sure she's not dead. We were on the phone when the alert came through and I just figured I didn't have anything to live for up here if she wasn't with me. So, I'm going on a likely suicidal trip to try and meet up with her because... well... I told her I would. And that's that."

"You've got guts, kid; I'll tell you that. I wouldn't wanna go out there. The only reason I'm up here at all is because I heard you bust in the door."

"Five floors down you heard that?"

"I guess so. Must've traveled through the vents." She squared herself to him straight. "Look, hon. You can take the truck. I even stocked several containers of gas in the back in case I ran empty on the road one day. But I'm not leaving. I got lots of non-perishables and water in that storage area along with means enough to cook it. I was going to take the truck and get out if anyone got rough around here, but it's calm, so you need it more. Go get that sweet young woman back."

Will smiled. "Thank you so much. I'll try not to bang it up. But I thought the storage area was closed down? Did you sneak your supplies in or something?"

"Not really. I just slipped a twenty to the superintendent. No one really cared about that place. They just didn't want anyone using it who might move out and leave a bunch of junk behind that they had to deal with. So, I just loaded up with a hell of a lot of spring water which I got on sale over the years and added a couple extra things to my shopping cart every grocery run I did. To be honest, I thought it would be a biological attack through the water supply. I didn't actually think they'd drop the bombs."

"Holy shit, Rayne. You would have been called crazy, but now you're not, I guess." They both chuckled at the thought of it.

"So, hon, did you find anything of use up here or is it all toast?" she said, scanning her apartment.

"Well, some of your clothes aren't actually burned completely if you feel yourself wanting a change of clothes in the future."

"Oh good."

"Yeah. There's no good food left, but I did find this. I don't know if you want to keep it or not. But it seems to be pristine." He handed over her wedding photo from earlier.

She gazed over it longingly for some time. "I didn't realize I kept that up there all this time," she lied, "but I'll take it for old times' sake. Thank you."

"No problem. Look, I only have so much in this filter, so I have to go. But I just wanted you to know that I'm really glad you're okay. I seemed to have this waking nightmare earlier that... well, that you didn't make it. So, it's good to see you."

"Aw, thanks, hon. You're alright. You know, all this time I've been telling you that you really got lucky with Rachel. But I also thought she's pretty damn lucky to have you too." Rayne wasn't the outwardly sentimental type, but she obviously figured she had better say it before he left in case he never came back.

Will hung his head in appreciation. Then he had to say goodbye to the only bit of sanity still standing on two legs. "Goodbye, Rayne. I'll come back up to Canada if I find her... if it's safe."

"Rachel's a tough one, I think. You'll find her. See you later, hon. And don't lose yourself out there. The world is one thing, but your mind is another. Don't push it too far or you'll lose something you may never get back. Just be careful."

"I will, thank you."

And with that, Will left her to her old place. He was relieved and concerned at the same time. Rayne would spend a long time alone. He hoped she would be okay. But the major concern was over himself. What on Earth did he see in there? It was a daydream or, as he put it, some kind of "waking nightmare" indeed. But it was so real and so vivid. He had no idea what to expect now. It wasn't just a vision. Because it was wrong, and Rayne was alright. She was actually doing much better than he could have ever predicted. The ghostly figure jumping off the balcony might've been the manifestation of his fears, sure. But his mind had never done that before. And was it merely a coincidence that there was a skeleton at the bottom of the building? Or was the skeleton merely a part of the hallucination? He had more questions than answers after his exploration.

CHAPTER 5

WILL ENTERED THE carport. He wiped his Geiger counter over himself to see if the poncho needed washing and it was surprisingly unaffected. He guessed that materials had a hard time sticking to its slippery surface. Water was going to be an issue going forward. He debated going back to ask Rayne for some of hers for the road. He hadn't really considered that water out in the world would be irradiated. There were going to be very few good sources. So, he doubled back to ask her and to procrastinate against having to leave.

He peeked his head in the door. She was still standing where he left her. She seemed quite troubled. She was staring at that wedding photo silently. Will didn't immediately know how to ask. She had been so gracious, despite the stress of being in this new world.

"Hey, Rayne." She didn't move to face him. Certain that she heard him, he continued. "One last thing, if you don't mind. Do you have any spare water in your stash? I could use some for the road, but if you need all of it, I don't mind.

I'd hate to impose and ask you for more than you've already given." He was being very careful around this subject as though he should not disturb her thoughts. However, his mission was a resolute one and he needed every advantage he could get.

She gave him the key to the storage area without looking at him. Will took this as permission but knew enough about her to not pry about her feelings. He backed away quietly to not disturb her thoughts and went down to the basement storage area. After loading up the truck as much as he could, he returned the key to a crying woman.

She was standing in front of the balcony window, which was shattered inward. It wasn't difficult to see what she was crying over. But it was impossible to know the history of it or the particular reason. Still clutching the photo, she wasn't hysterical. Rather she seemed regretful and painfully powerless. It was like she recognized the past was gone and far behind her, and perhaps rightly so. But there was a latent wish breathed out amongst the mild huffing that wished things had worked out differently after all. That maybe if there had been someone here with her, then it wouldn't all be so bad.

A terrifying idea struck Will all at once. It was difficult to see at first, but Will felt very uncomfortable about the similarities here. The similarities between where the ghostly image was standing when it jumped off the balcony and where Rayne was standing now. She and the ghost seemed to have roughly the same body shape as well. He didn't want to act on his hallucinations yet, at the risk of seeming crazy to her. She hadn't noticed him come back, so he simply watched, cautiously.

Then the worst came to pass. She reeled back suddenly, dropping the wedding photo and rubbing her face frantically. It looked just like when the blackened ghost had done it. Then she let out a yell and Will jumped into action. He bolted towards her, minding the furniture as she dashed for the balcony free and clear with surprising speed. His long legs were able to close the distance, but when he grabbed onto her, he lost his balance. She was much stronger than she looked. Will shuffled his feet, regained his control and got between her and the edge of the railing. He grunted and lunged forward, tackling her to the floor on the inside of her apartment.

She lay there, squirming like a child throwing a tantrum. She grabbed onto his arm and squeezed it hard in a fit of powerless rage. Her face squeezed itself together and blushed red with emotion as her arm shook under the pressure of gripping his arm. Then she breathed and it was as if all the emotion bottled up in that face burst out at once. In one long protracted attack, she cried and hollered and grumbled something inaudible. Will got off her, certain now that he could handle it if she tried that again. He waited until she was exhausted from her episode. He was pretty sure she wanted to kill him, but surprisingly, she simply let out a very weak, "Thank you." And she hugged him around the shoulders.

"What the hell was that?" he asked in the softest way possible.

It took her a while to gather the breath to respond. She rubbed her eyes with open palms and felt her forehead and cheeks as though checking for fever. "I have no idea what's gotten into me," she said with disbelief and a twinge of loathing.

"The world. That's what's gotten into you," he said. He was very confident that the ghostly apparition had something to do with this, but he didn't know how. All he knew was that she was not prone to this kind of self-destructive behavior. But then again, sharing a sofa with a six pack of beer might have indicated that she was a lot more vulnerable than he thought.

She nodded in agreement with Will's diagnosis. "Will, could you..." She stopped as if dreading the question. "Could you throw that... god damn picture off the balcony for me?"

He was surprised at the question at first, but then thought it would be better if she did it. With him standing guard at the balcony just in case. "Why don't you do it? It'll probably help you more that way."

She agreed and when he was at the balcony, she threw it out the broken balcony door. She remained inside the apartment, afraid to go near the edge. He looked down and noticed that the blackened skeleton that he had previously assumed was Rayne's body, down on the pavement, had vanished.

"Are you going to be alright?" Will asked, not wanting to leave her to her fate, but needing to, nonetheless.

"Yes, hon." She sighed. She was partly in disbelief at her episode, but she was also exhausted from it. "Thank you. But I have no desire to do anything but sleep at this point. I haven't slept but four hours a night since the bomb."

He helped her down to the storage area where she would be hiding out for the foreseeable future.

"Don't worry about me, dear, it's just memories now," she claimed as she stood among the doors of the storage area.

"Oh, it's alright. I'm no stranger to the weight of all of this, either," Will reassured her to the best of his ability. "But we must keep on living. We cannot give up just yet. Not only are we the only people alive that we know for certain, but we're both sane enough to talk. That might be a rarity too." He left the key to the basement storage area in her hands.

"Good luck out there, hon," she offered.

"Thank you. The surface should be safe to traverse without a mask in five weeks maybe. You should try to go for limited walks to avoid rotting down here."

"Good idea." She smiled weakly. "See you later."

"See you, Rayne."

He found it difficult to leave this conversation. He knew he likely would never have one like it again unless he found Rachel. He didn't really know Rayne that well. They spoke like longtime friends now. They acted like they went way back. Before the war, which was what he was calling it, he saw her once a month, roughly. They spoke for five minutes at a time and that was mostly it. It's funny how things change in these circumstances. Will made his way to the old carport for the last time.

The motor to the garage door of the underground parking was left unpowered like most everything else. It was a crude contraption. An electric motor, a bike chain and a rope were all it took to lift that door along its tracks. After trying and failing to get it open, Will wondered if the door locked in place as a security feature. Or maybe it was due to the warping from the outside heat right after the bomb. Despite being below ground level, the door itself was facing outside and would have been cooked pretty well. Will looked at the contraption and realized that its crude architecture did not allow for a complex security system. He hit the latch that was pressing against the side of the bike chain with his small prybar, knocking it out of the way. He was then able to lift the door.

After that, Will hopped into the truck and started off. The truck had a good feeling of torque to it. It wasn't sluggish getting up the ramp and was plenty responsive on the right turn to escape the lot. The carport was behind the building, so coming around, he paused to get a better look out at the front of the building just to satisfy his curiosity. He felt nowhere near satisfied, gazing at that skeleton that was most certainly not there anymore. It even looked like it fell from Rayne's balcony. He shook his head, not sure what to make of the ghostly shape that he saw before starting his journey.

CHAPTER 6

THE REASON FOR Will's apparent sluggishness on the road was that, with all the wreckage and debris, these speed limits basically enforced themselves. He drove for a few hours without any particular event. More wreckage, lots of pretty much open road in some parts. Will was surprised to find that there was plenty of forest untouched by the effects of the bombs. But the sky was quickly becoming wrong. The sense of wrongness only increased as he headed towards the border. The sky resembled a disease of green and blue mixtures and terribly unsettling currents hidden behind contemptuous clouds of nausea.

It was deeply unsettling looking up at a sky of that disposition. The leaves that remained on these untouched forests took on a different plethora of colors as well. Some of them showed the gray, brown and black disfiguring like you'd expect, but as he moved along, a lot of them were muted and dark colors of purple, orange and blue. These colors were not simply random in their distribution but were dominant in waves mutating from one color to the next.

The long drive turned out to be a catalyst for thought and worry once he got past the 'looking for danger' phase in the first hour or so. He thought a lot about his parents. His father was a retired tradesman. An auto mechanic who was really more of a general mechanic, as many of them are. Will could swear by his father's ability to fix anything. Even without much experience with the object he was able to figure it out quickly. There are very few everyday things that are more complicated than cars. His father had retired too young by his own opinion. He was sixty-five, yes. But he always felt that his job, which was comfortable enough, could last him into his seventies if he just took it easy. The arthritis in his hands said otherwise. Still, he could tinker with things which made him happy. He wouldn't admit to it all the time as he seemed to grumble when his wife asked him to fix anything or explain to her how he did it. But she was smarter than that.

Will slowed down as he came up to a congested part of the road where three cars connected haphazardly right across it. He didn't feel like taking the risk of going off road, so the only way through was to push them out of the way. He slowed down and approached to push the back end of the middle car. The truck succeeded pretty easily, and he was on his way.

His mother would sometimes break things on purpose. She did little things like that a lot, she created puzzles for Will's father to solve. It was a careful dance of whatever would keep him from going crazy with complacency. Will's mother was a totally different kind of woman out there in the world, possibly even a benevolent one. She was the editor in chief of a national news firm. She was opinionated, strong-willed and tactical. She was the kind to always know her market value. But she also kept it thankfully separate from family affairs. She wore her opinions like a jacket, by her own words. "Wear it around town, show it to anyone you like, but leave it at the door when you get home and for god's sake don't sleep in it."

When Will was a kid, he always reveled in his mom's stories of her job. He could swear she put on a superhero cape when she left, though it was just a mink coat in the winter. You see, her job was rather complex. She was the editor in chief, sure, but beyond that she was also partly an advertising executive for her ability to choose the stories that would draw clicks. She was part secret agent, as her prominence in the industry led to her meeting very influential people on occasion. She knew how to pry and sly her way to leads on where new stories might be found through conversation alone.

She knew many figures who would actually tip her off to things that were happening in their respective industries or businesses. It wasn't a paid exchange. For thirty years she cultivated many partners in the business by holding true to a policy of "first come, first served". What that meant to her was that the first ones to give her good leads on where a story might develop were covered positively if it involved them. The power of spin opened many doors and closed the ones of her enemies and competitors.

There really wasn't much competition left against his mother and the industry knew it. She made damn sure her salary and bonuses reflected it too. Will thought that people might think of her actions as immoral or that people like her were evil or dishonest or maybe even the problem with media in Canada. They might be right, but only a little. You see, she didn't remain this cruel and manipulative in this industry. When she had Will, it changed. She was always a competitive spirit, sure. She had to learn how to get by on her own at fourteen. She was kicked out by her parents, who apparently didn't care either way. Her puberty was rough on the family and after a few years of negligence, they decided they couldn't do it anymore. She stayed at her aunt's place for a time and then became roommates with the closest thing she had to a friend at seventeen.

It was rough on her. For a long time of her sixty-three-year life, she didn't really care about anything. She acted, yes. She didn't collapse or implode. But it was very unfeeling. Forced to grow up quick, she had a certain hibernation of her very soul. She met Will's father at an auto shop and put up with his advances only barely in the beginning. And only because there was no one else who cared to compliment her. But also, she needed her car back. She didn't mind that bit of leverage, though, and he didn't do it on purpose. She could tell that. This was just the only place they ever met. She got plenty of compliments now, but that was just business. She warmed up to him slowly every six-month checkup and eventually decided this was the best she could ask or hope for. She didn't have her sights set very high.

That was not a mark against Will's father. He was a good enough man and better than most. He was patient, knowledgeable and thick-skinned. He kept himself out of trouble. They didn't have the perfect marriage. No one does. But unlike some, they were smart enough to know it doesn't get any better than this, really. They stuck together because he was the very last bastion of security for her real self. He was the valiant knight who kept the dragon of her career at bay, lest it eat up her whole life.

He was a simple kind of man. He loved her because she was pretty to him. She was smart and caring. Everyone else was so rough and he went through enough roughness at his job. He needed a softer personality, but one that wasn't useless. And he felt compelled to love her after she confessed her childhood to him. He thought he found the diamond in the rough. He was right. Will's mother was good for him in every way he could reasonably want. They didn't fight much. The father was too patient and the mother's job itself was confrontational and dramatic by nature.

Will's mother had a certain way of being protective of them. A lot of mothers start to take it easy after their only son is born. But Will's mother decided that was all the proof she needed that she couldn't afford to take it easy. She saw the world through a different lens. She started making moves. She reasoned that the world had been unduly rough to her. Not just by her lack of fortune in childhood and by birth. But there was also a severe reluctance for anyone in this world to help her going forward. Neither governments, nor companies, or even individuals would step to the plate to give her reasonable opportunity to move past the basic covering of her bills. Everything she had she had to fight for, almost clawing. Every time she asked, they would say, "It's not policy to pay out an extra dollar an hour to people who haven't been here five years" or "Not our problem" or she would get preached at by the old "personal responsibility" trope.

She was young and understanding through her frustration at first. But as she grew older, she realized that policy wasn't the law. It could be changed by any person, any time. Exceptions could be made, and franchisees had the power to decide if she was given a raise or not. The world was a lot more flexible than their laziness and nonchalance permitted. Then she realized that the very same people who told her to take "personal responsibility" (whatever that meant given her situation and that fact that she was trying her best) couldn't hold themselves accountable at all when they got into trouble.

She was mad then in a sort of passive-aggressive cynicism for many years. She kept up a rather well-written column in a local newspaper under an alias, exposing practices of certain businesses. It was a hit in her small, gossip-driven city. And that was how she started editing for a national network just before the internet became a popular way to digest news. She decided that when she was successful, and she would be, she would decide that these same people were simply "not her problem" and would not benefit within the terms of *her* new "policy".

It wasn't her problem that they never learned or cared how to fact check a news story. It wasn't her problem that their business had some scandal. If they didn't serve her purposes, she would bury them and never look back. It wasn't her problem that millions of people enslaved their "dumbasses", in her words, to her cultivated news feed and hung on every word of her personal militia of reporters and investigators. She commanded a certain power that you only get when you're ready to do anything to get what you want. It was sinister, yes, but not totally.

She not only had control over resources herself. But she was rather particular about businesses that donated large sums to charities that help young women out of tough spots. It seemed, for some reason, that those businesses that donated never got the stink eye from her goons, no matter what. Funding had never been better for those charities. Will's mother maintained that weak spot perpetually. Businesses knew about it and used it to get on her good side, which was her plan. Many of the charities had used the decades of stable resources to grow regionally, with one growing into a national outreach.

Was his mother a hero, like Will thought as a kid? "Damn straight," he defended with certainty. Every time he thought of her, he became enamored with her story, and what the latest business was about the country. She had decided that if the populace couldn't be motivated to help girls like her on their own, then she would simply use them to do it herself. Make no mistake, she farmed these people. Businesses and viewers alike. She created a nearly agricultural practice out of it. There were seasons for news like elections, seeds to be planted and a harvest to be had along with a nice profit and lots of open space to plant whatever she thought most profitable for her and the network for next year's bounty.

Her absolute priority was securing her enormous salary to set her family up for life. She'd rather be damned then leave her family vulnerable. They were the only ones she didn't have to put on appearances for. It was the only place she could really be herself. But her power was in domestic politics and business. She never had her fingers very deep in the international politics pie. She could never have prepared them for what was to come. In fact, as Will drove, he realized that nothing was prepared. Not even the government.

He hated not knowing if they were doing alright. Not many people were after the bombs, apparently. Will hadn't seen anybody since he started driving. No scavengers or looters, confirming what he thought earlier. The people likely to go outside and cause trouble were dead already. Will hoped that they got his text and that they were far enough away from any blasts.

Will was nearing the border at Buffalo. He decided to take the route north of the city of Niagara Falls. He hoped the checkpoint was empty as it didn't look likely that a manned presence would be sustained. Even if there were people here, would they really risk exposure just to ask for his passport and his reason for visiting? It wasn't particularly tourist season, but that doesn't mean the border traffic would be calm. Still, there was a particular order in which the cars were arranged. The chaos of the normal streets didn't seem to reach here as much.

Maybe it was because everyone was sitting in their lineup of cars, and not actively driving. Regardless, with some clever maneuvering around cars, pushing smaller ones out of the way, driving up sidewalks and through blocked-off areas which were guarded by nothing more than traffic cones, portable metal fences and tape, he successfully made it through the border using these weaknesses. This truck was perfect for bulldozing small obstacles. It could prevent much of the damage to itself with those rails on the front and had the heft and the power to move things.

It was odd, though. As he passed through the border, he could have sworn he had seen something. Just over to the right of the vehicle. Partially obfuscated by the fog that occasionally condensed on the inside of Will's visor as he breathed. A hitchhiker. A silhouette of an undefined person sticking out a thumb. However, the person did not appear in the rear-view mirrors. Will brushed it off as he had to pay attention to the road. He was officially in the United States.

It normally didn't take very long. In most of Ontario south of Toronto, he was only really a couple hours' drive from the US at any given time.

It took a little longer to do it now because of the complications on the road. Will glanced at his watch. It was now close to five o'clock and he decided that he didn't want to leave the building of a campsite too late, in case it took him longer to find good firewood than he'd like. He drove south to try to find the least dreadful spot to set up camp. But, as he approached Buffalo, New York, he noticed the trees blackening as he moved closer and lurching away from the epicenter in a much larger and more pronounced area of effect than he experienced in Canada. He spotted a fog in that direction as well.

He figured it might be rain over there, as it often resembles a fog from afar. Moving even further south, he saw that the rain was green and yellow. Then it took on the shape of a large dome. And then it wasn't actually rain at all. It was an enormous cloud that resembled gas with the source being unknown, but definitely fixed on the center of the city. And then he witnessed the curving architecture of what looked like highway overpasses and skyscrapers which were only visible in that smooth cloud due to their extreme corners and unhealthy leaning and bending. He felt a disturbing wonder wash over him as he realized that this was what remained of Buffalo, New York. He stopped briefly to get out his binoculars and look. The wonder twisted into confusion as the shapes rendered themselves a little better. They were not overpasses or buildings but pipes of incredible interwoven structure. Will was completely transfixed in his now halted truck.

It was like a giant cage that engulfed the once populated city. It didn't have the definite shape or structure of one that was built, though. And it bent at such odd geometries in towards itself. It was a completely alien shape to this world. As Will's view got better, he noticed individual elbows and joints in the layout. But it definitely wasn't built like that.

Will continued to move towards a place to camp, thinking that his tiredness was making him see things. He felt compelled towards a rather enchanting bit of forest. He drove off road for a bit down a secluded trail as branches intrusively scraped the outside of the small truck. He found a comfortable opening and went forward without the truck for some time in search of water he could test. There was a small creek maybe half a kilometer away from the campsite. When tested, the Geiger counter told him it was decent water. He would still need to run it through a cloth filter and boil it, but it seemed good otherwise. The point of this, he thought, was to save his good water in the truck for times when he would not have access to radiation-free water. He was far away from Buffalo, but the water being so clean was still puzzling.

The creek was secluded, and its source came from a direction farther away from Buffalo. It was flanked on both sides by a large ridgeline of dirt and exposed roots, about three or four feet tall. He gathered the water up in his mylar pouch and went back to the potential campsite. He didn't have to build a shelter, as he could sleep in the truck, and proceeded instead to make a firepit depressed into the ground. He built up crude dirt walls on all sides so that it wouldn't be visible from afar and decided to light it immediately. He gathered and shaved sticks so they would take flame better. In a small bag he had a ferrocerium rod and a steel striker. He lit the dead leaves on fire instantly and started stacking the sticks in a blueprint for the rest of the fire-building. He chopped and processed larger wood with his kukri and made up a pretty good pile to last a few hours. He wouldn't need it in the night as it was summertime.

He boiled his water in a small pot that he grabbed off his main bag and didn't have much time before he was tired. The sun was setting, and he wanted to be up early again. But he couldn't believe his luck, a rabbit hopped into the open area just twenty feet from Will's fire. It seemed to not notice him but smelled the fire. Will quietly drew his bow, which was leaning against a tree. The rabbit might have been deaf and blind from the bombs, the poor thing. He fired and killed it in one good, clean shot. The Geiger counter approved of the kill and declared it good to eat. He cleaned the animal out, skinned it and checked for parasites as are sometimes common in small mammals.

He gave it a quick wash with a cloth just to be sure he got rid of any fly eggs or anything else that might have used the poor rabbit's body as a host. It was very strange that this rabbit was clean. Will knew that the Geiger counter worked because it warned him about Rayne's furniture back in Canada. He had guessed that the rabbit was affected by the bombs and was possibly unable to perceive him because it was completely abnormal for a rabbit to approach an active campsite. But if it was affected, why wasn't it radioactive? This was all very strange, but Will knew better than to complain about good food after surviving on meal bars down in the carport.

He cooked the thing a little well done, just to be sure it

was a thorough cook because the temperature of an open fire could fluctuate due to wind or the dampness of the wood. It felt good to eat it. He hadn't had meat in probably more than a week. It was gamey and a little weird, but it was protein. Much-needed protein.

But there was something terribly wrong and ominous about that metal structure over Buffalo. It wasn't natural.

CHAPTER 7

WILL SLEPT SOUNDLY that night in the truck due to his emotional exhaustion from the day prior. He awoke in the morning to the flickering of the sun in his eyes and the sound of stones and dirt falling next to the truck. He squinted. And then, once his mind realized it, his jaw shuddered in disbelief. A giant metal pipe bent in an unhealthy, molten curve of cooled steel which reminded him of the metal structure over Buffalo. It had human markings indicating numbers and dates. The red line of spray paint had long faded down to a barely visible strip. It tried to dictate something about the pipe to service personnel. But it was only one part of an unbelievable structure which covered much of the sky. This new metal sky was mangled by natural trauma of force and heat and turned at dedicated elbows at various angles and was strapped together by metal frames. The pipes were not clean. Dirt clumped generously at various locations along the maze-like puzzles of twisted steel.

Random intervals of green and yellow clouds swung from pipe to pipe like a monkey through a jungle. Everything they touched seemed to burn, and steam escaped at the nearest opportunity. And then there was that lumbering sound. It was a decadent, heavy, aching sound of stressed metal trying to carry the weight of a city. The structure broke the trees when they were caught in the geometry of the heinous steel trap. And it left its hefty footprint in the soft dirt of the forest. Will scanned the structure for signs of anything. He read more on the noisy pipes and finally found some words that meant something to him.

BUFFALO WATER DEPARTMENT

Will was completely beside himself as he pressed his face against the window of the truck door. The entire damn underground pipe network surrounded him. Every pipe that connected every house, apartment building or business to the water supply in a city of a quarter of a million people was currently over his campsite. Will was stupefied. He thought of the fact that the bomb that hit the city must have been enormous, given how far away the trees in their black cloaks leaned away from the impact site in an immeasurable circle of death. Could it really have vacuumed up that much dirt into the mushroom cloud to unearth the city's entire water infrastructure? The evidence for this idea growled and twanged all around him. The true scale of this cage that blocked out the sun suddenly hit. Those guttural sounds of steel thunder were much farther away than he thought, and louder than he cared to imagine.

It was truly a maze, even on the ground. Will knew he had to find a way out of here before something fell on him. He wasn't about to wait for this thing to move. But that was just it, wasn't it? The proverbial elephant in the room. How the actual hell did it move all the way to his campsite in the first place? And *so quietly*. He was thinking about the fact that nothing could have pushed this monstrosity anywhere. But even then, he was proven wrong.

These green clouds of burning and boiling were moving around the structure at random, causing many sounds of stress. But this time they moved almost deliberately towards the south side. Their combined effects caused the water in the pipes to boil and steam to thrust out of the collars of these pipe junctions. They collectively changed the water pressure and caused the monster to rupture, with an almost ear-splitting sound. Will covered his hearing organs desperately. If he wasn't protected at least a little by the truck's windows being closed, that would've hurt even more.

The colossus moved much easier than Will thought it could. It lurched southward in one heaving motion, tearing up the ground around the truck. Pipes bent at incredulous angles to accommodate the changing pressures. They acted like millions of legs contributing their small share of its acceleration. It slowly gathered up the necessary momentum to roll like a tumbleweed. It shook the ground with uneasy vibrations and left a path of broken trees in its wake. This was easily the single most dangerous thing on land, he thought. And it was going south.

Will decided to watch it with his binoculars. It didn't get far before he saw it veer eastward. And Will thought it looked as though it was trying not to. It was pulling away from the source while continuing in a compromised southward general direction. And it was then that a beam of light from the east appeared to connect to the monster. The light became more and more vibrant until it ripped off an enormous chunk of pipe infrastructure with the scratching thunder of shearing metal. Almost a quarter of the beast was taken in this way. This seemed to relieve some of the traction that the beam had on the monster. It was wounded. Water and steam sputtered and exploded out of the open parts as it tried to run away. It was now moving slower. The beam of light dragged the pieces it stole across the land at uncomfortable speeds and seared the ground it left behind.

The monster tried to fix itself by fusing the leakages, but it was too little, too late. It bled sewage and water all over itself. It tried to move, but the water pressure likely wasn't there anymore. The structure sagged in defeat, waiting to collapse from the unsupported weight of empty pipes. It wouldn't get the chance to die peacefully. The beam came back. Or perhaps it was a second beam. Even more intense than the first light, it found its prey without having to search for it and tore it apart as it dragged the hundred-thousand-ton carcass eastward without further resistance from it, destroying the beauty of the countryside in its path. Will felt awful. He felt guilty that the most amazing thing he'd ever seen just got torn to pieces by a force he couldn't understand. It was some kind of cosmic injustice that wasn't simply settled just because the Buffalo pipes wouldn't pose a threat anymore.

He shook his head to ensure that he wasn't still sleeping. Something about all of this was horribly wrong, he thought. He decided he could think about it more on the road. He wanted to head south and go far away from this place. The truck crawled along the ground, retracing the way out of that spot that used to be lovely, before the tumbleweed. And then, just as he turned on the road, there he was. The hitchhiker from before. Will couldn't be sure it was the same guy, of course. But he had the same dark silhouette and stuck his thumb out rather obviously. Ordinarily, Will wouldn't think that stopping for a stranger at the end of the world was a good idea. But he just had to know one thing. He rolled down his window slightly.

"Hey, did you see the same thing I just did?"

"That… depends… on what… you… did see." The man's voice was heavy and slightly confusing. It wasn't threatening or sketchy. But it was very strange in a way that couldn't be defined. He spoke very deliberately, almost like he didn't really speak English. But he had no other accent.

"Umm…" Will was struggling here. He didn't want to seem crazy by explaining it if it might've just been him that saw it.

"You mean… big… metal?" The man labored to find the words. He didn't seem to be on drugs. He stood perfectly still, like a statue. His eyes met Will's directly and held there. His face did not hold stress or anxiety.

"Yes!" Will was too excited about this new reality to worry about this man's particular condition. He breathed a large sigh of relief. "Yeah, like what the hell was that, eh? It almost crushed me while I slept, but I didn't hear it until I woke up."

"Yes… it was… very bad." The man took a breath for the first time in this whole conversation. It seemed like he only remembered to do it when Will drew in that large breath and expanded his chest.

"Are you alright, man? You seem a little off, no offense," Will prodded. He finally let the discomfort win against his politeness. And tensed up on his driving foot just in case the man proved violent.

"No, it is okay… I am… it is… speech im-ped-i-ment."

The man was correcting himself almost like he was reading from a book on how to use conversational English. He certainly put in work to say the words correctly, but he added emphasis in very strange places.

"Oh! Sorry about that..." Will didn't want to pry about his condition anymore. He seemed like a well-intentioned guy and Will felt sorry about his position out here.

"It's okay... every-one... ask." The man smiled for the first time too. It was an awkward smile that didn't really understand how the mouth works, but it wasn't overinvested, and it got the job done.

"Where are you headed?" Will said while unlocking the door. The man very strictly adhered to a stock animation of "human getting into passenger seat". Will got the feeling it was more than just a speech impediment, but considered no harm done and accepted the man's strange animation to be some kind of OCD or maybe even an injury or something. He didn't want to pry anyway.

"New York City," the man said deliberately, as though from an old recording. Will suddenly felt as though he really should go to New York City.

"Why? What's there?" Will objected but could only bring himself to slightly disagree with the direction. He remembered that was the same way that the monster was dragged off too.

"My... wife... and... son," the man lumbered out from his memory. Upon the word "wife", Will saw a picture of a woman in his mind. She was beautiful with light skin and dark hair. Upon the word "son", he was given a mental image of a boy who was a different nationality than both of them. He felt the kid was probably adopted. Will felt even more compelled to go now. This man was essentially on the same mission as him. He couldn't really leave someone hanging out to dry when he knew damn well the twisting feeling of being far away from your loved ones and whether or not they're in danger. Will started to drive forward and turned eastward when the man interrupted.

"Wait... roads... blocked... east. Try... train in... Buffalo." Will immediately stopped to absorb what the hell had just been said to him.

"Uh, we can try other roads instead. The trains probably don't work. Especially in Buffalo. You know the giant pipe thing? That used to be Buffalo. That was all that remained when I came through yesterday."

The man seemed to search for words. "That was only... part of... Buffalo. Depew... is not... as bad. Train is... Maple Leaf line. Arrived in... Depew... never departed. All other roads blocked. New York City was... busy." His English was improving. It was becoming more like Will's. At least that last part he said made sense. New York would have been bad.

"But still, unless you know how to drive a train, we're shit outta luck, bud."

"I do," he said confidently.

Will decided that this guy's story was fixing itself. He thought it was weird that some random hitchhiker knew exactly what train was in exactly what place or that all the roads were busy. But if he worked with trains, this made sense. His proximity to Buffalo also made sense if that was his normal route. But just one thing stuck out. If he was a train conductor, why did he need Will's help to get to a train?

"Oh. Well, do you know how long that train usually took to get to New York?"

"Eight hours," he said dryly as a matter of fact. "But... we can do it... faster."

So, Will turned the truck around and made for the direction of Buffalo. He got directions from this guy but realized he didn't know his name.

"James," he said, even though Will didn't ask yet.

"Sorry?"

"My name is James. What... is yours?"

"Will. It's a pleasure to meet you."

"Yes, I... agree."

Will thought that was a good-hearted kind of funny.

"Where are you from, James?"

James seemed to struggle with this one more than with his own name. "Buffalo," he finally let out. "How about you?"

"I'm from Canada." Will decided to name the country rather than the city because he expected that to be clearer for Americans. "This might sound like a weird question, but did I see you up near the border hitchhiking?" Will couldn't resist asking that anymore.

"No... that was... someone else," he answered.

The only thing suspicious about that in Will's mind was that he insisted it was someone else, like he knew it had happened at all. That suspicion was quickly overrun by a wave of single-minded determination to reach Depew station, which was still a little way away according to James, but rapidly approaching. They had been driving for all of ten minutes.

"So how long have you been a train conductor?"

"Twenty years," James said. Will thought this was strange as he didn't think the man looked any older than twenty himself. He looked over to James, who was now sporting graying hair that he did not notice before. "We're here."

Will stepped on the brakes to bring them to a gradual stop. He had no idea how they crossed so much distance so quickly. On top of that, there were no cars in the road the whole way here. But there were cars everywhere else. The station looked to be in good condition. Actually, it was the only good-looking structure around them. The rest were all half collapsed, fully flattened or burned out. The windows were broken on the station, but that was the extent of it. Will felt something he shouldn't have.

"How did we—" Will began to ask, but he was then overcome by an intense feeling that they need to get on that train quickly and he shut up and picked up his pace. They crossed the platform towards the only train engine that was actually sitting there. Again, it was in good condition. James told Will to get on the engine while he disconnected it from the rest of the train. James appeared a few seconds later, claiming the job was done, and studied the controls.

"Wait, I have to grab my supplies from the truck," Will said. The urge to get onboard the train had been too distracting for him to remember his food and water that he had been so careful to save while camping.

"You… should get some sleep," James suggested flatly.

Will really felt like he needed some sleep. He curled up on the floor and fell asleep immediately.

CHAPTER 8

"**W**E'RE HERE," WILL heard as his eyes opened stickily from a sleep that he wasn't tired enough to have. He tried to rub his eyes but hit the face shield on the gas mask he didn't remember putting on. Glazed over and humbled by the bright light, he looked at his watch. It was 10:30pm, which was strange. It must have been perfect daylight out, given the brightness. He looked behind himself to find the total inventory of his supplies. James must've grabbed them. He didn't see James in the front of the engine. He gathered himself up and looked out the side window to the west. He just wanted to see if there was perhaps a late sunset that was causing all the light. What he saw was not that at all. He saw a painting of a sky that would be perfect if it wasn't moving. Burning orange streaks foolishly flailed in the west to slice up the predatory darkness of a night that was supposed to happen everywhere on this hemisphere.

The dark of night was cordoned off in the west, arrested by a light from the east so powerful it was like a resurrected sun. The deep black of the west mixed irresponsibly with the blood-red hues of the light over the dark gray clouds. It was gorgeous. They were at the train station in Yonkers, northwest of The Bronx and on the northernmost outskirts of what you might call New York City if you really wanted to lump it all into the same place. They couldn't get any closer than this, though. Not on the surface. And then, pivoting to the windows up at the front of the train, facing south, Will saw the source of all that light.

The thing towered taller than the Empire State building, even though the building itself was nowhere to be seen for comparison. Spearing out in all directions, it was an angry orange and yellow eminence. It looked like it was a giant mushroom cloud that decided to stick around after the rest of physics knew well enough to disperse. But this one was awfully different from how he thought a mushroom cloud should look. It had a core of brilliant white which drew up material from the ground and poured it into the air, creating the mushroom shape.

But the matter didn't simply fall back down elsewhere. It looked like it was draining all the buildings it could find their essence and soul. Pirouettes of dust stripped from the faces of those buildings that, just a week ago, had been bustling with the regular business of New York. It created a sort of sub-atmosphere cloud when they all combined near that white ball.

The materials that got thrown out of the top of the singularity seemed to circle back and orbit the white core briefly before falling into its gravity. Along the elliptical orbit of concrete dust and molten slag, there were eyes. Many towering ovals for eyes that shifted randomly like a lava lamp across the surface of this mushroom cloud which made it really look more like a jellyfish or a squid standing upright.

The eyes sprayed light over random metallic objects and lifted them towards itself for consumption. It wasn't horrible to look at so far as brightness goes. It was quite mesmerizing. Will thought, in all his excited yet disoriented grogginess, that they were too far away for it to get them. But then he remembered that Buffalo tumbleweed of pipes. He didn't believe his own thoughts at first. Could this thing really have devoured that beast? Could it have grabbed it from across the entire state? If it did, then presumably it was because of how much metal was in it.

New York was flat in a large radius around the Inferno. Sucked dry by this singularity of light and energy. Will knew that they were in danger. As a matter of fact, they might just be inside the most metal thing in the vicinity. The train engine. Will scrambled outside, checking his poncho and mask to make sure it was covering him well enough. He found James at the front of the train, standing in his normal statuesque pose. He was studying the anomaly with his eyes.

"James? Buddy, we've gotta get underground or something. We both saw what that thing did to those pipes in Buffalo. And we're in a metal train."

"The air is… clean, no need to wear the mask. That… thing… sucked the… pollution out of the air."

"How the hell did bombs make that thing?" Will asked, incredulous.

"They didn't," James said matter-of-factly. "But the… bombs… provided energy. Sometimes that is all you need. That is my… opinion, anyway."

"Alright," Will said, not actually accepting the story. He felt as though James was holding back a lot. Literally nothing about him made sense. He wanted to ask what they were really doing in New York, but he felt like he couldn't ask that for some reason. He loathed the fact that this man took him far away from his truck and prevented him from going south. "But it could also suck us out of the air if we don't move soon. Do you know where the nearest subway entrance is? To go underground?"

"Right this way." James and Will hopped on the train and pushed it through the bend of the Spuyten Duyvil creek, which is just about the most New York name for anything, ever. They proceeded to the Marble Hill train station and then walked into what used to be the Marble Hill stop on the number 1 line subway. Will tried to carry his water on his belt to free his hands for this new excursion.

"Don't worry. There will be... water where we go," James reassured.

Will didn't know how he could possibly know that. But he felt like he was under the influence to believe him no matter what. Like it or not, he was stuck with him for now. He grabbed his other things. The wind was steady and only hit hard when that giant squid-shaped cloud of Armageddon pulled some mass of moisture from the creek and river into its sphere of influence. The platform of Marble Hill is a raised one, over the streets. It connects to a bridge going south into Manhattan proper. They walked south, braving the winds and the wet before Will thought of something.

"Hey, James. Why do you think this thing grabbed the Buffalo pipes, but hasn't grabbed our train or the metal of this bridge?"

"Opportunity."

"What?" Will thought maybe James didn't understand the question. But he did.

"The... anomaly had to grab that one before it... got away. But it can grab this... stuff... whenever it wants."

Well, wasn't that the most horrible thing Will had ever heard.

"It... eats?" Will asked, prepared to flinch at the answer.

"It hunts... yes," James said. "It needs metal."

"So, wait..." Will said with a giggle of disbelief. "Wouldn't that mean we're trapped here? That if we tried to leave on that train, it would grab us too?"

"Yes," James declared, but he was not laughing.

"You can't be serious, man... You mean to tell me that it let us come here without disturbing us just because it knew we would bring it a snack?"

"Possibly... the other... option is that we're insignificant. We're... hiding from it."

Will contended with the fact that James was serious. And that it was the only explanation he could think of for such a difference in the priorities of this thing. That idea sat on Will's empty stomach uncomfortably. But he didn't allow the thought of this thing being intelligent to settle for long. It wasn't possible for a ball of fire to be aware enough to have priorities. It could have happened upon the great steel beast of Buffalo's pipe network randomly, after all. Just a random reaction of something that was obviously a little new to physics. A one-in-a-million spooky interaction. And that was such a nice cop-out. The concept of random chance has protected us from so many unbelievable mind-shattering horrors that would come to life if we didn't think random chance was more likely, more reasonable. He gazed at the anomaly between the buildings still standing when he could, minding his feet on the subway tracks. The thing was located in the middle of the big four. It was south of The Bronx and east of Manhattan Island across the East River. It was a good way north of Brooklyn and far west of Queens.

They dove underground at their earliest opportunity, and Will sighed at the new sense of safety. They proceeded further south along the subway lines, unafraid of the trains that weren't running anymore. The tunnels still retained their colors, but not their lights. James didn't seem to have any trouble seeing, but Will had to turn on his flashlight. Will commented about the little details and signs he noticed on the way. James just looked at things. It was in there that they met the first person as they moved through. A young guy was walking in the other direction, going out of the system. He was packed up to leave.

"Woah, hey there," Will said, tensing. James didn't seem to care. They were still a way off from each other, but Will learned just then that he didn't need to shout as the quiet subway walls carried his voice.

"Hey. Did you guys come from outside or something?" the kid asked in such a way as to betray his youth.

"Yeah... Are you going outside?" Will didn't believe so, but he asked out of amazement as there was nowhere else to go beyond that direction.

"That's right." The kid was grinning ear to ear, but he meant it.

"Are you aware of what's out there, my guy?!" Will quipped, not minding his tone.

"Yeah, 'my guy'. I was here when it happened," the kid said, offended.

"Oh, right. But... I guess... Why go out there?" Will struggled with that simple question.

The kid put his pack on the ground to talk a bit. "I'm going west. Early last week, I think the day after everything happened, we started getting weird radio signals, I guess. Over the subway intercoms I heard some weird shit." The kid paused in place.

"Weird shit, huh?" Will said, crossing his arms. "About out west?"

"Yeah, something about interceptors. I heard they were able to shoot a lot of them down." The kid was wistful, with only a small register of hope, as if he himself knew it was a long shot.

"And you heard that the day after? I thought everything in telecommunications would have been fried by the EMP…"

"That's what I thought!" he declared, vindicated. "But if the bombs never went off out there…" The kid led the statement on as though he wanted them to finish it.

"Holy shit… they could broadcast." Will trailed off to think about that as the kid nodded in pride. "Tell me the whole message. What exactly did you hear?"

The kid shuffled his feet. "A lot of it was garbled, I guess because of the range. But I heard a lot about the western coast. The signal kept interrupting, but it was like: 'We (static) managed to (static) stop many of them (static) it looks like (static) we're done (static).' It was static for a long while after that. So, I managed to pack up and now I think I'm finally brave enough to go."

"Wait…" Will paused to think out loud. And then copied back what he'd just heard. "We (static) managed to… something's not right about that. If it was that choppy… Then how do you know that they didn't say that they *never* managed to shoot many of them down? It sounds a lot like that static might have cut off words in the sentence."

The kid basically deflated, and his eyes rolled back. "I guess that's possible. But it's also possible that it was true what they said. It was said kinda fast."

"And you're willing to risk it all to go out there?"

The kid rolled his eyes as if he'd been through this conversation before and hated making this point. "Look, man. I don't know about you. But my mom was at work when that fucking thing invaded the city. I've got no reason to stay. There's a hope out there. I know what I heard."

"I'm so sorry to hear that." Will lowered his head for a moment in the pain of realizing that there used to be real people in these cities. "For me, my wife was stuck in Florida when it happened. I was on the phone with her, so we had warning on both ends. I have a good reason to believe she took cover and lived, but like you, I guess I'm just on that hope. I don't really know."

"I'm sorry to hear that too. But you're willing to risk coming down from Canada, so I can't be that crazy." The kid smirked.

"How—" Will began, unsure of how the kid came to know his country of origin.

"I heard you reading the signs here to your friend as if you were lost. You sorta sounded like that accent, so I guessed." The kid was proud of his reasoning ability.

"Oh. So, weren't you afraid we were armed or something? You just kinda came right through," Will said.

"No. Nobody is that willing to kill each other. Except for what's called 'the Worshipers'. Basically lunatics, but that's all I know. I haven't seen one yet and I plan on getting out of here before they get brave. Other than them, though, meeting someone else out here is like... your last chance to be human and talk about shit. That's why it was hard for me to decide to leave, but I know the subways were going eventually. That thing out there is eating New York from the ground up and out."

"Yeah, and Buffalo, apparently," Will added.

"Uh… What?" the kid asked flatly, eyes wide. Surely, he just misheard that.

"The city of Buffalo," Will said in a regretful manner. "Did you guys hear any kind of commotion within the last day? Like giant metal pipes clanging across the ground?"

The kid was clearly caught off guard by the description. "Yeah! We heard some of that and some rumbling and Jeremiah said the thing found new food from somewhere, but he couldn't believe the amount."

"Jeremiah? There are others?"

"There's a few of us left. But the fiery mushroom cloud got way bigger after eating… whatever that was…"

Will and James looked at each other. Will looked with horror. James didn't look that disturbed, really.

"Huh. Yeah, that was basically all that was left of Buffalo," Will said, slowly turning back towards the kid.

"Not… all. Some," James added sort of randomly.

Will thought about withholding the fact that it was a semiconscious tumbleweed, hydro-powered by its own water supply. He wanted to keep talking to this kid and thought sounding crazy was not the way to continue. But he felt pressed to be honest with him since the kid was going to go out that way anyhow.

"Look, this may sound crazy, but I think we're past that label, seeing as how there's a giant bomb monster eating New York." Will inhaled in preparation. "The pipes were lifted out of Buffalo by some crazy powerful bomb several times the power of whatever hit my place in Ontario. They were curled into a ball and basically rolled around like a giant tumbleweed. It tried to roll south but was caught by your monster there and you know the rest. I'm only saying that so you're aware that the bomb monster is not the only fucked up thing you're going to see out there."

The kid was thinking about this for a while. His eyes were staring through the ground at nothing in particular. "Shit," he said, as his only input.

"Can't you leave at daybreak? It's night outside and you mentioned those Worshiper people…"

"Nope. Everyone else has this fucked up idea of waiting until the tunnels start shaking before they move. I want to be far away from here before the Inferno gets that big." The kid pointed towards the exit of the tunnel.

"That makes sense, I suppose. So, you said there were others?"

"Uh, yeah. There's Jack, Dave and Ruth, who's his wife, and Jeremiah. They're down in there a ways but if you keep straight, you'll get to their camp. It's in the service door to your right. Just announce yourselves first. Dave doesn't want to shoot anybody, but everyone's scared, you know?"

"Yeah, of course," Will said. "If you don't mind me asking you just one more thing, what happened immediately after? You said you were waiting for the train, but what happened to the rest?"

"You pick up quick. I never said I was waiting for the train, but that's an interesting guess. Anyway… um…" There seemed to be some trepidation on his part. "Now it's my turn to sound crazy. Everyone who wasn't wearing fully ear-covering headphones dropped instantly and died. And then the bombs went off like five seconds later."

Will's eyes chose to roll back in his head. It took him about five seconds to physically recover from what he had just heard. "What?" was the only word he could eke out from his grimace.

"Yeah, I know. All of us that are here now were wearing some and listening to music when it happened, and we all heard the same thing. Our music was replaced by static that sounded like the ocean at a beach. Waves lapping and sort of grinding on the sand, you know?"

"And then the bombs went off?"

"Exactly. Then the ground rumbled and felt like an earthquake, and I heard the sound about five seconds later I would say. Something hit before the bombs that turned everyone off like robots. Jeremiah was a physics researcher at a lab somewhere. He's been trying to figure it out. He thinks it had something to do with the ears, but nobody in our group went deaf. If it was a sonic bomb, we'd all be deaf. That's what Jeremiah says."

"I think we have a lot to talk about with this Jeremiah guy," Will said.

He suddenly felt a cold breeze pushing him from deeper in the tunnel. The kid moved back against the far wall as Will moved his back against their side of the tunnel. There was a gust of wind that was powerful. It felt like an object was moving in front of them, but they couldn't see it. It was as if one great rectangle of air moved along the tracks all at once. Will's flashlight revealed windows rolling by them; their frames, and the train they were installed on, were translucent. They were a dark gray and a generally smoky texture, much like what Will thought was the ghost of Rayne up in the apartments. The train was perfectly silent but cold. Awfully cold.

After it passed, the kid goes, "Oh yeah, we also have ghost trains. They don't hurt you, physically. But one of them passed through Jack as he was smoking on the tracks. It put out his cigarette. But then he just kind of knelt there and cried for a while. He wouldn't answer us when we asked if he was okay. He still doesn't want to talk about it. So, watch out for these things."

And then there was a silence as they tried to find anything else worth discussing. There was nothing that came to mind just now. "I guess we'll let you go, then. Be careful with the water that you drink. Radiation loves that stuff," Will warned.

"Wait," the kid said. "How exactly did you guys get here?"

"James here found a train that could run, and we took it here from the north tracks. But don't take it back to Buffalo. James suspects that the Inferno can hunt opportunistically. If you try to leave with its food, it might target you."

"Oh, fuck off. No way," the kid said with a start of laughter. He saw James' expression and dropped the laughter off a cliff.

"Yeah. I'm not sure how we'll get out either," Will said despondently.

"You will," James assured.

"Alright." The kid started to leave. "I'll probably cross the bridge over the Hudson into New Jersey then. See you, guys. And good luck."

"Yeah, man. Thanks for the goodwill. Good luck to you too."

Will thought about those being the last words he said to the young man. He was about to die, probably. New Jersey wasn't a fun place before the war, and now it would be worse. But were those even his greatest concerns? He would have to trek across the whole country to find anything even close to "out west". The middle of nowhere could be promising, but America kept a lot of its missile bases in rural stretches of the country. They may have been hit worse. And then if he got there and he was wrong? If all the sands of Utah and California were glass? Well, Will didn't want to think about what the kid might do.

But he seemed hopeful enough. That would probably change. Will already felt fatigued. He had felt something akin to disgust and hate when the kid mentioned how the people dropped instantly without something covering their ears. As if Will thought that it was just another mystery that would only barely be solved enough to haunt your dreams.

Will and James continued on in the tunnels, making sure to keep to one side of it just in case. And then they saw a light flickering a way down. Will did not like that they had to learn more about all this, but he mostly had a chance to breath and relax as they walked down the tunnels. When they were sufficiently close that Will thought his voice would carry, he announced their presence. There was no response.

Coming up to the platform, there were bodies. They had fallen where they stood but slumped over each other as they had no free space to fall, as huddled up for the train as they were when the bombs landed. Their legs were all bent at the knee and their torsos straightened out. Evidence of a group of standing people who died before they hit the ground. Their carcasses toppled each other outward from the center of the group like dominoes. It smelled bad, but not terrible as long as they kept their distance. The light flickering was someone's flashlight running out of battery. They were limp on a bench and looked like they were taking a nap and that they didn't have the time to choose where to lie, with an open book by their feet with the flashlight beside it.

Will decided, for no good reason, to mount the platform and look at what book it was. He didn't smell as much through the mask, so he put it on. It was a wonderful story. *The Call of Cthulhu* by H.P. Lovecraft. On the page that was open, there was a red mark at the beginning and end of one sentence in particular, which was fairly well-known:

"The sciences, each straining in its own direction, have hitherto harmed us little; but some day the piecing together of dissociated knowledge will open up such terrifying vistas of reality, and of our frightful position therein, that we shall either go mad from the revelation or flee from the deadly light into the peace and safety of a new dark age."

That was particularly eerie. Almost anything Lovecraft could say would be eerie, though, given the circumstances. Putting the book down, they continued on until they saw another platform in the darkness of the tunnels. Will shone the light and noted that it was in a similar state as the first one. Bodies. Maybe a hundred slumping figures obscuring and wrapping themselves in clothes with a collage of fashion senses which used to be relevant.

But this time, as he turned away, he noticed some of them standing. That wasn't right and he whipped in the direction of what he thought he saw. The flashlight proved nothing more than the slumping bodies he knew were there. He turned slowly away and caught it again. He stared at them through his peripheral vision. Only, it wasn't a few of them standing. It was all of them. Translucent black, smoky figurines of people. The same look as the false image of Rayne at the apartments or the train they dodged at the entrance.

He was in awe. People looking at watches, phones, and waiting for the train. Then he saw them shuffle and gather closer towards the loading parts of the platform. That was not good.

"James, train's coming!"

James was already at the edge, where Will joined him. The ghostly train stopped at the platform and loaded the people on it. About a hundred people got off and then the train started down the tracks to maintain its schedule in the afterlife. All of those who got off simply stood there, waiting to get on again. Everything happened without a sound other than Will's breathing. It was there that Will wondered if the same smokey people existed at the other platform. The answer was probably yes, and he just didn't notice them as he entered their space directly. He shuddered at the thought of passing through one by accident. But if what the kid mentioned happened to this Jack character, then Will would expect some kind of psychological disturbance if he did cross the same space they occupied. Luckily, he felt nothing. Nothing yet.

CHAPTER 9

OVING FORWARD AGAIN, they found a service door into the maintenance hall. Upon opening it, Will announced them and they were greeted by a small service light still lit on the wall and a man saying, "Who's there?"

"Oh, I'm Will, this is James. We were told about you guys from that kid who wanted to leave here on his way out."

"Oh, yeah?" He had his handgun already out. "Give me proof that you talked to him and didn't kill him. Speak clearly and stay right where you are for now."

Despite the fact that he was pointing a gun at Will, who had his hands up, and James, who didn't, he did not come off as mean or aggressive. He was sort of soft spoken and his voice hitched with hesitancy and stress. He was a bulky and stout fella a little shorter than Will. Will decided to play it as cool as he could. He didn't believe Dave would shoot, and he believed this was Dave. And that was exactly their ticket.

"You're Dave, right? And you've got a wife named Ruth—" Dave seemed to tense up and trained the weapon hard when Will mentioned the wife's name. Will blinked rapidly in distress and felt he should hurry it up. "—and a researcher named Jeremiah and a guy named Jack, who I heard could be doing better." There was a little pause and then the gun lowered, but only a little.

"Yeah, alright. Sorry about the gun, but we've been getting Worshipers snooping around lately trying to deceive us into believing they're just strangers."

"Worshipers? Worshipers of what?" Will confounded.

"Uh, really? Just where are you two from? I can't believe that you haven't had problems with them and their 'holy conversion' and shit."

"Ontario, for myself. I'm heading south to find my wife in Florida, who was there on a business trip when it all happened," Will answered.

"Buffalo," James added. "I too… lost a wife. But also… a son. Here in the city."

"Holy shit, man. Were they on the surface when it happened?" Dave implored.

"Maybe…" James answered uneasily.

"Well, unfortunately we have yet to see that anyone on the surface survived. And you—" He looked at Will. "Aren't you a little far east for a man going south?"

"Tell me about it, but I'm helping James. He was hitchhiking and I picked him up on the way and figured I had to help."

There was a silence for a few seconds. "Oh, that's good of you," Dave said, lowering the weapon but still keeping it firmly in hand. "Well, do you have any news about the surface? Jeremiah's been looking for clues that life still exists outside of the subways. If you know anything, he's on the surface now, but he'll come back later. He always does."

"I haven't seen any humans, but the trees still live outside of cityscapes. But a lot of them are strange colors. I shot a rabbit with my bow, and it was clean of radiation."

"No shit? You guys had better talk to him then. He's up observing the surface again. You'll find him up on what's left of the Empire State building. Go down the line and come up on 33 Street. It'll just be west a couple a' blocks."

"The Empire State building survived?"

"Only the bottom half. Whatever hit Manhattan was powerful enough to peel off the top of the building and sent it crashing down. The bottom of it is still usable, though. It's got that old-century construction, yeah?"

Will picked up on the fact that he said something hit Manhattan, specifically. "Don't you think it's weird that something hit Manhattan Island, but that thing out there is across the river?"

"Well, the way it happened, by Jeremiah's account, is that several bombs hit New York City itself. One for every major area and then something bigger than death itself right in the bloody middle. He said it was possible there used to be five such mushroom clouds like that one now, but that all merged together on the middle one, which might have been intended. He can see the impact zones and the trails of their movement from up there, if you see him."

"Wait, hold on. Worshipers, right? What are they? The kid mentioned them before." Will needed to remember this if they were gonna go anywhere else safely.

"Alright, so Jeremiah has some idea that the people who worship the Inferno (that's what he calls it) were struck by the bomb's initial effects in such a way that they dropped all notion of sanity and self-awareness. They became these cult people, many of them burned pretty crispy. Their worship involves breaking down parts of the city with heavy tools to make it easier for that thing to feed. They're fuckin' wild. They don't normally have anything other than hammers as weapons, but that was yesterday, and that bow won't get you very far anyway if they swarm you. Jeremiah sneaks up there just fine, though, you guys should too. He thinks he may have a way to stop the Inferno."

"To stop it? How?" Will furled his brow.

"That's all I know, I swear. He just mentioned it before leaving."

"Alright, thanks. I guess that's our next stop," Will said. "Oh, by the way, do you know anything about those smoky-looking ghosts?"

Dave shrugged and threw his hands up. "Ask Jeremiah, man. He thinks it's a sickness that we have that makes us see shit. But if you're seeing it too, he might finally listen to what I've been saying. We saw the train hit Jack. Or not 'hit' but... you know what I mean. And then he randomly has a mental breakdown on the spot?" Dave chuckled in disbelief. "You know what Jeremiah said? 'He could be deathly afraid of trains and feared for his life.' Fuckin' bullshit. If you're asking me, and I guess you are, then I think they're real like you and me, but differently real. Like they're the same people who died, but it's like a looping recording of the last thing they were doing. Just replaying the same thing for all eternity because they never got to finish doing what they were doing. You know, unfinished business."

"Hmm..." Will grunted.

Will pondered this for a second. At this point, he had to accept anything as possible. And really, ghosts would be the least strange thing he had seen all week. It's just that they weren't white like bedsheets with an agenda of poltergeists like in the movies. Instead, they were blotchy puffs of cloudy black smoke making incredibly rough outlines of a person and repeating what they did before they died. But that didn't even come close to explaining Rayne's situation. In that situation, the ghostly apparition happened *before* her attempt to jump off the balcony.

Her attempt looked like it could have been rehearsed after that ghostly premonition. He supposed that it could either be the future or the past which was being shown by the ghosts. Or perhaps it was the future for the living and the past for the dead. After all, when he intervened, the skeleton on the ground disappeared. It was as if that future was severed. That made enough sense to him for the time being, and he found it strangely comforting that it might just be a recording of time and not conscious apparitions with a vendetta.

"Well, how have you guys been surviving?" Will asked to finally break the silence.

"Vending machines. I'm gonna get diabetes from all these candy bars, and on top of that I'm fuckin' sick of them, but that's sort of a long-term problem. The sugars and calories are short term and I need those if I'm even going to have a long term. The chips are alright, though. Not too sickening yet."

"Wow. Well, that's... interesting," Will said, feeling sorry for their predicament. "We've gotta get on with finding this Jeremiah guy. But thank you very much for not killing me."

"My pleasure, really," Dave confided. "I'd rather not ever have to do that again. Killing a Worshiper is something that has to happen, but it's still awful."

"Thanks," Will concluded.

Will decided to go and see this Jeremiah despite his impatient need to find Rachel. He knew they couldn't leave if what James was saying about the Inferno was even close to true. If it could reach across the whole state for some pipes, it could probably pick up a car without any issue even a couple states over. They bid farewell to good old Dave and went back out the way they came. They carefully trod through the tunnels, avoiding the occasional trains which sprinted silently through the subway lines. Will thought quite heavily about Rachel and his uneasiness about her predicament. He had just seen two of America's most recognizable cities destroyed by an incomprehensible power. He had no idea what the rest of the east coast would look like.

Initially, when he had nothing better to do in that underground carport and he was waiting to run out into the world, he tried to calculate Rachel's chance of being alive. He considered what he knew. The end had actually happened and that was unbelievable enough. But bombs were survivable. Unfortunately, not for most, but for those who were in a position to act on the news of the incoming threat, there was a good enough chance of living to hear the explosion. And you could hear it. Even though Will thought it was the most disturbing and widespread boom he had ever even conceived of, he knew it was contained to a particular radius. He knew the bomb had particular properties, though he couldn't fathom exact numbers.

He knew the bomb was hot, incredibly so. He knew it had the power to crush standing objects in its wake, undeniably. But this? Bombs so powerful they could tear up an entire city's worth of old waterworks and roll them up like a foil ball? And what of the weapons so strange that they turned off every human like a light switch unless they just so happened to be wearing headphones? And finally, that fireball. Eating metal like a power source to maintain its mass. This wasn't what he signed up for. When people talked about the end of the world, there were statistical projections of the percentage of ICBMs brought down by interception. It was always a horrid fifty or sixty percent success rate in simulations. It was possible to shoot them down, but it wasn't enough to violate the principal of mutually assured destruction among nations.

And everyone felt so safe with the knowledge that nobody would actually ever use them. It would be insane to do so, after all. But maybe there was another function at work. Maybe it was the murderer's idea to kill people as a form of suicide. People do insane things when they find the world no longer worth inhabiting under its current ruleset. How many homicides turn into suicides by the end of it? And that is even without the guarantee of mutually assured destruction. The murderer could run, hide or kill more. But instead, they decide to end it on their own terms. What if one of the many dictators on Earth felt the same way? That the world would never justify them. That they were likely enough to die in some revolution, ruining everything anyway. And for that matter, who started this war?

It didn't matter now, in the end. But the methods were so strange. And what if the function at work here was a disgust of a collective batch of humans? We know that such hysterics can lead to insanity in a collective led by a narcissist who considers himself a prophet of the true human image. Hitler is the example that comes to mind. What fits the Nazis best is the description of organized insanity. And Will wondered if Auschwitz was still standing. Maybe it wasn't. But if the cities were the primary target, then ironically, the very structures of human insanity lasted longer than the people who built them. There were always talks of lasers. If we simply had better or more abundant lasers, then we could shoot the missiles down. Will guessed that someone in Congress thought the survival of human beings was too expensive or unrealistic. It wouldn't be the first time. His thoughts were all over the place. Searching for answers he could never truly have.

But could lasers really have protected them from these effects? They obviously weren't told about all of the weapons being worked on in secret. The death bomb that shut off every New Yorker like an unplugged computer was nowhere to be found in any publicly available document on the planet. Not even theoretically. They had a working model without even a hint of theoretical research in the public. If we weren't told of the weapons themselves, then we certainly weren't told of their delivery systems. Normally countries would brag about their capabilities on paper, but actual performance is the hard part. All of this led Will to the conclusion that the world wasn't very well understood. So how could he calculate Rachel's survival? If anything like this hit anywhere close to Florida, she likely died before she could wince or blink. And that was gut-wrenching to think about.

Will thought intently on his mission. And about just what the hell he was doing in New York. He'd wasted a day following the directions of this James guy, whom he still didn't understand, to find his wife and child that were certainly dead. And now he was pretty sure he was stuck here, with that Inferno threatening to grab him if he left in any car worth driving. He resented James a lot for this, but then he thought that he and this guy actually had a lot in common, if he considered motivation. He was likely holding on to the same stupid shred of hope as Will. Seeing the world as having befallen a previously-thought-to-be impossible fate actually opened up a lot of possibility. Who says that horrors have free rein over the impossible? What if miracles snuck their way on to Planet Earth with the rest of the universe's impossibilities?

There were also those ghosts of smoke and repetition. Will figured maybe that's what James was after. Maybe he was searching for where his family could have been when it all happened. To find their smoky, blackened recording sitting in a hotel room, just to say goodbye to something other than that Inferno which almost certainly consumed them. Perhaps to see the smoky outline of his young son playing video games one last time. To ask him if he was winning. Maybe it would be enough for him to know that his son died having fun. The shadow wouldn't know he was there, but maybe James would stay with them anyway. He seemed like a man who was at the end of his rope. Will tried to open up a little.

"Hey, James. Do you have any parents?"

James spun around on his heels and glared at Will, not in anger, really. Just surprise. He took a long pause of about twenty seconds. "Not... anymore. Let's... keep... moving."

His words were deliberate and carefully selected, despite their simplicity. As if it would be too complicated or too personal to explain. Will allowed himself to think freely of James. What on Earth was it with this guy anyway? He was a complete rock. He didn't put his hands up when Dave pointed the gun at them, he didn't seem disturbed by anything, and he knew things or at least assumed things that no other human would. He walked like he couldn't be touched and at the same time he walked with purpose. It was like he'd been here and done all this before. He didn't talk much either. Was he an alien? A ghost with more physical presence than the others? Traveling with him was an odd experience. He didn't want to elaborate on anything personal and Will could sense he was hiding something big. Yet, despite all of this, he couldn't bring himself to dislike him personally. He always found a way to justify being with him despite his own priorities. To be fair, James was one of the only other humans, if he was human, so Will thought he might just be clinging to James as a companion for this dangerous world. Exactly like the feeling he had with Rayne. That they were basically strangers before the war, but now it was so difficult to leave her behind.

But, of course, there was the matter of himself. He felt awful about all this. Uncertainty was something you went to the movies for. It wasn't actually that fun waking up in your truck to half of Buffalo's pipe network burying you alive. It wasn't that fun being trapped in a city with a monster of strange physics. It wasn't fun being threatened with a firearm. This whole expedition reminded him of the world they lost. The ground provided them with anything they asked of it, like Eden. Humans could plant crops, harvest trees, build structures of business and residence and actually trust the ground to hold all of that stable. And then they cursed it with an occult power that they had no business messing with. Did they even deserve the Earth they were born on? Did they deserve an Earth so eager to give life that it grew even now after the end of days? In fifty years, Human legacy will crumble without maintenance. The vines and trees and grass will reclaim the land that was borrowed from them. They will hug and remember those tombstones of concrete and glass diligently and gently, until the weight of forgiveness and forgetfulness tears them down and erodes them back to sand.

Will felt a certain sickness. Not a cold of the head and throat, but a sickness of heart and mind. The world was a destabilized mess now. And Rachel was caught somewhere in it in Daytona Beach. He figured he had to complete the mission, whether or not she lived. Like James, just to say goodbye. He would probably stay with Rachel's body as well if he could stomach it. And if not, he would dig a grave for the both of them. There wasn't anything left otherwise. There were no adventures, not really. Will had the freedom to go anywhere in the country and see everything he wanted to see. But for what now? What actual purpose was there to go and see death everywhere you looked? To see the skeleton cities. To chronicle new monsters and anomalies in a bestiary of sorts. Really? That was the only other option. A speculative zoological... physicist with only a notebook and no degree. That's what he'd become. And something told him that wasn't a job you could sustain yourself on in this market.

CHAPTER 10

THE DARKNESS OF these tunnels was the perfect storm of thought-inducing oppression. It smelled like lubricant and concrete, partially. But most of the time it smelled like nothing and looked like nothing. Will's thoughts and observations were limited to a twenty-degree cone of light in front of him. The only feeling of note was the cold breeze that warned you to move to the left a little to make way for the trains. They were making their way to the 33 Street exit, following the signs. There were bodies and ghosts to avoid at the exit if you wanted to keep what was left of your sanity.

Coming out of there was like entering a portal to an alien landscape. They were closer to the Inferno, here, and it felt like it. There was a shortness of breath for Will, and he was breathing heavily climbing the stairs to the station. The air was speeding past them as it tore over the streets and around the buildings.

The buildings had this rounded look. Every edge, every corner was eroded cartoonishly by the high winds and the Inferno's gluttony for raw materials. Will donned the mask back on when he saw the wisps of dust leaking off the buildings toward the epicenter like watercolors. Will saw the Empire State. No wonder he hadn't seen it when they got off the train. Even with the top half gone, it was still one of the more imposing structures. Not much was left standing. The air smelled like a forge burning metal and it whistled hard like a high-performance turbo. The violence of the area was increasing with every passing hour. Will and James made their way to the Empire State. There wasn't any rubble on the roads. The Inferno probably picked all of it up. The other half of the skyscraper had fallen behind it and had been dragged a little farther east. They trusted the remaining building had enough structure left to support them.

Taking the old-century stairs to the top, they finally met the legendary Jeremiah. But it was a precarious situation. Will didn't want to start shouting their presence in case Worshipers were listening. The researcher almost met them with a bullet from the handgun he had pointed at them, but he also didn't want to draw attention to himself with the report of the gun. He lay in wait for them to come into full view and made sure they were normal before proceeding.

"Greetings, gentlemen." Jeremiah introduced his presence with his handgun still trained on them in case they were bad actors. He was a man in his mid-fifties with an unkempt goatee. On his head were a few valiant black hairs fighting off the hordes of gray around them. He was shorter than Will and slightly overweight, but his business casual attire fit him well. He cast a gaze of caution behind thick glasses.

Will was not getting used to having guns pointed at him. "I'm, uh, I'm Will, this is James. We came to find you on the advice of Dave and that kid who was leaving to go out west."

"Ah, you mean Charles? Good kid. I hope he makes it out there." Jeremiah lowered the gun.

"We don't have much time left that we can spare, Jeremiah. Do you know of any way to move past this Inferno?" Will had a new sense of urgency after his thoughts in the tunnels. He really shouldn't be playing detective to the end of the world while his wife's fate was still unknown.

"Unfortunately, not without destroying it."

"Seriously? I can't just leave?"

"I'm dead serious. If it was possible to leave without consequence then we would have done it already, don't you think? I tried to convince Charles to stay. He's a brave kid. He would have made destroying that thing easier."

"And how do you suppose that happens?"

"I've spent some time watching the area and I've noted a particular building that's being taken apart piece by piece by Worshipers. It's obvious enough that they want to maintain the stability of the Inferno. It ate a much smaller building all at once a few days ago and I could see the core of it destabilizing. At least, that's what I thought I saw. Our only real shot, in any event, is to give this new building some 'encouragement' to fall into the core."

"Okay, woah, woah, woah…" Will clutched his forehead in frustration. "Hang on. You mean to demolish a building? How? And why would we gamble on feeding it?"

"There's a lot to unpack here," Jeremiah said, positioning himself to explain the thing in the distance. "First of all, I need you to do it. You look young and healthy. I have a bad hip. I was going to get Jack to do it, but he's not well. And he might not get well in time."

"I'm not a demolitions expert and I'm not taking dumb

risks to get close to that core and try to kill it without being crushed by a building or killed by those Worshipers. I'm sorry, I can't. If my wife is still alive, she's expecting me, and I have a responsibility to that end." Will was very blunt, flat and no nonsense about this. He had just about had enough of New York in the past few hours.

Jeremiah was shaking his head very certainly from side to side while Will was explaining all that. "You don't understand the gravity of this."

"Really? Try me," Will challenged with a cutting edge of annoyance.

"Do you see over there?" Jeremiah pointed to a path that was made right through the buildings between the Inferno and the rough direction of Buffalo, west. It was an enormous path that cut off just about every standing structure in its way at the base. "That wasn't a bomb detonation. That was something the Inferno caught from some place far away. You see how everything is gone at the foundation? Something was dragged through there. We heard it underground."

"Those used to be a large ball of pipes from Buffalo, maybe half or a third of the city. I saw it happen basically next to my camp out that way."

Jeremiah's demeanor changed from the matter-of-fact nature of a teacher to the shock and horror of a student who has been handed a failing grade. "Buffalo, New York? Yes, of course you mean New York. So, that's how it is. What happened?"

"There was a beam of light that got more vibrant every second that seemed to latch on to it and drag the beast here. It basically tore it to pieces."

"Yep. That does it then." Jeremiah turned around to look at the Inferno. Its "eyes" were shifting in an uncomfortable excitement. It gave it the look of having gained energy. "We're all fucked without trying something tonight."

"What do you mean, 'all'? If it is growing, you can just leave. It'll eat New York and then sit here. Besides, if it ate all those damn pipes at once, then throwing a building at it will just make it angry. There's no way to kill it."

Jeremiah became very somber. "Fortunately, you're wrong. It does gain size even from random debris that's not metal. But it is a lot less stable than when it absorbs metals. And with increased size, it gains increased magnetism. I never dreamed it would be able to do that. Even just three days ago. There used to be a lot more left of New York then."

"Have you seen it actively seek out random materials or does it only seek out metals?" Will asked.

"It seems to go after metals ruthlessly. Probably because of the high density. It'll take random stuff too, bricks, sidewalks and the like, but I've only seen it hunt metals. Just tonight, I've seen it get more advanced. It will tear the metal out of whatever is left. It'll rip the supports out from a building like tearing out the skeleton of a person. That's probably why its little zombies, the Worshipers, are out there right now trying to break it all down."

"How much has it gained?" Will said, his patience dwindling.

"I'll tell it to you straight, this thing used to be a third of the size it is now. If it doesn't stop at the edges of New York City, it'll rip the land apart looking for new scrap. If it gets so large that the biggest building cannot destabilize it, then I believe we have just guaranteed hell on Earth. And then it won't matter if you find your family. It won't matter one bit. It might even find her first."

Will had just about had it with him. His over-dramatization, his know-it-all demeanor and his desperate insistence to push this onto him. It was overwhelming and Will felt every bit of the stress of all this. The capstone, however, was him claiming it wouldn't matter if he found Rachel. That burned much hotter than Jeremiah might have intended.

"Oh, so, you're saying I should've killed myself in Canada then if it didn't fucking matter. Nothing matters to you people besides your fucking predictions and your graphs. It was the same thing before the war, too. I'm sick of people not having common sense. If it eats metal, it eats metal. Go find a place that doesn't have metal and call it a day. It hasn't shown itself to be a threat outside of that, so let it recycle the old world." Will sighed, realizing he shouldn't have raised his voice. "Look, I'm leaving. Even if I have to find a bicycle, I'd rather do *that* than die here and let down the expectations of her memory."

"But you have to. You don't understand—"

Will was experiencing quite a bit of physical discomfort every time these survivors talked to him, he was beginning to realize. He took a second and then said, "As I said, no. I have to find my wife in Florida, and I can't do that dead. I owe her this much. I told her I would."

"You don't understand how grave this actually is. It'll reach out and take any metal it can find from anywhere in the country—" Jeremiah begged.

"The thing can't touch us directly. Eventually it'll run out of metal to catch and then it'll fizzle out. I'm sorry. But there's other places to go to get away from this thing. I'm sorry about New York. But I made a promise."

Will turned to go back out and down the stairs, but

before his foot could touch the first stair on the way down, Jeremiah said something. It was by far the most disturbing thing Will had ever heard. And it wasn't even that crazy. It was just a simple biological fact that everyone learns in school. It was such a flat and simple sentence, but it sent chills down Will's spine that met with his feet and froze him into place. What Jeremiah said was just a casual observation. But it changed everything.

"There's iron in our blood."

Will backpedaled into the room as though he were walking on eggshells. "What..."

Jeremiah cut him off. "There's gold in our brains. There's trace iron in the ground. The mountains are full of aluminum, uranium and other metals in entire veins. Do you want this thing to get big enough to where those eyes can find you and rip the fucking iron out of your veins from across the country? Do you want it to topple mountains? Do you want to live in peace with your wife? Do you want to have an undisturbed burial if the worst has come to pass? Think, motherfucker! Before you try to tell me how this thing works, tell me there's no risk! Tell me you know it better!" Jeremiah looked Will right in the eyes and held it there, concentrating like the eyes of the Inferno itself until Will looked away.

"How do you know that will happen?" Will was still critical of this plan.

"I am a man of evidence and caution. Evidence says that it's getting bigger and more powerful and hasn't stopped and hasn't slowed. Caution says we should kill the goddamn thing before it's too late to find out. Besides, with the plan I've got, your chances are alright."

"Alright, he says," Will mocked. "Look, I'm not dying

over a hypothesis." Upon Will saying this, Jeremiah was visibly defeated, and he held the sides of his head in grief. Will continued. "I'm sorry. If I knew my wife was dead, I might do it. But as it stands, I've done enough. James," he said, switching his perspective to him, "I've done what you asked. I brought you here. The rest is up to you."

Will could tell that James was trying just as hard as Jeremiah to come up with a reason why he should stay and do this. Which was strange to him. Will remembered that the only thing James wanted was to hitchhike to New York. But then again, James basically brought himself to New York with Will in tow. Either way, Will wasn't having any more of it. His mind was finally starting to completely reject the craziness of the situation. He turned to leave, just like before, and was halted in his tracks by another statement.

"You want to know about Rachel?" James asked bluntly.

Will likely needed a lifetime to recover from this whole episode. But he didn't have time for that yet. There was only one burning statement on his mind. "I never told you her name."

"No... you didn't," James said.

Will came in from the doorway where he was originally going to leave. He looked over to see Jeremiah's reaction, only to see that there was none. Jeremiah was still clutching the sides of his head and oddly staring at the doorway as if Will was still there. "What do you make of that, Mr. Scientist?" Will said, addressing Jeremiah. Jeremiah did not move. Not even a millimeter of change or expression. He was frozen in time.

"Will," James said. "I can't... reveal too much now. But I can offer you... answers at the end of your road here. I cannot... influence you too much as that would make the proof... incomplete. Just know... there is even more... at stake... than you realize. But do not ask any questions now... just yes or no. It is how it must be."

Will was still distracted by the statue of Jeremiah, even though he was listening intently. He knew that James had information on Rachel. He wouldn't know her name if he didn't. It was also becoming crystal clear that he wasn't human. So, Will agreed. He needed answers, sure, but he needed hope even more. Thinking about Rachel's death dampened his spirits. There was also still the problem of transportation. He would be wasting time trying to walk far enough away from this thing to find a car and then hope he found a good one. In truth, there was more to this.

He wasn't happy that he had to help, but he also didn't really fancy his chances of surviving all the way down the coast anyway, given what he'd seen so far. He likely couldn't drive down there without being caught up by the beams of light. Without a good method of transportation, he fancied his chances against exhaustion and running out of edible food and drinkable water to be terribly depressing. He looked out at the Inferno, concentrating on it for the first time since they climbed the stairs. It was much larger than it had been when Will first arrived in New York. And it wasn't just because he was closer here. The air was pure, but stiflingly hot for nighttime. "So, what's the plan?"

Jeremiah looked at him as if he was never frozen in place. "Wait, what changed your mind? I thought you were walking out?"

"I was, but I'd rather have some answers about all this." Will spared a glance toward James, who seemed more relaxed now.

"Thank god, at least you'll listen." Jeremiah sighed with relief. "Okay, we have maybe ten hours to get this right before the Inferno's growth overcomes the point at which it can realistically be destabilized by the building I've selected. The building is on the other side of the river just outside of Queens Plaza station. You'll see it, it's the biggest one still standing. It has remained there stubbornly due to an incredibly strong foundation for starters. But it is also close enough to the Inferno that if the supports were to give out, the core would essentially eat the whole thing too quickly. Therefore, it would be unable to maintain its own stable mass."

"How close are we talking?" Will said.

"Danger close. Wind speeds that will pick you up off the ground. If you're in direct line of sight of the core, that is. And temperatures hot enough to leave first-degree burns on any exposed skin in fifteen minutes with worse burns the longer you're exposed."

Will nearly fainted. He regained his balance on a wall. It occurred to him that he hadn't eaten in over twenty-eight hours. He had been much too queasy and there was too much going on to get an appetite. But now his body had given up. "Hang on a minute." He breathed out in sudden exhaustion. He had his bag and, like he assumed before, not enough food to hoof it to Florida. But he had enough for right now. He ate a couple of bars for a thousand calories and Jeremiah gave him a room-temperature sandwich wrapped in plastic he had pried from the broken glass front of a vending machine down in 33 Street station. Will ate gratefully. It was a shitty final meal if this plan failed.

"Okay," Will said, his mouth still chewing. "How do you intend on collapsing the supports?"

"I've got some homemade pipe bombs. I cut off some of the metal tubing in the subway tunnels with a hacksaw and filled them with rust from the dilapidated system. I took my pocketknife and shaved some aluminum cans into a fine mix."

"Oh. So, thermite?" Will knew that from a video game.

"Yes." Jeremiah was shocked at his knowledge. "I've already tested a small amount and it works well enough. It burned right through the concrete platform for a few inches. An insulated reaction in a tube will allow the temperature to build much higher before eventually losing it to the environment."

"And you think this is enough to level a building that big?"

"It's not about leveling it outright. This building is majorly unstable. The Worshipers have been scrambling to keep it standing while also breaking off as much as they can to feed it. I think they fear the same thing we want to capitalize on. They've been adding concrete to the supports, I think. I can see them move in buckets and buckets of something. I don't think they actually know how to make it in the right proportions, though, so luckily their reinforcements might be worthless."

"I'm still not clear on what the hell these Worshipers are. I was under the impression they were sorta zombie-like. But now you're saying they're mixing concrete."

"They're bringing it in from hardware stores. I don't know, really. They used to be like zombies in the first few days. They walked around, hobbled, and didn't really do anything much. But then they started using random sledgehammers. They organized themselves like ants initially. Doing their part and then moving to the back of the line to refresh. Then they graduated to jackhammers and other equipment taken from dead city crews. Then, just yesterday, we had some wearing masks and trying to convince us to let them in."

"And why didn't you? Like, I don't really get what makes them an outright threat if they're getting intelligent. Have you tried talking to them?"

"Oh, we did. Yes. We did. Did Dave tell you about their religion?"

"Actually, he did, yeah. But he just said, 'Holy Conversions' and didn't elaborate."

"Alright, so I'll just state it simply. They worship the Inferno. I caught them praying to it when they were still basically zombies. It was some creepy shit. Even when they were close enough that their faces started to boil and crisp over. Something has infected their consciousness without killing them."

"Or maybe it did kill them," Will interjected. He didn't really know why he said it, but he felt like some pieces were coming together.

"What do you mean?" Jeremiah was very curious now.

"What if these people were the victims of the same initial event that dropped people where they stood? What if these people are resurrected?"

"I can't tell you for certain that they aren't," Jeremiah confessed. "But that would be inconsistent with the evidence. There are still so many bodies around that haven't moved an inch since doomsday. You saw them on the way up here."

"That's true. But what if it works in a radius like everything else about it? What if the Inferno is saving them for later, like our train or the buildings in the surrounding area? What if it couldn't have all those zombies at the same time feeding it materials because it would have choked? *What if all those bodies are waiting to be called on?*" Will said, surprising himself.

And with that, it was official. They had all said truly awful and terrible things that day. James with his idea of the opportunistic hunter. Jeremiah with the idea of iron in our blood being targeted for harvesting. And now Will with the idea that an army of zombies had been sleeping in those tunnels for a week, waiting to activate. Add that in with the background observations that had been made so far. They had religion. They were organizing. They were advancing in technology. And soon, there would be millions. Well, now Will was a lot less begrudging of the duties laid before him by the researcher.

"Alright, how do I get to this building?"

"I'll show you." And with that, Jeremiah left his post up on the remains of the Empire State and led them back down into the tunnels under 33 Street. He took them north towards his stash of homemade thermite bombs. After a ghost train passed them by, Will asked Jeremiah about them.

"So, Dave seems convinced that you're full of shit on these trains."

"Yeah, Dave seems to think a lot of things are full of shit."

"Heh." Will gave a singular chuckle. The tunnels refracted their voices to a deeply preserved echo that bounced back and forth a few times before dissipating. The crunch of random articles of wrappers and other trash passed underfoot as no one was ever paid enough to get down here and sweep it properly.

"Yeah, if you guys are seeing it too, then that probably means I'm wrong."

"Wait, really? You're just going to admit you were wrong just like that? I had taken you for a stubborn man, Jeremiah." Will was thoroughly amused for a moment before remembering where they were heading.

"Yes, well... I used to work as a researcher on particular projects. They used to be top secret, but that doesn't matter. We were shit at intercepting asteroids. Did you know that? We had no plan at all if we saw one coming. I was working on the private details of making that plan while the public releases were meant to encourage faith in us. It was part of my job to pump up numbers and tell comfortable lies that people mostly didn't care to listen to. I don't really feel like doing that anymore."

"That's respectable. Everyone has to put up with the conditions of their role, right? My mother was the same way."

"She was a researcher?"

"No, she was in media. She could be downright manipulative of a news story when selling it. But money always found its way from industry into young women's resource charities. Sometimes you gotta do what you gotta do with the skills the world gives you."

"Sounds like a good person at heart. I'm happy to meet someone who understands that the world is complicated. Lies are not so much lies as they are responsibilities in some sense. Misdirection can be your best friend."

"I might agree, in some sense."

"Exactly," Jeremiah concluded.

"So, what do you think happened to Jack?" Will's mind had been percolated by the revelations they had up on the surface. What if everything was connected to this Inferno somehow?

"Yes. Well, I mainly told them that Jack probably had a fear of trains to keep Ruth calm. She trusts me as the most educated of us to know what I'm talking about. Whether I've got her fooled or not, I don't know. But I can at least lean on my credentials to give some legitimacy to her desire for peace. Dave's speculations were harmful. There is no point in dwelling on the horrible possibilities of things you have no ability to change."

"I agree. And that's what's so unfortunate about our position." Will thought of his position in hoping Rachel was still alive and dreading the possibility of her death. "We've gotta look this stuff in the mouth to change it."

"Will, you are right. It's so refreshing to be able to talk about how it really is."

They would be walking and talking through the tunnels for quite a long way through the darkness. They would have to be careful enough to avoid the trains while they were conversing, however. Or there would be no more conversation. James was walking ahead of them, listening diligently.

"Listen, I'm sorry about what I said up on the Empire State. It's been a long week and a half," Will said, admitting his rush to get to Florida.

"Don't mention it, Will. It's been long for everyone. Besides, you aren't nearly as bad as the critics I faced before the war."

"Maybe so. What is it, really? This thing with Jack?"

"It's difficult to say. Being scared doesn't really cover it, I know that. There's something about crossing the same space with these entities that causes distress of a very deep kind.

Perhaps these dark recordings of people carry their memories, their suffering. If it can preserve their movements and their body shapes and heights, why couldn't it preserve emotions of pain?" Jeremiah wondered.

"But the one problem there is that there was no suffering. These people dropped instantly," Will protested.

"That's what I do not understand. What could make a grown man cry? I couldn't get a word out of him since the incident. He's stopped crying now, but he rocks back and forth in the corner like a troubled child. You know what? Let's go see them first. It will be useful for them to know what we're doing so they can evacuate to a safer place."

"Good plan," Will said. "What if they aren't really dead? Like what if their bodies are being held in some kind of stasis and they are projecting the recordings themselves? Tormented souls not being allowed to die fully because they're trapped until they're called up." He knew that this contradicted the ghost at Rayne's apartment. But he wondered if the cause of the ghosts was different in different places.

"That's the second worst thing you've said, young man. You're on a roll," Jeremiah quipped. "Anything seems possible. The only thing we know is that we have to move quick." It was clear that Jeremiah meant what he said earlier and didn't want to speculate about how horrible the circumstances might be when Will was already doing everything possible to change them. And the added stress wouldn't help him do it. "But be careful when we go back. I have a bad feeling about it."

CHAPTER 11

THEY CAME UPON the maintenance tunnel after some time and went in. Dave greeted them same as before but put the gun away after he saw who it was. They walked in farther than Will and James had gone previously. There was a gray room full of lights and switches and gauges and pipes. It smelled like bad food. It was small, but cozy now that nothing rang or buzzed or clicked without power. The only thing heard were the soft and humble whispers of a very small fire they had going underneath a ventilation shaft in the ceiling for some warmth and the ability to heat up the garbage from the vending machines. There was a stack of old deli sandwiches on the wall opposite the fire. They felt old and terrible but toasting the bread over the fire and heating the toppings in a can tricked their brains into eating it without throwing up. Whether their stomachs would take the bait was a different matter. The candy bars and other things would last for months, so they sat there as dessert to look forward to.

This was Will's first time seeing the Jack he had heard

so much about. But he didn't really get to see much besides a balled-up man in a red long-sleeve shirt and khaki beige pants. It was obvious he was on the younger side. He had long black hair that curled at the ends. Ruth was leaning on the wall near the fire with Dave running interception between the group and her. Will only got a glimpse of her hazelnut hair and a single curious eye of rich brown color that had a warm glow by the fire.

"How's he doing?" Jeremiah asked Dave for the update.

"He stopped crying and as you know he went silent for some time. But now he started talking to himself. He just says the word 'no' on repeat sometimes. It's very rapid and sounds like he's warding something off. I tried to ask him, like, 'no' what? What are you saying 'no' to? And he still won't answer."

"It's a damn shame he's like this about it. If we got him to open up, we could probably help him."

"Honestly, Jeremiah, he scares me. I've moved past the idea of helping him and I just keep my gun ready," Dave said, gesturing in the direction of poor Jack.

"Yeah, well, don't get too eager to discharge it in a small room like this. Concrete and metal will guarantee some permanent hearing loss," Jeremiah warned.

"If I have to, I have to," Dave said with a shrug.

This was a strange mix-up from the kind of character Will thought he had figured out in their first encounter. He was pretty sure Dave said he didn't want to shoot them. In fact, looking back on it, Will reasoned Dave was hoping he would never have to. Maybe Will misjudged the man. Maybe it was just fear clutching at him and not humanity in that moment. Or maybe it was the last few hours that had changed him.

Spending about three hours in a box with a man in the fetal position repeating "no, no, no" in succession would increase the anxious toll on anyone. Jack looked like a mental health case ready to snap. His boney fingers clutched through his dark hair all the way up to the knuckle. And the few glimpses you could catch of the side of his head showed a grimace, as if a clownish smile was assaulting the borders of his face. The stress marks were like veins. He was not healthy at all.

Another small detail Will noticed was the fact that Ruth squirmed uncomfortably against the wall. She had stood up after they mentioned Jack's "no" habit. Her face was now in clearer view. It was a face that almost any forty-year-old has when they've been sleeping and waking up on concrete for a week straight without the makeup to hide their fatigue. She was tired, awfully so. But the main feature was the panic she visibly showed when they mentioned the gun going off. She stared at the fire while they were speaking as if not wanting to be caught looking at any of them. She stole a glance at Will. In the fire, her eyes were strikingly light brown, which contrasted with the shadows dancing over her hair. And just about the second that her eyes met Will, Dave's meaty forearm ended up blocking them as he pressed and splayed his hand against the wall.

Will looked at Dave in surprise and he was looking back intently. As if saying, "Oh, no, you don't! Those are my wife's eyes and only I get to look at them!" It was just a split-second thing. As if Dave had plenty of practice. This put off Will from his other thoughts and he glanced at James. James wasn't just looking at Will, he was studying him with a penetrating concentration. That was disturbing enough for

Will to cast his gaze into the fire just like Ruth. He had one screaming thought above the others, *What the fuck is going on here?* It was funny to Will that, despite never sharing a word with Ruth in his life, they came to the same opinion. They'd rather not be caught looking at any of these weirdos right now.

"You don't have to discharge it," Jeremiah continued to Dave. "He's probably had some terrible experiences as a child, and he'll get over it in a peaceful, controlled environment like this."

"It's not his fucking childhood, Jeremiah! He's possessed! Look at him!"

A clearly annoyed Jeremiah rebutted. "Yes, it is. As I've said before, there are other things to add into the equation besides the ghosts you have seen in movies."

"Oh, my fucking god—" Dave's voice had risen a good bit.

"Let's just please listen to him, okay?" That was an odd new voice. Could that soft, high and quiet emission really have come from that big woman on the wall? Her voice was unsettlingly soft and scared. It wasn't necessarily about to cry, but it was begging Dave to not give her a reason to. But yes, Ruth did interject.

He whirled around to face her, and she never budged from looking down at the fire. "Honey, there is no fucking way that mess in the corner is childhood trauma. That doesn't happen to people."

"Yes, it does! You're being insensitive!" Now, surprisingly it was Jeremiah's turn to raise volume.

This was an interesting experience for Will. Witnessing someone tell what they know to be a lie is something else.

What Jeremiah was saying wasn't technically false. It would be a perfectly valid opinion for anyone to hold if anyone actually believed it in this circumstance. Childhood trauma is real, and yes, it can curl you up like a dead spider and make you pull on your own hair. But the only person worth lying to here was Ruth. Literally everyone believed that there was something otherworldly going on here but her. She didn't know who to believe but trusted the credentials of Jeremiah to keep her basking in the better of the world's possibilities instead of the dark, foreboding reality of those tunnels with the stench of expired humans.

Maybe that's why Dave was so competitive about this. He was jealous of how his wife saw Jeremiah as a guardian of sorts. Sometimes men want to be right for all the wrong reasons. Was Dave this kind of man? Probably, if that little arm trick he did earlier said anything. Will glanced at a part of his vision that had continued to bother him. Jack was rocking back and forth harder than before.

Dave had started shouting something else at Jeremiah, which was quickly perforated by Jeremiah's smartly preconceived comebacks. Will wasn't really focusing, though. He was looking at Jack. He noted how terribly he shook. Like every word that they shouted hit like a small rock being thrown at him. He flinched as if fighting some danger away. And then there came a voice. It was difficult to get at it clearly. It was like trying to find the exact frequency of a radio station that was too far away. You had to get it just dead on or you'd lose most of it in the static of other indescribable nonsense. It might have been Ruth. Her voice was quiet but that didn't sit right with Will. He heard the same thing over and over and over. After the sound repeated almost on a loop, Will decided to risk another quick glance at Ruth's face. Her mouth wasn't moving.

A process of elimination said it was Jack. Will strained to listen carefully. Dave was gesticulating in the way, so Will couldn't see him clearly either. It wasn't like a "no, no, no", it was more like he was saying: "I won't do it. I won't do it. I can't do it. I shouldn't do it."

At this moment, Will did something that he really didn't have the time to think about too much. Ruth and Jack were both clearly degenerating because of this argument. Jack was genuinely starting to freak out. Ruth's lips curled as if she was beginning to sob a little, but it was almost like she had nothing left in the tank. Will spoke up. And he did so with authority.

"I think Jeremiah's right." And, surprisingly, they shut up for a second. "We all saw what passes by us in those tunnels. But I think trauma can produce what we've seen from Jack. I saw it in Canada. The same smoky ghost shit happens out there. I thought that a woman I knew had jumped off her balcony. That's what the smoky ghost thing did. I was reduced to a crying mess, like Jack. Then she, in the flesh, found me and I realized it wasn't true. But if it can happen to me, and you're talking about a potentially much deeper trauma for Jack… it seems to me reasonable that he's suffering and just needs a chance."

Ruth took a heaving gasp of relief that there was now a majority who thought it was just a normal thing to have this much trauma. It was beautiful. Jack became completely still, which was odd, but it was the desired goal, so Will didn't think it was creepy. It wasn't technically false, either. Will didn't make it up. But he didn't believe it. It was a constructive lie. And it turned out to be the wrong approach to de-escalation. It was a nice attempt, but Dave wasn't just in this for the truth anymore. It was maybe a matter of competing with Jeremiah before. That's speculation. But it was certainly about being cornered by the both of them now.

"I can't BELIEVE—"

Dave started up again. This time even higher pitched than before. Jack was practically vibrating in the corner of Will's eye. Dave moved back and forth in his varying mannerisms, now aimed at both of them. And Dave moved out of the way enough for Will to catch a glimpse of the most horrifying human face he had ever seen. Jack was looking up at the back of Dave's head. His face was a pale white, like wet paper. His long locks of black, greasy hair now partially covered and infected his dark eyes with a new blackness of shadow. His face was longer up and down than any face should be and it nailed a strained smile almost up to his temples. His crooked nose was long and slender at the bridge and never lifted up off his face.

It all happened so fast after he stood up. To start with, he had to be nearly seven feet tall and thin like a twig. His beige khakis were now flood pants that rode halfway up his lower legs, and his sleeves were nearly up to his elbows. Nobody wears clothes that small. He used to fit those clothes. Just two days ago. Before Will could blink, he was on Dave like an ambush predator. Dave squirmed and shouted his way into looking at his attacker. Dave had a gun. But there's a difference between having one and being trained to use one. Dave let off several successive rounds. One into his own foot when he was startled. Another two into the leg of Jack on the way up and three planted into his stomach. Each shot became more difficult to hear than the last, due to the siren ringing of certain inner ear damage. As the disjointed fingers wrapped around Dave's neck, it became apparent that it wasn't enough to stop Jack. Dave gasped and grasped. Ruth was screaming her head off, but it was hard to hear. It sounded akin to a distant fire alarm.

She was a lot quicker than she looked, being the first to act. After the initial panic and scream, Ruth gathered the necessary momentum to push Jack from his side, but his fingers were latched on tight, and Dave was hauled with him against the far wall. Jeremiah scrambled for the pistol in the small of his back, looking for a clean shot. Will was completely stunned for a couple of seconds but drew his kukri and tried to get an angle on Jack's arms. Ruth had a swing at Jack as she was behind him now. And she hit him with the meanest left hook Will had seen in years, right above his ear. The giant stickman stumbled, then Will pounced from the side, coming down hard with the kukri, built for chopping as those things are, and cut clean through Jack's arm. Jack swung around as Will was hauling up for another strike and put Dave between himself and Will. That cleared the line for Jeremiah, however. And he ended this thing with nine millimeters of jacketed hollow point, in one temple and fragmented out the other. A final, stinging ring pierced all of their ear drums.

Will held the kukri to Jack's lifeless neck in case it wasn't as lifeless as it looked. Jeremiah had the dignified task of peeling dead finger bones off an unmoving Dave one at a time. Ruth stood there huffing and puffing some terrible emotions and rocking on her feet uneasily as if ready to throw another of those heavy hands of hers at the drop of a hat. Dave wasn't responding. Jeremiah felt for a pulse on the neck and the wrist but there was nothing. Nobody there actually knew CPR, but Jeremiah tried it anyhow. The man would be dead without it. It turned out he was dead even with it. Dave's neck wasn't aligned properly. It was broken. Those long boney fingers of Jack actually cracked the vertebra completely apart. Nobody said a damn thing for five minutes. The only thing they could hear was the tinnitus in their ears and their own thoughts.

Will thought about his lack of action in the first two or three seconds. It was possible, he thought, to sever both arms if he had started swinging immediately. Dave's neck might still be intact. Will wasn't sure if James tried to do anything to help them. He was the farthest one away and didn't even have a weapon. But he looked disappointed. No doubt the others were regretting their individual contributions to this mess. It wasn't even a good death. They died arguing and mad at each other. Ruth never got to kiss him goodbye or anything. It was odd, though. Because she could've. Will had been to funerals where the widow kissed her husband on the cheek or the forehead. Ruth made no such move. Dave's golden watch kept ticking in the silence. Eventually, Will had to open up.

"Ruth, I'm so sorry."

She didn't budge. Not an inch. She just blandly confessed, "Don't be. You did what you could. He was a bastard anyway. More than either of you know."

Will and Jeremiah gave each other a look like they had each seen a ghost. Will thought it was her way of coping with the immediacy of the loss. She was probably angry at Dave for dying and not paying attention when he should have, which is really not as crazy as it sounds. She was probably alluding to abuse as well. Dave did seem remarkably jealous and possessive, which are the typical signs of emotionally manipulative people. But should he be so quick to pass judgment over the dead while their bodies were still warm? It didn't quite seem like his right.

Ruth squeaked something out with that soft, high voice that didn't fit her body very well. "I would've killed him myself... *eventually.*" The last word emphasized by a sudden drop in tone.

Will and Jeremiah glared at each other with sudden concern. Will had picked up the gun Dave was holding earlier without realizing it and was now very glad he had. Ruth's remark was a terrible thing to say five minutes after her husband's death. And then there was a smell. Yes, that smell of death when the bowels and bladder see no point in impressing anyone anymore. Ruth remarked: "Fuck, Dave. Couldn't have held that in until we got home? Fuckin' pig."

Her voice cracked when she called him a pig and Will thought he heard a faint giggle of frustration. This was getting disturbing, quickly. Jeremiah rushed in, salvaging what he could of the situation.

"Ruth? Will, James, and I are going to go stop this thing up there. We should leave you alone for a few hours anyway, so you can... mourn properly." Jeremiah then motioned them to leave. Will really liked the idea of not being in that room anymore. Ruth simply nodded her head slowly in a way that could only be taken as ominous, given what she had just said. She paid special attention to the hand that hit Jack, massaging it greedily.

They departed the small room silently and entered the

subway tunnels yet again. Will's hands were still shaking from cutting the man-thing's arm off. They moved on without speaking for half an hour at least. They walked, crushing the same trash underfoot as when they came through there before and Will's flashlight held them straight on their way. They moved towards a station that was like the others when they passed it before, and Jeremiah stopped abruptly.

"Holy shit…" he said, like it was in disbelief. It wasn't hard to imagine it, given what they'd talked about before. But it was hard to come to terms with it. Will's flashlight pivoted to the platform. There were no more bodies. Will tried to see the ghosts in the corner of his eye and there were none of those either.

They felt the overwhelming sensation that they weren't moving fast enough. This anomaly was getting ahead of them. They sped up considerably as Jeremiah tried to assure them: "The thermite is close at hand. I didn't want to keep it in the same place as the others. Just in case they got any ideas of using it. I didn't know if Jack would end up deranged. I needed to keep a stash of it somewhere. I wasn't sure how much we might need."

"Good call, given how it turned out in there," Will said.

"It's hidden in a vent in the next station," he said, pointing. "If the bodies and ghosts are both gone, it should be even safer to get at it."

"That depends on where they went," Will protested. No one had a response for that.

CHAPTER 12

THEY MOVED ON to the next station. It was not any safer. One hundred bodies, each seven feet tall, stood at attention like gangly soldiers. They were unmoving. Will, Jeremiah and James didn't dare make any sound they didn't have to. If they were loud, they might wake them up. Will also kept his flashlight out of their faces for the same reason. It was good for his sanity as well. He could tell, based on how the peripheral light played shadows across their crooked faces, that they were the same kind of ugly as Jack. He probably never used to be that ugly before... whatever it was took him over. Jeremiah moved very carefully along the outer wall, making sure not to touch any of them. James studied their awful figures carefully.

Jeremiah guided his careful hands into the vent that he left unscrewed. The vent entrance was above his head considerably and squeaked lightly when opened. He flinched at the sound but continued his reach and grabbed the box of thermite tubes. They ran away from there as silently as they could, nearly tiptoeing until they felt safe enough to stop briefly. Will had so many questions, but he didn't dare speak in these tunnels anymore. No one did. He didn't want his voice to carry.

Jeremiah turned back and showed Will the devices he'd be using. Their design was interesting. When Jeremiah built these things, he clamped and sharpened one end of the pipes to make them into spikes and then flattened out the other to obviously be bludgeoned with a hammer.

He guessed that would be more effective since nobody had a drill to plant the pipes in the supports properly. Will didn't know what the supports looked like for this building, though. He didn't know how many of these tubes he needed for each support nor even how to identify the most important supports. His factory job never taught him how to demolish a building. He hoped dearly that he didn't have to be fully accurate with any of this.

If the building was as unstable as Jeremiah thought, he might not need to be. He took one out of the box to examine the fuses. They were heavy-duty rods. There were shoelaces which were cut in half and frayed on the open end to facilitate easy igniting. Seeing Will's uncertain expression, Jeremiah whispered carefully as they walked, "I've tested them. They should give you roughly two minutes each, give or take."

"I hope so," Will replied.

They moved on and were nearing the East River Tunnels. Will put his mask on and took it off depending on how close they were to the bodies. They planned on taking the tunnel closest to Queensboro Bridge to cross from Manhattan Island to the place where the Inferno held itself suspended in the northwest of Queens. However, Will had a really bad feeling about staying underground, even if they were still moving faster than before.

"Is there any way to get above ground from here?" Will said. The echo of the tunnels unsettled him more than usual. Like the walls were watching him.

"Well, we could take Queensboro Bridge itself. But it would be extremely dangerous wind combined with an unknown amount of heat."

"I like our chances better against the elements," Will said without hesitation.

"I actually have to say I agree," Jeremiah concluded.

They turned onto the line that would take them up to the bridge and that was when Will felt it more clearly. That sensation of being watched. He turned around and shone the flashlight behind him. He saw something, but he didn't know what. The darkness was distinctly moving. But it could just be another trick of the light. He banged the flashlight, wondering if it was a battery problem. He turned forward again to address James and Jeremiah.

"Hey, do you guys see something behind us back there? I can't tell what I'm looking at."

When he turned around to face the darkness again, his heart almost exploded. He screamed like hell and stumbled backwards when he realized he was eye-level with Ruth's chest. She *had been* much shorter than him before. But you didn't have to look up into her new, wretched face to understand what she was now. Will couldn't stop his body from looking up anyway to meet the face of horror itself and Will's screaming rose violently in pitch to that of a girl.

Oh, poor Ruth. Two weeks ago, she had been not-so-happily married to a supposed bastard and living her normal life in the Big Apple. Now, she towered over the team and glared at them with a stitched-together face of plaster and jagged lips that stretched unnaturally behind her eyes. She was pale and veiny in the glare from Will's flashlight. There were bruises where the veins could not keep up with her rapid growth and burst under the strain. Jeremiah pulled his pistol and aimed it center-mass.

"I thought you might want some meat. We haven't had any in a while..." She trailed off chillingly with her voice that was still recognizable as Ruth's. But it was strained across the new length of her neck. Her teeth were far too tiny for a mouth like that and somehow even more jagged than her smile. She held up a severed human arm in offering and it had... Dave's watch on it.

"Ruth? What the fuck, Ruth!?" The words were pushed out of Jeremiah in a desperate plea to not have to shoot. He and the others backed away slowly. She took one step for every two of theirs and still kept up with them. Imagining what she would be like in an all-out sprint was soul-rending.

"Don't shoot me, please!" she begged with a sudden desperation. *"It's not as bad as it looks in here, aligned with His glorious light. Let me say something. You owe me for Dave!"* She lunged forwards and stumbled over the name of her deceased husband, either like she forgot his name for a second or as though the pain of his memory wasn't completely gone from within her skinsuit of awful terror. Jeremiah almost shot her for that lunge alone.

"Don't come any closer then, stay there!" Jeremiah urged.

"Please..." She did not stop. And her tone changed suddenly, like a machine searching for the optimal tone and the right things to say to pass the test. *"Just let me show you the light of Him. Let me touch you and show you how it feels to be aligned out of your squishy little bodies. You'll need all the strength of all you could be for His new world!"*

"Ruth! It's a lie!" Will said suddenly, finally breaking free of his paralysis. "It's going to consume everything! Even your blood when there's no more metal!"

"*Oh, darling...*" She switched to a seductive tone and brushed her hair back behind her ear. Seductiveness was an odd new strategy considering any of them were more likely to piss themselves than believe her. "*Metal is only a means to an end... Stop moving!*" she shouted all at once, lunging at Will. She went to grab his unmasked face, but only grazed it before Jeremiah dilated her eye with a nine-millimeter projectile. She collapsed backwards like a folding steel chair. The report from the gun echoed throughout the tunnels.

"God damn it, Ruth!" Jeremiah screamed in desperation and dropped to his knees.

Will thought his reaction was strange. He didn't react that way with Jack. Given the hideous monster she was, and the threat she posed, Will thought it was undeniably and unfortunately good that she was dead. But then he also considered, as they all stayed in place for a minute, Jeremiah's goal to protect her from the horrors of what was really happening in these tunnels. The lies he told that tried to abate their complete cluelessness about whose reality they were subject to, because it sure as hell wasn't the human one. But then she succumbed to this and transformed into everyone's worst nightmare. Will reached up and touched the spot that she grazed. It was bothering him. He massaged the spot she touched on his cheek. Then he realized he was rubbing it in the same way Ruth was rubbing the hand that touched Jack. Before she changed.

Will decided to keep this to himself for now, or Jeremiah might turn around and shoot *him*. Jeremiah was not a man of half measures, it would seem. But where did he learn to shoot that well? Will allowed Jeremiah to slump with regret for a minute, but then he had to intervene.

"Jeremiah, you did what you could for her. But we have to move." He went to help Jeremiah up but stopped short. He suddenly remembered his last glance at Ruth before this. How she cradled her fist like the future itself and then became what she became. Will had been touched by her. *Maybe that's all it needed.*

"I killed for her. Worshipers," he sobbed, releasing the burdens of his masculinity to cry with commitment like a child.

"And you would do it again, right? Then let's go kill that fucking Inferno, yeah?" It was a nice thing for Will to say. It lent Jeremiah the willpower to stand, at least.

"They're evolving faster than we're moving. We gotta go," Jeremiah said, shakily, wiping his face. He made for the station exit.

Then James, for the first time in a long time, said something so awful it was dumbfounding. "They are coming. On their feet... and their hands. The bodies are... sprinting for us."

Silence fell over them hard as they tried to swallow that pill. "Oh, fuck," Will said finally, with a catch in his voice. "They must have heard the gunshot! Jeremiah, let's go!"

Jeremiah was gazing down the tunnel. After a small pause, he said, "Nope. On second thought, I got nobody to see now, and I'll just slow you down. Give me three of those tubes so I can keep them at bay." He traded his pistol to Will for three tubes of thermite from the box James was holding and held his lighter at the ready. There were ten of them left in the box now. His voice still trembling, he rushed the words out of his mouth. "They used Ruth as fuckin' bait. Distraction. Slowed us down. They'll catch us if I don't distract them here."

Will was looking at one of two Jeremiahs. The first option was that he was suicidally depressed and traumatized deeper than he looked on the outside, wasn't thinking clearly, and figured he would throw his life away to try to do the kind of good he might never live to appreciate. The second option was an honest-to-god hero. Willing to sacrifice himself for the greater good. Will didn't have much time to decide who it was he was looking at. But whoever it was, Jeremiah was certain of his own choice. The last choice. Will looked at James and started to run toward the stairs up to the bridge. He turned around only to say good luck, but he couldn't. He was shut up by the faint, trembling sound of hundreds of heels slamming on concrete and fingers clawing at the walls in the distance of the tunnel. The tunnels carried that kind of sound far. They didn't have long.

Will and James ran for it. Will was an excellent runner. He could keep up a fast pace for a long time. James kept up. They made it to the surface and Will immediately wished they didn't have to cross the bridge. When they crossed the north bridge into Manhattan proper last night, they encountered a wind heavy with water and humidity, hard and strong. This was twice as bad. It was morning time. Will barely noticed it as they struggled to run across the bridge without getting swept right off it. It was suffocatingly hot and dense out there. Any amount of air that hit him felt as if it were searching for a way to pick him up like a wrestler that could be all around him at the same time.

They ran hard. James was doing really well. Too well.

Will didn't hear him breathing hard despite the fact that he was carrying the box of thermite. The wind was too strong, he guessed. But it was impressive for a guy with gray hair to be doing this pace. Will looked over at him and was only half-surprised to see that James' hair was black again. They were going to have a long, serious talk when this was all over. James owed him answers. They made it to the other side of the bridge after just a couple minutes. Will chanced a look behind them and saw that they were clear. He knew the things were likely on Jeremiah by now. Hero or not, he would be torn to shreds as easily as string cheese by those man-things. But would they take Jeremiah's bait? Or would they mostly ignore the distraction and start chasing after the two of them?

It was a question of an evolutionary arms race. Did the two of them still have an evolutionary advantage in intelligence over the man-things? Will knew they wouldn't have one for long at this rate. The fact that Ruth was conscious enough to try to manipulate them, even in that form. It was beyond puzzling. Did Ruth realize that she couldn't convince them in that horrid form? Dave mentioned that Worshipers had tried to convince them they were normal before. But surely those ones would have looked more normal than Ruth, comparatively.

Perhaps the transformation into those gangly, crudely designed messes of superstrength and horror were involuntary. Perhaps their communication skills were not yet a mature weapon. Whatever the case, Will knew one thing for sure. If they started pouring out of that tunnel, they would catch up in no time. Will and James would have lost the arms race and they'd be strung out by their tendons across what remained of Queens with their bones clanging together in the breeze like wind chimes.

It was easy to tell which direction was north towards the building. The rising sun in the east told them it was on their left. The wind pounded at their backs when they turned north. And the temperature increased with every minute of running. Will thought back to the tunnels. And to Ruth. She touched him. It was just a light grazing, so maybe it would take longer to spread. But it would happen, same as Ruth. Who knew how long it took for her to become what she did? It could have been just thirty minutes, maybe less.

They were coming up on the building now. Jeremiah was right, it was easy to recognize as the only one stubborn enough to remain standing. But it canted hard toward the Inferno and even now, it was being stripped slowly by its forces. In just one hour there would be no building left. It was just down the street on the next block. They had to slow down. Wind ripped its way around the structure and threatened to throw their feet out from under them. It became a wrestling match to move at all. Then, they were ambushed.

It was just one of them. The original kind of Worshiper with the charred hands and burnt face. But it sprinted hard into Will, throwing him down and skidding Will's pistol across the pavement. The Worshiper turned around and came down on Will, fast. Will flipped over to his knees and grabbed the lower leg of his assailant, driving himself up onto his feet and toppling the Worshiper with a single leg takedown. The Worshiper squirmed away with surprising speed and stood up. Will punched him good while running at him and he stumbled. Then, Will drew the blade. That nearly two pounds of steel a foot long and half an inch thick at the spine sliced open the neck without any trouble at all. The Worshiper died very quickly, due to the loss of blood pressure. Will was stunned as it bled out and the wind raged. This was the first time he had killed anyone. Even if they were some kind of ugly monster that needed to die, this wasn't like hunting.

CHAPTER 13

I T WAS OVER in possibly ten seconds and Will picked up his pistol again. But a new trouble began. He heard a skipping sound like rocks being thrown at a pavement at high velocity. It was a rapid sound. Apparently, the Worshipers had evolved in technology yet again. Just as before, getting a gun and having the training to hit anything with it are quite different, especially at any kind of range. Luckily the Worshipers had no training for the rifles they were bringing to bear on the two of them.

Then, Will saw another smoky gray ghost sprint out in front of him. It was a tall and lean silhouette with a backpack and, when Will squinted, a machete on its hip! Will was astounded to see his own blackened, smoky ghost. It ran forward into cover up ahead. Will decided to copy his ghost's strategy and James darted for cover behind what remained of nearby buildings. This was a strange situation. Will heard the bullets skipping on the pavement when they hit, but not the gunshots.

They must have sighted the two of them from far away,

he thought. Sniping is not a trait he would have attributed to these freaks, but their lack of proficiency was understandable. Correcting for windage would also be impossible. He knew they couldn't stay pinned down forever. It was either death by stray bullet if they ran for it or death by Inferno if they stayed. Will watched his ghost get up, sprint around the corner and then dive for cover just ahead. Will thought that was brilliant. He could get ahead by moving from cover to cover. Will decided that he had good chances of not being hit, due to the kind of range they were at. But he forgot about one thing. Following her own ghost would have killed Rayne if Will hadn't stepped in. The ghosts were not good.

Will decided to move, still making progress toward the objective building which was now so close they were in its shadow. He rounded the corner and was exposed to their front line, not twenty yards away. He felt an unbelievably sharp pain lacerate his leg and he went down, throwing himself into the cover of the building, just like his ghost did. Here's where he messed up. He had not considered that they were using suppressors, that they would close the distance on them while they were in cover, or that Will and James were upwind of their suppressed shots; making it less likely to hear them. And his leg felt every bit of those mistakes. Will thought it was below the knee and he clutched his leg. He was blinded by the pain, however, and the wind made it difficult to hold his eyes open and he couldn't get a clear view. What he saw next was caught in snapshots between the shocking pain closing his eyes and the will to open them battling each other. A group of three Worshipers had come to finish him off. Life was cruel that way.

Nobody had any guarantees of surviving before the war.

After it? You'd be lucky to not kill yourself before someone else could do it for you. It was an already harsh world, made even harsher because human hatred understood how to do things that the mind couldn't keep up with.

Will had been through quite a lot and he did really well. He was a hero, just like Jeremiah was. He ran headfirst into a blazing Inferno on the off chance he could stop it with homemade pipes of thermite. He could have easily run away at any point. That might have been a worse option overall, but at least that might have allowed him to see Rachel one last time.

At this point, though, excluding his fear of their guns and their bullets, he was exhausted. He spent the entirety of last night hoofing it through haunted tunnels that were preserving a corrupted recording of the human race just to harvest them into monsters. He had to come to terms, within a few hours, with the fact that a ball of fire had invaded his planet and was actively building itself up to hunt down the human race. He had to watch people he had conversations with die meaninglessly. He had killed in self-defense. There wasn't very much more actual emotion you could squeeze out of him at this point. There was only that animalistic fear of death, which was uncontrollable.

His face right now would tell you he didn't want to die. He just wanted to find the love of his life in sheer denial that everything worth living for had ended. But when they pulled those triggers at him, any second now, it would have to be over. James would have to carry on his mission if he could. He was the one holding the box. He knew what to do just as much as Will did. But that was it, he thought. In the midst of the pure chaos of his fear, he saw his death coming. The harshness of the universe had spoken.

But that was precisely the point. The universe was harsh. There were apparently creatures roaming it which lacked any real definition even if they had a body. There were entire civilizations that completely eclipsed the narrow cone of human vision, understanding or empathy. There were things out there that simply looked like empty space when you stared at them. They had a form, but never triggered any kind of recognition. And there were beings in reality that could look at you and all your life choices and all of your emotions as nothing more than the random wriggling and writhing of bacteria under a microscope. So yes, the universe was tragic. But it was tragic for everyone, not just humans. There was a force that exercised itself over the street just then. And it must have *hated* Worshipers.

There were things in this universe so powerful that it might break your mind to even witness them. That was why Will saw only the beginning of it. The Worshipers who had come to end him lurched up in the air as they rounded the corner. They were suspended like props with their backs arching at unhealthy angles. Their heads started turning, slowly. Whatever had caught them was taking its time and enjoying this. It was the only sound you could hear above the wind. The moment their necks snapped, Will blacked out.

He woke up to James shaking him. "Will. We do not have much time... you must have... sprained your ankle."

Will couldn't believe what he was hearing. He had been shot. Sprained ankles don't feel like what he felt. But he sat up and, sure enough, that was the pain in his leg now. But that wasn't it before. Will was too exhausted to think this through. He winced at the pain.

James continued. "I know this... trick. Here." James

grabbed Will's foot and twisted it. He cried out in pain for a moment before realizing it was all gone. The pain was gone.

"Where the hell did you learn that?" Will pried.

"My... mother. She knows... things."

"I thought you didn't have parents anymore," Will said.

"You have had a lot of... thoughts." James didn't even try to make up a story.

"Yeah..." Will trailed off. At this point, Will was simply happy to be alive. He didn't care about the details too much right now. He would get them later. He had even more questions for James now.

"Can you walk?" James asked.

"Yeah, I think so," Will said, holding on to the wall and flinching with the expectation of pain. However, there was no pain anymore.

They left the alleyway and Will noted the bodies scattering the streets like a warzone. Not simply the three Worshipers who came at Will directly. No, the streets were littered with more. All of them were contorted at unhealthy angles. He remembered what he saw before passing out. "What the hell happened? Did you see it?"

"Let's go," James said, blatantly avoiding the question.

Will nodded and made for the building with an unbalanced walk. He was still disoriented, and the wind was still unforgiving as it rushed into the Inferno's maw. James picked up the box of thermite tubes and followed Will. The inhaling breath of the Inferno nearly dragged them away from the entrance. The doors were gone; sucked out long ago. They saw what they were after. There were many thick pillars of reinforced concrete of whoever's ground-floor lobby this used to be.

The building made this constant sound of gunshots as the metal stressed to the pressures exerted on it by the Inferno's hunger, heat and mass. The concrete and remaining drywall cracked under stress. Will could see seven large pillars on the southside. He reasoned those would be the optimal target as they would be primarily responsible for keeping the south side of the building stuck to the ground in defiance of the rending pressures from the north. They had more stress marks than the rest of the building and in some places, the concrete separated to expose the rebar reinforcing it. Those would be the easier and faster targets.

Then there was the matter of actually doing this. Was it better to give one to each pillar and a couple extras randomly slotted in for good measure? Or would he rather concentrate them into five pillars and hope the other two went as a result? Or perhaps he should put three rods into the three strongest-looking pillars and one into the weakest one. This was a hard decision for someone who knew nothing about these things. He ultimately decided he was going for the last option. These pillars would need three rods. There looked to be four strong pillars on the east side and three on their last legs on the west side. The Inferno was slightly to the east of the structure. So, the ones on the west side would have more pressure exerted, he thought. If he crippled the ones closest to the west, they would probably collapse under the pressure.

The best-looking pillars still weren't completely solid. There were some stress cracks throughout them, and the concrete would fall out in chunks with a little encouragement. Then Will realized something rather unfortunate. "Shit! We don't have a hammer to drive these things in, do we?"

He looked at James and rushed for the box. He dug

around and sighed with relief that Jeremiah was a logical man who thought of this detail. He pulled a mallet out from under the spikes and got to work. It was easier than he thought as he first chipped away the material, then hammered the spikes in like nails.

Without warning, Will felt that he didn't want to destroy the structure and the Inferno, and he paused his work. But then he realized that his infection from Ruth's touch had advanced. It was making him think that. He resumed his work. Tears began to form under his eyes as he really didn't want to do this. The Inferno was so beautiful in the sky like that. So much promise. A new world. A new life! Then Will thought of Jack and Ruth. They were friends to him, ended unjustly. They all could have lived forever.

The Inferno was manipulating his thoughts and desires, just like it did for Jack and Ruth. He snapped himself out of it and realized that Jack lasted quite long with his psychological infection compared to Ruth. It was a long shot, but he started to mimic what Jack did in the hopes that resisting it verbally would give him more time. He chanted "no, no, no" repeatedly and he was relieved to find that it worked. It took some of the pressure off.

Speaking and hearing himself speak seemed to anchor his focus into reality. It wouldn't last long, though, being this close to the Inferno itself. But it gave him that slight edge of control that he needed right now. He tapped the stakes of thermite into the first pillar. And then halfway through the second pillar, it spoke to him. Not through the air, but in his mind.

"*Greetings, Will. You have come far. You are among the saved. I have prepared a place for you in my kingdom of heaven.*" The Inferno's voice was magical and god-like.

Will wasn't that easily fooled. He figured that the Inferno was playing its tricks. He thought it was trying to manage human expectations by posturing itself as the routinely celebrated Christian god. The Inferno was clever when it tried to get one to listen. Will would soon realize just how clever it was. He cast away the sly invitation and thought that the only place for him now was beside Rachel, dead or alive. And then he moved on to the third pillar. Will could feel the Inferno crawling around in his mind, searching for Will's weaknesses.

Then, Rachel spoke.

"Will!" Her image ran towards him with her arms extended. She was beautiful. The kind of beauty only she could have and only he could deeply appreciate. Her image meant more than simple beauty. It was the beauty of change. The beauty of salvation and forgiveness. The promise was an end to his journey and an end to the nightmare. But he wasn't stupid. He looked dumbfounded, sure. The expression on his face was one of awe and the tears drew lines of hope down his face. Maybe it was the dust getting into his eyes.

But he didn't believe them. The look on his face masked a different kind of feeling. The betrayal. The idea that her image could be dug out of him to suit the purposes of the being in the sky was too much. Rachel didn't fool him as much as she proved to him that he was fighting a god. He suddenly became hopeless. If it could control perceived reality to that extent, how could Will be convinced that what he was doing wasn't somehow helping that god of fire and wind? *What if he was a Worshiper already?* And just like the Worshipers before him, working together with people he couldn't see to remove the god's only remaining obstacle? To feed it like the other savages. To break down buildings for its consumption.

He decided to drop the remaining thermite rods and embrace her. When his skin contacted hers, she felt so real and warm. He lost all hope of fighting this thing for just that moment. He knew he had been compromised at his core. It was in his nervous system, making him feel. Surely it could make him think, too. But he hated the damn thing. Rachel was a nice sight, but hugging a lie felt like a kick in the groin that he didn't feel he deserved. Then, his own words came back to him. How he told Ruth it was a lie and that, "*It's going to consume everything! Even your blood when there's no more metal!*" And then he found the willpower. Just because he had been fooled didn't mean he was totally controlled, especially if he could remain honest to himself. He felt the power in him to pick up the rod and bring it to the pillar. Rachel moved to block his way.

"Will. Please don't do this. I just want us to be together again," she said. And her face meant it. It was so hopeful and real. *Just how resourceful was this being?* No wonder Jack eventually turned, and no wonder Ruth tried so desperately to stop them. Will was on a mission to kill the only source of heaven that gave a damn about visiting Earth. Will was here to extinguish the only thing that cared enough to make sense to Ruth after Dave died. Will thought about it only briefly. This creature, this infection, or whatever you wanted to call it, was the only good thing to happen to these people since humanity betrayed them and the planet was ruined. It saved them from death in a way. Or maybe it didn't save their lives, but it at least saved their dreams.

It was then that Will knew the thing had to die. He

didn't know completely why it had to. But he knew there was something unbelievably violating about a being of that nature tearing up the planet and tricking people's nerves and giving them the illusion of heaven. No matter how sweet those proposals became, the source had to be eradicated. If only to let the dead rest properly without twisting into monsters. And really, if this were any heaven worth visiting, would there be all this burning, twisting and violence by the apparent citizens of this new heaven? Why weren't they happy until you were dead? They must be controlled by it and so it must die. Those were Will's thoughts on the matter.

He stepped forward to finish the job and she stopped him. She stood in front of the pillar like a guardian. But Will realized something. A way to possibly beat this thing. If the Inferno got Rachel from his memory, could it make her do something Will never thought she would do? More specifically, could Will think his way into making her move? These were his memories, after all. She spoke again.

"No, Will. Please. It's heaven, it really is, baby. You won't find me in Florida anyway. I'm dead. Please, just relax. I know your paranoia can get you so worked up. I'm in heaven and I want you to join me. Your parents are here too. Please…"

That crushed him. It didn't crush the fight out of him because now he was just spiteful towards it. He would take his revenge on this beast for violating the memory of her. But he felt himself splitting into two parts; the one that wanted heaven and the one that just wanted to escape hell. He looked at James, who was right beside him, for some ideas. There was a concerned, studying look across James' face. But Will noticed something weird. He didn't remember James being that short.

Oh no.

He had to think of something quick. He was growing to the height of Jack and Ruth after their transformation. He was becoming the same kind of man-thing that they became. He didn't know how much time had passed compared to Ruth's manic transformation. Maybe he had even less time. He remembered that Rachel would never say anything to him if he needed to think. It was a long shot, but he had to try it. He was really banking on the idea that the Inferno was accessing memories and needed them to be convincing. He thought there was a slim chance that the Inferno could not create anything new. The images were slaves to the person's memory. He had to try.

"Baby, I need time to think, okay? I just need some space for a few minutes. And no, it's not you," he said to his wife.

He chuckled at the inclusion of that last sentence. He remembered the last time he said that to her, she got upset because she thought he was sick of her. But that's not really how it is with introverts. They sometimes just need their own bubble. After talking about it with her back then, he promised that it wasn't her. He also promised to say that clearly the next time it happened. That was the ticket. If Rachel tried to stop him now, the Inferno would risk alienating her image from the memory of her, which would make her less convincing, and the trick would cease to work on Will. On the other hand, if the image just stood by and gave him the space he requested, then she wouldn't be a useful weapon against his progress anymore.

Then, his mother walked up in front of him. It had been months since he last visited his mother. He was shocked to see her for a split second, but then he remembered the situation he was in. There was a story he always wanted to know from her. She never finished the story, so his memory of her would never be able to tell him an answer.

"Mom? What happened with the oil spill in the Pacific? What made you change your mind about covering it in the news?"

"Oh, well... You see..." Will's little scheme was working. "They donated a lot of money to the young women's charities you know I love so much."

"Oh, yeah?" Will was taken aback by this answer. He didn't actually expect an answer. But it was too general and flat. His mother liked to relish the details of things. It was either a part of her editorial background or the editorial side of her grew from a natural fascination for the details. Either way, that answer did not come from her. "Then what company spilled the oil? You never told me that."

"No, I didn't, honey. It was the... Control Co. oil company."

"Hah!" Will exclaimed. His voice was strained due to the new length of his neck. This thing was crafty. Whatever it was, it was definitely operating with a full deck of cards. There was just one issue. There was no such thing as the Control Co. oil company. The Inferno would have no way of knowing which companies existed and which didn't. It appeared that the thing could only really use emotionally loaded memories. It probably thought those memories were the only useful ones to convert people with.

The name of a random oil company would never make it through. And with that, his mother faded to the side where Rachel was. Will suspected his father was next. And that's probably why it didn't happen. The Inferno would have to develop a new game to trick him. Will had cracked the code. But still, the Inferno's evil silence was unsettling. What was it planning to do with him now?

He was just about to finish hammering the last rod of thermite into the last pillar when he noticed his arms and fingers were longer and slimmer than he remembered. Then he noticed something else entirely. It was out of the south side windows of the building. The horror of it paralyzed him briefly. This vision wasn't like Rachel or his mom. This was definitely real because there was no promise of heaven to be seen in it. There was no trick of the eye and no happy, inviting sensations.

They came. Hundreds of the man-things, as gangly and ugly and pale as they were, sprinting at highway speeds over the bridge and turning to face his exact position. Many of them slid around the corner like dogs on laminate flooring, except that it was boney human heels on concrete. They had either outgrown their shoes or had taken them off for better traction. Both options were equally terrifying.

He hurried for his lighter in his bag and started lighting. He lit the one tube while remembering what Jeremiah said about the timing. But Will did not have two minutes. It took him and James at least several minutes to run here. It would not take the man-things that long. He had maybe a minute. He lit all the makeshift fuses at the halfway point and then ran outside. He knew then that he had a problem. He was stuck in the worst possible way.

He had to get away from the building, which was now sandwiched between the Inferno on the North-east side and the man-things quickly closing in on the south side. He had to split between them and go west for now, praying he could stay away from the man-things long enough. James followed and they sprinted harder than ever. Their feet punched the ground for traction, but the feet of the man-things were like sledgehammers on the pavement. They were completely devoted to the image of heaven that Will had the good sense to reject.

Then, Will chanced a look back at the building. A minute had passed. And Jeremiah's legacy of thinking ahead was to be preserved forever. He saw a bright glow at the base, and then there was a sound not even the howling wind could keep away from Will's ears. It was a grinding, crunching, lumbering breakdown of concrete. Will prayed in the only part of his mind that he could still think freely with.

He thought of Rachel, and she appeared before him, standing silent. She was flickering like a lightbulb about to go out. He reaffirmed the promise he made for her in his mind. *I will come and find you.*

The building lurched forward all at once in a matter of a few seconds. It entered the Inferno's large, fiery body. Will felt he had company, and he did. They stood all around him. He never heard them get there because of the wind. He was nearly the same height as them at this point. But they all stared up at their god just like Will did. The building was crushed into awkward portions and fed to the Inferno all at once.

This was the decisive moment. He put on the mask, which was now a little small. The nearly white core fluctuated violently and then finally dropped like a rock. The wind stopped dead and the ball of fire plummeted into the Earth. Its density ensured the ground rumbled with uncertainty. It felt like the ground was sick and concrete streets became waves like water. The ground buckled, throwing perfectly dry dust into his thankfully protected face. The core sank into the ground like a bowling ball into memory foam. The man-things dropped dead, just like they had during the first impact of the war. They collapsed in place like the corpses they had always been. Will saw the smoky, gray ghosts again in his peripheral, but they were staring upwards too. After a few seconds, they blew away skyward like smoke untethered from a fire. And then there was nothing but the distant banging racket of cooling metal and the sound of Will's heartbeat.

CHAPTER 14

WILL SLUMPED AGAINST the halfway gone brick wall nearest to him. He absorbed the sound around him. He realized that this was the first time in well over one hundred and fifty years anyone had heard that kind of quiet in that city. That creaking, cooling metal ball a few hundred yards from him produced a lullaby rhythm, like a distant thunderstorm sounding the funeral of a dead god. He fell asleep for a few hours. When he came back to reality, the dream he remembered was a fuzzy recollection of the Worshiper he killed, Rachel, his mother, and James. He couldn't distinguish whether that was really the dream or just the immediate memory before the dream. He looked for James. Will needed to have a talk with him about everything. He also needed to compare his height to James. He had to make sure he was back to normal. It was close to noon already.

James was studying the cooling ball of metal when Will approached him. "Hey, James." Will still felt gangly and upon getting closer to James and confirmed that he was still about half a foot too tall. "You need to explain everything right now," Will demanded. "But let's talk while we're getting out of here. I need to get to Florida and I'm not letting you drag me around anywhere else."

"Yes... I believe you have earned that right," Will heard, in his head. He was startled beyond his own comprehension. Then he heard the voice again, "Don't worry. It's me, James. It is so much easier to talk like this. It is better than pausing all the time. The human mouth is clumsy."

"You're not human," Will accused now with very good reason.

"You are correct," James said, again speaking in Will's own mind.

Some time elapsed after James said that. Will was terrified. He meant to get out of New York while the conversation was happening, but he was frozen in place by what he was hearing. Although he figured that if James was here to cause harm, he would have done so already. So, he was eager to hear what he had to say. Will turned and started to walk eventually. James followed and Will was about to remind him of his obligation when James decided on his own to continue.

"I was the one that sent you the dreams that you went to your therapist about," James said.

Will was completely shocked to hear those words. It was validation for him to know that those dreams were messages like he thought they were. But at the same time, it was a bit unbelievable to hear that the man that he had been traveling with was the one responsible. The implications of that sentence were stupefying. It was becoming clear to Will that there was much more to this.

"You weren't the only one that I sent the dreams to," James said. "As you know, there were many others who had

had the same dream. I was simply trying to ensure that some of you survived so that you could do what you have just done. It never had to be you specifically, but you seemed to be the most prepared out of all of them."

Will led James back to where the Worshipers had attacked them before with suppressed rifles. The place where he was shot in the leg. James had said that it was a sprained ankle. But now that the wind had died down, he could see quite clearly where he had slumped over in pain just after getting shot. There was blood on the concrete.

"Did you... save my life when we were under attack by Worshipers?" Will asked. Will's head was still very groggy and unclear given his recent bouts of unconsciousness and the meddling of the Inferno on his mind. Perhaps it was just James' telepathy that made it worse.

"Yes, I did," James said. "Because it was irrelevant to your mission."

"What? I don't understand," Will said. "How was my death irrelevant to my mission? It seems like it would be completely relevant."

"Maybe I had better start from the beginning," James offered. "Your species was being watched. When it became obvious that humanity was violent enough to cause great harm to itself, a debate began among our kind. Yes, I have helped you complete this mission, but I don't believe that I've crossed the boundary into interference, because any human could have helped you in the capacity that I did."

"I'm very sure no one else could have saved my life in that way," Will said, remembering the way those Worshipers who were about to kill him lurched up in the air and had their necks broken.

"It could have happened if the person with you had made different choices. If they had merely killed them before they got to you. It was possible for you to complete this mission without my intervention. Therefore, yes, saving your life was irrelevant in the grand scheme. It cannot cross over into interference because that would involve helping you in a way that nothing on Earth theoretically could. I am the one who sent you the dreams because I needed someone available who could complete this task. It was all done to ensure that I had the evidence to make your case."

Will thought about this while he walked over to where the Worshipers lay dead. He saw the suppressed rifles that they used to get the drop on him. He grabbed one for the journey ahead. They were strapped to the Worshipers with a sling. Will took the time to notice that these guys were not just ordinary people turned occult. He never had the time or conscience to notice the details while being shot at. They wore tattered uniforms and armored vests. Their guns were of a military style with various optics, and grips. They had a few extra magazines in the vest of each and all of them were of the same standardized cartridge.

They could have been national guard or swat team. The uniforms were just as charred as their faces were. He took as many magazines as he could fit into his bag, then grabbed a rifle he thought he could shoot best. It had a nice open red dot sight and a comfortable foregrip. He decided it would be wise to steal a vest off one of them. It was heavy, but not as much as he expected. He could manage until he found a working car at the edge of town.

"Did you make that fireball in the sky?" Will said, meaning to accuse James of setting him up.

"No. That was an opportunistic species of EM Hunter. Their world is very different from yours."

"EM... electromagnetism?" Will asked as he put on the vest he got from the Worshipers.

"Yes," James said. "It is very complicated. But the premise is that they use electromagnetic force to hunt for what they call food. It is not as crazy as it sounds. Your own Earth had creatures that can do that, but on a much smaller scale. Electric eels, hammerhead sharks, and the list goes on. Birds and spiders can sense EM charge in the atmosphere. Life can do a lot more than you realized here on Earth."

"But how can a lifeform exist in that state? It was just metal and fire, right?"

"The Inferno wasn't the EM Hunter. It was a trap set by the EM Hunter. Think of a trap that you might make for a rabbit. You set up a metal cage, which the rabbit cannot understand because it is not natural to the rabbit's environment. Then, somewhere in that trap, you place something that the rabbit wants more than anything. A carrot or a few nuts. You want the rabbit's meat, so you set the trap. The rabbit wants the food and so it falls for the trap. The EM Hunter wants accessible conductive materials, so it sets the trap. You want paradise, so you provide some for the trap."

"Holy shit..." Will said, clasping his face, trying to understand. "But how did it control thoughts and memories?"

"Electromagnatism is inherent to how the brain works." James said. "Action potentials rushing through synapses are charged and can therefore be manipulated. It doesn't even have to be very precise. The trap caused more activity in the parts of your brain that hold memories, then it simply created an impulse of need and reduced the activity of your amygdala response. Your brain did the rest. Your brain thought of Rachel when you felt the need. You thought of heaven when your fear was reduced. Your memories made you see your family in front of you and feel that they were present. Unfortunately, most of that mind control process was your brain rationalizing and trying to create a clear picture. The trap didn't need to provide reasons or themes or narratives. Your brain does that automatically."

"You're saying mind control can be automated, then," Will said, incredulous.

"With the right formula, and for a short time, yes," James said. "It's an effective trap set by the Hunter."

Will was trying his best to absorb this information. He knew now that humans were not alone in the universe, but he never expected that a nuclear war would provide those answers. He was not comfortable with the thought that his own brain could be so vulnerable to a trap like that. After some seconds had elapsed, Will realized that the nightmare was over and that he should go find Jeremiah. He knew what he would find. He knew it wouldn't be pretty to see him torn apart, wherever he was. But regardless, he had to tell him that his plan worked and to say thank you. The dead man deserved that much.

"Why did the war happen?" Will asked, making his way across the bridge to the subway station they had initially come out of. "Why is this stuff only happening after the war?"

"The war was your own fault. Your planet was protected by a Veil while life developed. If we didn't do that for new life, then you would be hunted for resources before you even had a chance to fight back. We deem that the diversity of life in the universe is more beneficial than simply letting one kind of super-predator eat everything that ever develops. So, we hide you from them and hide them from you. We provide the balance, and the ignorance to make that happen. The war, caused by humans, set off an inquiry. You see, the planet was protected from outside destruction so that life could flourish. However, the development of those nuclear weapons was concerning. Upon launching them at yourselves, you became the greatest threat to intelligent life on Earth. So, The Veil was broken pending further review."

"What kind of review?" Will asked, his eyes wide.

"If the case for humanity fails, then it will trigger an extermination protocol. We will eliminate human life on Earth to give intelligence a chance to grow from other sources. We will eliminate the largest threat to the diversity of life."

"Us," Will said, finally understanding the implication.

"That is why the case is so important. I am trying to argue that your life is not merely intelligent, but conscious. That you can rise above definitions and circumstances to handle even those things which you cannot understand. Consciousness is more important than mere intelligence and they would have to reinstate The Veil to protect your future development from being interrupted by other species. If I can argue that you are part of the conscious category, then The Veil will be restored, and humanity will be given the chance to continue from here and rebuild the world. If I fail to convince them, then we will have to rely on other primates to become conscious over time."

"Have I done it then? Have I convinced you?" Will asked.

"You were compromised by one of the most effective

mind-altering traps in your galaxy, yet still you persevered. Many humans wouldn't. Almost no intelligent life forms can withstand its influence in the short term without equipment. This, to me proves the difference. However, there will have to be an argument and both sides will have to be heard. I am sorry for your predicament, but the test was necessary."

They made their way across the bridge. The New York City subway system must have had hundreds of thousands of people in it when those bombs hit at the height of the day. There were bodies everywhere. The bridge was practically made of them. There were few places where you could look down and see the concrete between the warped limbs and torsos. Will went down into the subway system through the same station they exited before. He climbed down the stairs, avoiding the bodies that littered them, and then he saw the nightmare Jeremiah had to endure for this plan to work. The bodies were stacked up and flowed like dominoes falling over onto each other from one end of the tunnel to the next. They were all motionless now, but they all had fallen forward. One had to wonder if they were so eager to get a piece of Jeremiah that they frantically climbed over each other like mealworms.

The man-things were aligned in such a way that Will thought that just before their death, they were running right past the stairway he took with James. They flooded down the tunnels that go under the river. Further down the tunnel, the bodies stopped and seemed to turn around and climb over one another in this chaotic-looking pile of nightmare fuel. They were trying to get back to the exit that Will had gone through. He stumbled over the bodies, cold to the touch. The body vest made it so much harder to balance himself. It must have been sixty pounds or maybe more. He noticed random fingers and toes and strips of Jeremiah's clothing. At the very end of it all, there he was. The collection of whatever remained of his parts. He successfully led the man-things down this tunnel before he was caught. "Misdirection can be your best friend," Jeremiah had said earlier. Will told Jeremiah's body about the success of the mission while trying not to look at his corpse.

"Jeremiah. We did it." Will started speaking carefully in respect for the dead, and was partially startled by his own echo. "The thermite rods you made did the trick, the building was the right size for the job, and it was close enough. And most importantly, you kept them off us while I did it." Will paused as if to let him take in the fact that they won the day. Struggling to deal with the air in the tunnel, Will said, "Maybe you'd like to know the details, right? You seemed like that kind of guy. Well, I wanted to attack the pillars on the south side because I thought they were under more strain. There were four good ones and three bad ones. I put three rods each in the good ones and then the last one in the—" Will choked up and gagged a little bit and had to breath in his shirt and close his eyes to compose himself. The smell of death and viscera plagued these halls of horror and the thought that Will was speaking to a man who had been ravaged by unspeakable beasts pushed itself into the forefront of his mind. How indescribably terrible it must have been to scream alone in these tunnels.

How awful it must have felt to realize that the last time he saw the sun, he didn't know it would be the last time ever. He didn't imagine dying in the dark. Maybe he had always thought that his excursions to the surface would get him killed one of these times. The Inferno had changed much more than the anatomy of people. It breathed life into dead bodies. It corrupted light into darkness and memories into brainwashing. Its death may very well have saved the world. Of course, Will had previously had his uncertainties about whether this thing was actually a threat to the globe or if it was just confined to New York City. There was no more doubt.

"The last one, I put in the weakest link," Will continued. "And then I saw them come out of the tunnels. I saw myself changing too and figured I only had half of the time that you set those things for. So, I lit them halfway up the fuse and we ran. It all worked. I guess I'm just here to tell you that it's dead. Your soul can rest easy. You're a hero, buddy. And as long as I'm still walking, I will make sure that you get what a hero is owed. A memory, and a story. I will tell others of exactly—" Will had to stop himself again. He had no more tears to cry right now, but his throat didn't get the memo. It still choked him up. "Exactly what a hero of humanity can do." And with that, Will set off. He climbed over the bodies and went west after consulting his map.

"James." Will turned around and looked hard at him. "Include Jeremiah in your case for humanity. He was the only one here who had a plan to save us. Not me. He was the one who was willing to sacrifice it all. Not me."

James stared at Will for an uncomfortable length of time. Finally, he said, "Yes, I agree. But do not discount yourself. You *are* willing to sacrifice it all. For Rachel."

"Rachel!" Will yelled, his senses finally coming back to him. He realized that James had promised answers. "Where is she? Is she alive?"

"She is still alive for now," James said.

Will felt an instant sense of reassurance but also a sense of emergency. He felt that he had to get to her as quickly as possible, but it is not every day that you get to meet an alien. They continued to make their way out of the city. "But what is your name? Your real one."

"I am known as Number One. You can continue to call me James. It is a nice name," James said. "My apologies for tricking you so much. But you must believe that it was necessary."

"Number One? How many of you are there? Are you the first? Their leader?" Will asked.

"I am the first, but not the leader. There are many of us. I am the first one to be assigned to this... section, let us call it. I cannot describe for you what the different sections are or how they came about because I need to avoid interference. The less you know of my species, the better."

"You manipulated me into coming to New York City to begin with," Will said. "Isn't that interference?"

"Believe it or not, it was your choice to help me when I claimed to have family in this place. I didn't create your sympathy. I just prevented your mind from generating too many questions along the way. I am not very good at impersonating a human."

"What are you then?" Will asked.

"I am not able to explain that right now. And you have a journey to continue," James said.

"So, let me get this straight," Will began. He was grinning involuntarily from the strain of trying to wrap his head around this. "There is an argument in space about the validity of our species as intelligent life. The argument was triggered by Armageddon because it proved our inability to let life flourish. Our protection from the harsh nature of the universe was revoked and now crazy shit is happening because we are being punished. If you fail in defending us from our accusers, we will be wiped out and the planet will be given another chance without us. If you succeed, we will still have to put up with this hellscape and try to rebuild. Do I have that right?"

"Mostly, but you are wrong in two ways," James said. "The argument was not triggered by Armageddon. It was triggered by genocides long prior. For intelligent life to diversify across the universe properly, genocidal races must be kept in check. The true nature of the universe must be shrouded from them, and they must not be able to conceive of faster than light travel. And you are not being punished. The Veil broke because you moved yourselves into another category. We did not do that. The Veil is only designed to help relatively safe species flourish before contacting others. You proved with certainty that your species only gets more dangerous as you advance. We thought, for some time, that you had turned a new leaf. You had nearly eighty years when your violence had progressively declined after what you call World War II. It turned out to be a false trend. Now, overwhelmingly, the consensus is that the violent trend is the true one. That was your last chance. That is why the only way to defend you now is to prove that you are in a different category. That you are all individually very different from each other."

Will realized at this point that humanity never could figure out faster than light travel. Of course they couldn't. They were marked as too dangerous. Like a convicted felon who is not allowed to own a firearm. Will wanted to test this idea, though. So, he said, "Then why allow us nuclear weapons? If we're so genocidal then why were we able to conceive of nuclear theory?"

"It is the difference between building a gun that can shoot others and a gun that can only shoot yourself," James said. "Without faster than light travel, those nuclear weapons cannot hurt anyone but you."

Will wanted to pressure him more about humanity. "Then why are you defending us at all then? Why are you telling me all of this? Aren't you defending our genocidal abilities?"

"Are you genocidal?" James asked, sharply.

Will looked around as if wondering who James was talking to. "You mean me? No, never. But why does that matter if everyone else has already decided that we are?"

"It is not normal for members of a species to have very different thoughts about things. It is quite rare, actually. Most intelligent life is collectively intelligent and those that do not have a collective mind at least have mostly the same ideas. It is irregular for a species with your level of advancement to have nuclear weapons at all. The fact that you figured it out without collective intelligence makes you either a conscious species, or the most dangerous intelligent organism in this galaxy at the moment. You are only held back from violating the galaxy's life by lack of technology alone."

Will recoiled at that statement. Science fiction would have you believe that aliens are the dangerous ones. They are the ones who would invade humanity and subject us to their will. He realized in this moment that humanity was like Jack, back in the tunnels, rocking back and forth in the corner of the room, unable to deal with their environment or inner turmoil. And just like they were all concerned with the threat that Jack posed to them down in that maintenance room, other species were concerned with the threat that humanity posed. Humans were the trembling psycho in the corner that no one wanted to deal with.

"But what about the EM Hunter? Isn't that thing a lot more dangerous than us?" Will asked.

"That is much more complicated than you might think. They hunt conductive materials, not life. Just like sharks that hunt fish, not humans. Yes, occasionally humans get in the way and suffer for it, but sharks are not a threat to humanity as a whole and never will be. They don't even understand you as food. Neither does the EM Hunter. It is just not that dangerous."

"What? But Jeremiah said that it would come after the iron in our blood. He said it would destroy the world! How is that not dangerous?"

"Jeremiah was a smart man, but he was wrong here," James said. "The iron in your blood would take more energy than it is worth going after. And the planet is too big to be prey. The trap you destroyed in New York, if it was trying to hunt the planet, would be like a house cat trying to hunt a moose."

"So, what was the end game, then?" Will asked.

"Simple. The EM Hunter will come and collect the trap once it is full."

"So, that thing was never a threat to Rachel, or me," Will said. "Then why didn't you tell me back when Jeremiah was telling me this? Why not correct him?"

"Interference," James said, clearly wondering how many times he was going to have to explain that. "Also, it *was* a threat. It manipulated people both dead and alive to help it consume more materials. You called them Worshipers. It was preventing you from traveling anywhere in a vehicle. It was doing its job of preventing metal from escaping. I needed to prove that you are able to handle something you cannot understand. It just so happened to be the right opportunity."

"Then what about the Buffalo pipe network? You said you saw it as well," Will asked.

"Yes, The trap of the EM Hunter had grown to become very powerful. The bomb that was dropped on Buffalo was of a massive size. It pulled the pipes out of the ground with the shockwave. The Inferno merely seized an opportunity. It is responsible for the movement of the pipes."

Will thought that answer was as reasonable as he cared for it to be. Then he asked, "The sonic attack that shut off the people of New York and killed them where they stood, the one that was avoided by the others in the tunnel because they wore headphones. What was that one?"

"The initial deployment of the trap," James said, calm as ever. "It is meant to paralyze and keep creatures very close to death for a long period of time. It is the initial EM pulse, it does something to the brain. The headphone wiring is a far better conductor. The technology ensured that the pulse went around their heads instead of through them. The insulated wiring prevented the frequencies from repeating back into the brain, converting them to sound instead. Hence the sound of ocean waves that Charles had claimed he heard. It was really static following a sine pattern of the information it was receiving. Converting electrical input into audible sound is the function of headphones, after all."

Will was stupefied at the coincidence. Regular old

headphones defeating the technology of an alien race was hard to believe, but it made enough sense for him to follow. Still, he felt he was short on time, so he wanted to get back to the topic of his involvement in this whole plan. "So, what you were saying before... I'm different from humanity then? Is that why you're talking to me?" Will asked after a long pause.

"Do you feel different?" James asked.

Will felt like he was back in therapy all of a sudden. "Why don't you tell me? You're the ones who are blocking our brains from understanding things."

"I think," James said, "that at the end of your journey, in the near future, you will have to prove how special you really are. You will have to show exactly how you deal with Fear, Death, Anger and Wisdom. I think that you will have to choose which truths become real and which ones are put behind you. You will have to prove your consciousness. You will have to know the difference between the threats that face you and the future ahead of you."

"So, the test is still ongoing?" Will asked, exhausted.

"No, you have done your test already with the Inferno. That is all I needed from you. But, if you want to add even more evidence to help your case, to prove that you can handle even more of those things which you cannot understand, then that is beneficial."

"Beneficial..." Will repeated. He felt as though he had been trapped in his thoughts for some time. When he looked around himself, he didn't recognize where he was. He wondered how long they were traveling for. The buildings were in better shape than the ones he had seen just a few minutes ago, as if the Inferno never had any influence here.

He turned around and asked, "Hey, James. Where are we—"

James was not there.

Will wasn't angry. James had fulfilled his promise to give some information once everything was done. He still couldn't believe this. All of it. The Inferno, aliens, the argument in the heavens. It was too much. But he would have time to think it over on the way south. He still had a promise to keep. After all, it was clear that this new world wasn't going to wait for him to be comfortable with it.

CHAPTER 15

WILL LOOKED AROUND and saw a shop sign for a "Newark Deli". He decided it must be Newark, New Jersey. He eventually found a car at the western edge of the city with its driver door open and keys still in the ignition. Will saw the driver, or what he thought was the driver, burned up in the ditch to the side of the road. He must have thought that diving for cover from his car was a good idea. The bomb that hit Newark must have been an airburst high up above the city. Will noticed on his way through the city that cars had been crushed flat and a few buildings too. But the destruction wasn't total. Unfortunately for the driver, ditches would then be worthless to protect from the temperature and pressure wave as it came in from above.

He sat down in the car, which was far enough away from the bomb to at least be in drivable shape, and the seat complained with a crunch. The interior was black as it likely caught fire. But the windshield was intact, and it looked like the fuel didn't explode on this one. It was hard to find cars that were intact. Fuel does not react well to fast increases in temperature.

Will attempted to start the car. It worked, miraculously. It was late afternoon at this point. His legs ached with the new weight of the vest, and he just wanted to rest his feet.

Will restarted his journey south. He passed by the empty buildings of Newark, then the suburban houses of the outskirts and then trees whose leaves had been burned off from that bomb above. Will thought about Dave and Ruth. He felt sorry for Dave. He seemed so stressed out. But Will couldn't think about Dave without also thinking about what Ruth said. That she would have killed him herself eventually. Will remembered the feeling of shivers down his spine when she said that. Something about the Inferno's influence was making her say those things, Will thought. But maybe that was wishful thinking. Maybe she was always like that and the stress of that situation in the tunnels made her finally show her true colors. Dave never transformed into a man-thing, at least not to Will's knowledge.

It was beyond disturbing to think about what Jack had gone through for a full day, trapped in his own mind. Will had to play the Inferno's games. He knew that there were puzzles to solve to avoid getting convinced of its heavenly propositions. Was that all that Jack was doing? Was he denying his family members too? What was the Inferno offering him for all that time? Even worse, what the hell finally made him accept its persuasion and give in? Was it just too much and it worked by brute force? Jack did get noticeably more tense and distraught with Dave's yelling going on. Was that the last straw? What if he wished for Dave to shut up? What if the Inferno offered Jack the power to shut him up? That would be why Jack didn't attack the people with guns, but Dave's neck was singled out as a priority.

Jack opened up far more questions than answers. But so did Ruth. She seemed like such a sweet person. She was soft-spoken and was clearly submissive in general. When she transformed, there were two options. Either the Inferno had full control of her thoughts and words and used her to try and trick them, or her quiet nature was carried over into that form. She was the only man-thing that tried to convince them with words before attacking. The three of them that remained never got to see what Ruth wanted to do when she lunged at Will. Maybe she didn't want to kill him, but just hold him in place. It was too dangerous to find out. Jeremiah made the right call by shooting her even if he hated himself for it. But one had to wonder how such a nice person could become such a monster. But that would depend on one question. What on Earth was she offered by the Inferno?

It wasn't entirely clear that everybody had been offered something to join the Inferno's heaven. But it seemed reasonable. Jack was resisting something. That was clear to Will when he used the same tactics to ward off his subversion to the Inferno. Will was offered an eternity with the image of his lovely wife and mother that looked and felt so real. He missed them both too dearly. That's why the Inferno caught on, he thought. But what would Ruth be offered? She seemed to change quickly and callously down a spiral of slight psychosis even before they had to leave her behind. Perhaps that was exactly it. She didn't need to be offered anything. She was in a vulnerable position, and it took full advantage of her distress and started to twist the open wound of her husband's death into something dark and sinister.

There wasn't any way to know. Maybe she wanted all of them dead for not saving Dave in time. In any event, it was time to reflect on Jeremiah. He was probably in love with Ruth. It's a little irresponsible to fall in love with a married woman over just a week of being in the same space. But Will couldn't judge him too harshly. She was quite pretty for her age, and she would have been a type of innocent that Jeremiah could protect. That sounds ridiculous, but men sometimes get protective of random women. Plus, if protecting her innocent mind gave Jeremiah one reason to say that there was still something to live for then it would have warded off hopelessness.

These kinds of things are not easy to understand. Will didn't have the full picture and really, it was doubtful that anyone did. Jeremiah was definitely a complex person. Probably due to his intelligence. He cooked up the most hare-brained scheme known to man. He wanted to collapse a building into a floating ball of white-hot mass using nothing more than the random scrapings off pipes and aluminum cans that were stuffed into tubes and using shoelaces as fuses. That part made Will chuckle quite a bit. It was probably insane to think that way. But, honestly, with the way the world was working now, insanity was just the new way of being "well-adjusted" to your environment. It was then that Will saw something in the rear-view mirror that made him slam onto the brakes and come to a screeching halt.

He opened the back seat and stared at it. The original driver of the vehicle apparently had a passenger with him. A small skeleton charred the same color as the seat. Will didn't see it immediately because the color blended in. The Newark driver must have jumped out and abandoned the kid in the back. It's crazy what panic can do to a person. To a parent. He carefully went to remove the skeleton from its fused position in the seat. He wasn't squeamish about these things anymore. After what he saw in New York, this wasn't that bad, it was just sad.

But then he touched it, and everything changed. The world became brighter, the trees were in full bloom and the world took on this nearly heavenly aura of normalcy. As if the bombs didn't happen. They were back in Newark, just outside that deli that Will first saw. Will and this child, now perfectly alive, found themselves in the world before the bombs fell. She was a little girl. She had a yellow bow clipped onto her hair and hazel eyes. It was midday and the world was normal. There were the many smells of a local bakery. The sun shone carefully on the skin. The wind carried a cooler feeling and was very welcome. Cars were driving and people were walking and talking about whatever. The little girl looked up at him and asked, "Who are you?" She was clearly distraught by a stranger opening the car door.

Will didn't remove his hand from her shoulder for some reason. "Oh! God, I'm so sorry—" he began but then was cut off.

"Hey! Get the hell away from my daughter!" A man came running out of a store, darting towards Will.

Startled, and preparing to explain himself, he backed away from the girl with his hands up. And just like that, he was back on the road, in the drab real world *after* the bombs. What the hell was that? Will stood there, slowly shaking his head and looking in the same direction the man was coming from. There was a catch in the back of his throat, then tears welled up in his eyes. Then he cried like hell.

This world was far too crazy for him. He was in a state of complete traumatic shock. He curled up by the fender of the car and hugged his knees for dear life, checking to make sure no one was watching him break down. People are often so concerned with not being sad in public. But now there was no one to see him, so he just let it all out. Everything came back to him all at once. The warning message he got on his phone and the sirens he heard on Rachel's end. The few days he spent hiding down in the carport. Seeing the world for the first time on top of the apartment building and seeing his first melted corpse. The situation with Rayne and her attempted suicide. The ridiculous metal structure of Buffalo. Being tricked by a damn alien to come to New York. Dealing with Worshipers, the Inferno, and the truth about The Veil. And now this? Touching skeletons that can make you hallucinate?!

He had had enough. At this point, he thought, he wouldn't mind it if he got hit by a passing car, if there were any, or just died from exhaustion. This was just too much. He was in the fetal position for a few minutes, but he eventually uncurled when the tears stopped pumping out. He sat there, legs and arms limp. He sat there for a long time just trying to make sense of it all. He couldn't find the strength to get angry at anything, or to blame James for not stopping the end of the world when he clearly had the knowledge that it would happen. He was simply drained, and he passed out from exhaustion, but didn't die from it like he hoped.

CHAPTER 16

WHEN WILL AWOKE, it was already nighttime. He got up, painfully, and looked inside the car. The skeleton was still there. How would he reckon with the hallucination? It felt so real, like he slipped into their timeline. But if it was real, that would bring forward even more uncomfortable questions.

Will shook his head, dismissing the thought. It wasn't logical. He was just spooked by a child's skeleton and hallucinated. *Rationality*, Will thought to himself, *you have to keep it together*. He stepped forward, convinced that the child could stay in the car. It would cause him less trouble than trying to remove her. He didn't want to risk another hallucination. But as he approached the car door to close it, he jumped back in a sudden fright and yelped. Her skull was looking up at him; just like in the vision. So, his decision was made for him. She had to go.

He was not about to drive around with *that*. The seatbelt was still buckled in. It wouldn't come out, so he reached for his kukri to cut it right beside her hip. It did a terrible job of cutting the seatbelt. The edge of the blade was polished, which lent to its toughness as a chopping tool, but detracted from its ability to slice anything. The blade just didn't have the roughness necessary to dig into that waxed seatbelt material.

He jolted back with a fright when he stood up to reach for his other knife in his bag. Her skull was looking down at where he had been working on the seatbelt. He tried to tell himself that her body moved with the seatbelt when trying to cut it and her skull just so happened to roll over that way. But it wasn't absolutely convincing. Rationality wasn't doing it anymore. He grabbed the knife, flicked it open and went to work. After a few hard cuts, it came loose. This time her hips had shifted, and her chest twisted as if to pay more attention to what he was doing. But those were hard cuts and he definitely jostled her around that way, right? He didn't want to touch her to actually remove her. So, he had the fancy idea of taking the small prybar from his bag, hooking it in and carrying her from under the ribcage.

It worked fine. Her body was light and easy to move without all the weight of muscle, fat, and organs. He wasn't likely to dig this girl a grave while she stared at him doing it. But he wanted to at least put her in a ditch, like her father was. He looked both ways out of habit before crossing the road and then went to drop her into the crevasse when he saw the problem. She was holding onto the prybar like a rope and looking up at him.

"God!" He shouted. Shaken to the core, now, he threw her in the ditch and the prybar with her.

Rationality was officially dead here. There was no explanation of jostling or otherwise that could explain her hands around that bar. He seriously wanted to leave the prybar behind and be done with this damn thing. But it was the only one he had, and it could be useful for locks or doors later on. He figured he just had to man up and rip it out of her hands. He stretched downward and grabbed the bar, being careful not to touch her directly. If only it was that easy.

He noticed that she was looking at him again with her head tilted to one side. Something about this look compelled him to speak.

"I'm sorry," Will said to the lifeless skeleton.

Then, for whatever reason, he felt as though he should comfort her. He did not forget about what happened the last time he touched her, directly. In fact, that was the goal. He thought if he could hold her hand, then he would go back and help her, somehow. He grabbed her boney hand, and he was immediately taken back to a time when she had hair and a face that could smile.

She looked up at him holding her hand while she was in a ditch. She sat up and giggled. "Your face is funny," she said as a look of concern came over her.

Will folded like a house of cards. "I'm sorry, I'm so sorry," He grimaced. "I don't know how to help you." His chest started convulsing as the emotion could no longer be contained.

"That's OK, mister. I don't need help anymore," She said, still smiling at him. She pulled her hand free from his grip and the illusion ended. Will had his prybar back and her arms were now crossed over her chest peacefully, pretending to be properly buried.

Will didn't know what to think of all this. Some part of him wanted to sit here all day, paralyzed. Another part of him wanted to actually bury her to the best of his ability. But the larger part of his mind simply wanted to continue on and find Rachel.

Will had the paranoid feeling of having walked into a spider web as he moved away from the skeleton. Typical supernatural fears like haunting or spirit vengeance plagued him as he continued onwards and thought more about the nature of death in this world. He never expected to be fighting the skeleton of a young girl to throw her out of a car, into a ditch, and then wrangle his prybar back from her. He never expected to be forgiven by her, either. He got back in the car and began driving again and thought more about death.

Death in general was just strange. Everything that died in the world was apparently just waiting to become something else. Memories were recorded in smoky ash, bones apparently held a record too, and what else now? This surely couldn't just be the psychosis of himself alone, Will thought. Ruth, Jeremiah and the other people in the New York tunnels saw them too. Well, most of those people turned into monsters so he could not be too sure if they weren't psychotic themselves. As for himself, he was fairly sure that it was real. Before the end of the world, he was convinced that death was a material definition for a material event. That is to say, when one dies, nothing remains to haunt the world or the heavens afterwards.

In general, one could say he was sad about it all. He was sad about that little girl. He felt sorry for the souls of that City of the Damned where he killed a giant ball of fire that could hack his mind. His gut twisted a little every time he thought about what Jeremiah went through in the tunnels. Foremost, he was sad that everything he knew before had ended. The old world was so comfortable compared to this *disaster*. He missed his family. He missed Rachel, but he knew she was alive so he could suspend that feeling for a little while. He didn't know if he would ever see his mother again. He felt like he needed her to come and tell him that things weren't as bad as they seemed or maybe tell him another one of her stories. Anything. And yes, that's right. A grown ass man wanted his mommy. But, more so, the idea of his mother was really just a stand-in for normalcy. He wanted his world back. He should have seen his parents more often. He should have done a lot of things differently.

But something inside Will had died back in New York, in the heart of hell. His willpower to find Rachel when he left the apartment building could be described in one word: commanding. He had the total and unquestionable desire to brave the world back then even if it was scary to think about. Now the word to describe it was "pleading". It wasn't that he had lost confidence in whether or not the goal was worth it, but he had lost confidence in his ability to do it. One would think that killing what was essentially a god with nothing more than sticks of thermite would boost his confidence to the moon. But Will knew the truth. He was damn lucky. Had he wasted even a minute, he would have been torn apart by the man-things. He didn't feel like a hero, yet. He felt lucky to have escaped with all four limbs and his life. He felt a little queasy.

BRAKES! Will thought as he slammed on the brakes. He came to a halt as a deer galloped over the road in front of him. He sighed in relief that he didn't hit the thing. But at the same time, he was happy to see something alive other than himself. It gave him the sense that the world hadn't stopped its natural processes. It wasn't entirely an alien planet.

CHAPTER 17

H E CONTINUED ON and had just crossed into Maryland. He was coming up on the Washington D.C. area. He had been driving well into the night and figured that he should wait until morning when visibility was better so that he didn't crash while daydreaming. He was also tired, which was odd considering how much he slept earlier. He guessed that being unconscious for eight hours isn't the same as sleeping for eight hours in terms of his health. He decided to camp up in the hills to the northwest of D.C. He would have to be quick getting to Florida. If he rationed it, he had four days of food bars. It would only take a couple days to reach Daytona Beach from here, but he would have liked a better safety net than that. He felt that he couldn't fall asleep in the car given the risk of more hallucinations or time travel or whatever that was that happened with the little girl.

It wasn't a terrible idea to sleep outside. He had a small tarp in the bottom of his bag that was thin, but it could protect him from wind and rain if it came to it. He held his flashlight in his mouth as he worked to fasten it. He tied it with paracord to two thin trees an agreeable distance apart. The other two corners of the square tarp were secured into the ground by a couple of tent pegs. It was crude, but effective. He didn't really feel like building a fire in the dead of night and it was certainly warm enough to go without one. He ate some food and fell asleep without realizing it.

He entered a dream seamlessly that tricked him into believing he had woken up for real. The sun was high, and it was late morning. He felt odd and almost like he lacked self-control. He picked himself up and came out from the tarp. He saw three Worshipers on their knees. They were raising their hands up and their burned faces were looking up at him. He didn't feel particularly startled, but he did feel rage. It all happened in such a blur. He couldn't control himself, but he liked what he was going to do. He lunged at the first Worshiper and started tearing him apart. He felt strong and a superhuman kind of powerful. It was easy. There was about as much resistance as wet clay mixed with the snapping of a small twig wherever there was the occasional stubborn bone. Will could feel his smile nearly overtaking his ears. The other two Worshipers looked surprised and betrayed and scrambled to their feet. But Will was a lot faster.

After dispatching those two by the very same method of mutilation, thoughts had overcome his mind, almost shouting at him from outside his body. What were they doing here? Why were they worshiping him? Will didn't take too long to figure out what he was. He was a man-thing. "Am I the next step in their evolution? Is that why they looked up to me?" And then he felt the call of heaven. The sun beat down on his elongated neck and he turned to face it. Ah yes, that was what they were worshiping. They weren't giving praise to Will. They were worshiping the sun, the greatest Inferno in the solar system. He felt compelled to worship it as well and he had no choice. He dropped to his knees, threw his hands up to the sky, and woke up.

Will must have been sleepwalking. He found himself in what yoga enthusiasts might call the "child's pose". He was on his knees with his hands outstretched in front of him and touching the ground. The dirt left a distinct print on his forehead. He was facing the rising sun. It was early morning, which meant that he didn't get the length of sleep he would have wanted. He was disturbed at the pose he woke up in. But he thought of a way to verify his height. He had to make sure he wasn't a man-thing. He had a thin tape measure of six meters' length in his bag somewhere that he forgot about earlier. He stepped on the metal hook end of it and extended it all the way up over his head. He pinched at where he thought the top of his head lined up to and gasped quickly at the number. He was six foot seven inches tall.

That was an unfortunate measurement. Normally, guys would love to be that tall. But Will examined his arms and legs and found them to be longer and slimmer than he had remembered. He decided, still in disbelief, to test his strength on one of the local small trees. It was just a little bigger around than the grip of one hand, even at the new size of his hands. He tugged at it a little with one hand before bracing his other hand against it for a real pull. He heard the wood cracking and stopped short of pulling it down. Checking the other side of the tree and seeing splintered wood, he marveled at his own strength. But he could never see Rachel like this. He was halfway to being a monster. He thought that he might be accepting of his new form if at least his face was normal, so he went to look at his reflection in the river.

It would have been nice if he had thought of packing a mirror in this bag of his before the world ended. A signal mirror would have been a sensible thing to include if he was ever lost before the bombs fell. But that was a different world. He could have clicked a button on a website and received a signal mirror in the mail in three days. Now, it was unlikely he would ever find one. In his present state he had one goal. Find his wife. He wasn't keen on exploring the unkempt skeletal remains of human society. Though it would have been fascinating to enter people's homes wherever the buildings still stood, he could not waste the time. In any event, the horror of the things he would see if he did explore the world was not going to help his mental stability.

It was already teetering on the brink just now and he didn't need another horror story. He didn't need to know what families clung together in the living room in their final moments. He didn't need to see the shadows of people burned into the walls. He didn't need to think about all the parents clinging to the cribs of their young children as the end flashed them all into burning wallpaper. He needed Rachel. He had almost refused Jeremiah's scheme to defeat the Inferno. In fact, you might say he did refuse and then changed his mind. He still couldn't believe his luck that he was alive.

Mental stability was the key. There was truly no sound that could compare to the sound of hundreds of man-things scraping their way through a pitch-black subway tunnel. There was no horror quite like the devil hacking your mind and body to produce your loved ones in front of you so convincingly that you could reach out and touch them. Feigning paradise when you need it most. There was no loss quite like a man who gave his life and died horribly on the supposition that he might buy Will a few minutes on the clock. He could have simply left New York, just like the kid had when Will first arrived. All of this had taken its toll. He would need a *long* time to recover, and he didn't know whether his body would be the same again.

But he guessed that his long journey of recovering from mental trauma had to begin with finding Rachel. He could only bring himself to see her if he was normal in the face. Looking down at his reflection in a nearby stream was interesting. He was actually mostly normal, even though he felt like an abhorrent freak. Especially after his dream last night. But the only changes were that his skin was a little tighter, eyes beadier and more sunken and jaw line more pronounced due to the skinny nature of his face. He was relieved, to say the least. He tried thinking about it objectively. If he was taller, stronger, and probably faster, then he had come out of all this more adapted to his environment. It would be a huge evolutionary success to change that much in the same body. Now he had to mix feelings of being cursed with the thought that this might be a blessing. It might help him get to Rachel after all.

He just hoped that his mind didn't break beforehand.

CHAPTER 18

WILL GATHERED HIS things and hit the road, trying not to dwell on all that he had been through at this point. He checked his map as he came out of the woods and into the clearing by the road when he saw something strange. Washington D.C. wasn't there. There was a large dark spot in its place. It seemed rather odd that it would be burned flat like that considering Will had passed many cities at that point and none of them had the same effects from any type of bomb. Though D.C. was home to the nation's leadership and harsher punishments were expected compared to the cities of the plebs. He got out his binoculars and zoomed them in as far as they could go. No, it wasn't a flat dark spot. It was a hole. Not a crater, a hole. The opposing sides of this hole went straight down. It was like a giant sinkhole swallowed the city, but Will knew better. It was possible that the bombs shook up enough of the Earth that a sizable part of it subsided and dragged the city down with it. But it was more likely that multiple nuclear bombs blew up on the same spot over and over. They were used as shovels, sucking up the dirt from the city and distributing it around the state of Maryland.

Will remembered what had happened to Buffalo. How the pipes from underground were brought up and curled by the force of whatever weapon descended on it. The same might have happened here, but multiple times. Not even the pipes remained. They would have been trying to get to the president's bunker under the White House and whatever other underground safety the representatives of America's government thought they had.

He saw the car by the road and thought briefly about the little girl and his trip back in time. He couldn't make any more sense of it now than he could last night. There seemed to be an internal pressure coming from the back of his mind to push down the thoughts of everything he had been through so far. To suppress them. It could have been stress or disbelief or both. But he realized how dangerous the radiation around a hole in the ground like that could still be. He lifelessly got in the car and headed south once again after eating the terrible breakfast of a meal replacement bar.

He went all the way to Charlotte, North Carolina that day with his mind silent, but alert. It was a long drive and he arrived in the evening. The trees had gradually differed themselves from the ones he left in the morning. Green and a few strange colors were replaced with a brown that was nearly total among them save for some evergreens. The gradual shift to these darker colors unsettled him like some ominous warning. The background was reminiscent of a dying world of forests whose life-supporting processes were cut. The city was in clear view, but it looked deceased and decayed from a way off. The brown jungle of forests had reclaimed large swathes of the city. It didn't look like it was hit with a lot of force. Certainly nothing like Buffalo. But the area around it looked sickly enough that Will was convinced a chemical or biological agent had been at work here in the last week and a half.

The city looked terrible. What was once a bustling metropolis in the south of the state had become sinewy with vines and overgrowth which stretched from building to building. He decided to stop near the outskirts, where the overgrowth appeared thickest. The rate of growth must have really been incredible. His request of this area was simply food. He was getting rather tired of mass calorie bars and his brain could really use a bit of diversified nutrition. He figured he needed a bit of self-care to keep his mind from breaking. He was going to locate a store that sold canned vegetables and canned potatoes. The kind that you merely have to heat up and serve for a taste of what the old world used to grant you for less than ten dollars.

Upon leaving the car, the smell was one of freshly cut grass. The air felt heavy and sub-tropical. He made his way into the overgrowth, watching his footing carefully. The lines of brown across the road threatened to swallow him up if he tripped, he thought. He looked down the street, which was flanked on either side with signs of stores amid the trees that came up through the sidewalk. Will really hoped that those trees had been there before the war, and hadn't just recently grown in. It was a strange thought, but something felt off about this place. The more Will stood still, the more he felt like he was moving ever so slightly. It was as if the ground was crawling around underneath him, oblivious to his weight and treating him as a feature of the street, not an obstacle. Will knelt down to examine the roots or vines or whatever they might have been.

He saw movement, to his surprise. These plants were growing before his very eyes. It was a general uneasiness that he felt on the road coming in as well. It was a sneaky thing, too. It might have been because of the dream he had last night, or what he discovered about himself that morning, or even that damnable lack of nutrition which was undoubtedly catching up to him. Hell, he didn't even know if he was really awake or if he was still dreaming. His dreams had felt so seamless lately. Not just in the last week, but for the last couple of months too. He certainly didn't feel like he was dreaming and yet this plant growth was impossible. It never could have set in that quickly after humans had gone. It would have taken decades. But then again, just how many impossible things had he seen this week?

He moved down a block and looked down that street as well. He should have seen the sign for a grocery store somewhere. He had been to the States on a few occasions before and he knew the brands, but there was nothing here either. Another piece of the puzzle stung him in the eyes as soon as he realized it. Where were all the people? There were a few cars parallel parked along the sides of the road, but no bodies in them. It was difficult to keep his balance on the apparently unsettled pavement. But he didn't even see the signs of human activity abruptly ending like he had seen elsewhere. It didn't look like a bomb went off here. At least, not a nuclear one. If this was a chemical or biological attack, then that would explain the absence of people that were out shopping along this road.

Then the thought came to him without solicitation. *Don't*

go to the hospital. He didn't plan on it, but if this was a non-nuclear attack then that was where all of the ugly stuff would be. He carried on searching block after block until finally he laid eyes on the sign for a supermarket. He approached it, maintaining his balance across the roots and vines of the road. He turned the corner of the building just before the open expanse of parking lot that spread out, inviting the consumers of the end of the world to browse its goods. Then he saw something more unbelievable than he could imagine. He thought he must be hallucinating again.

People were shopping at this store. It was a normal grocery store with a wide glass front. The parking lot was filled with cars, unlike the roads. Normal life was commencing right in front of Will's eyes. The sound of shopping carts rattling along concrete with their imprecise metal construction was perforated by the sounds of people discussing shopping lists and the slamming of car doors and trunks. All of the sounds of a normal place.

In the middle of this parking lot, there were three juvenile trees scattered randomly among the parking spaces. One of the trees had upended a car that used to park there. The scene looked as though the tree grew underneath the car with such force that it eventually toppled the car over and it landed roof first on the car beside it. Will locked his focus in on one particular family out of a dozen or so. This family was heading in the direction of the upturned car. Their shopping cart was closer to him than all the others were, so he kept his cover. He stared around the corner with one eye and noticed that their cart was violently shaking through the lot. The wheels were hitting every vine and root and tossing their groceries from one side of the cart to the other. They were a husband and wife and very happy. They laughed while saying something Will could not hear. The husband pushed the cart into position behind where their flipped car used to be and where the tree now commandeered the space. The wife brought out her keys and made all the motions necessary to pop the trunk and the husband started putting the groceries into nothing but air. It was as if they were pretending to still have their car there.

Will was puzzled by this behavior. If these people were aware enough to get groceries, why could they not see the obvious state of their car? Nobody seemed to notice the state of the parking lot or of the vicious war the land was waging on the otherwise desolate city. The grocery bags hit the ground, the woman closed the non-existent trunk, and the man returned the cart to the overgrown corral. They both opened the doors to a car that was no longer there and then tried to sit down in it and fell to the ground. They then got up quietly and stone-faced. Their disposition was no longer that of a happy family but was all business now. They stopped pretending they had a car. The man picked up the groceries from the ground while the woman grabbed the cart back from the corral. Then, like robots on a production line, they moved back towards the store for a reason that Will couldn't guess.

Will emerged from the corner and moved towards the store. He was emboldened both by his curiosity of this new situation as well as the fact that these people seemed oblivious to everything about how their environment had changed. He deemed them no threat. He caught up to them with a jog and simply followed. He knew he wasn't dreaming now. The sounds were too real and then there was the smell. The land here smelled the same as earlier, like fresh-cut grass, despite the fact that it was a parking lot. It was a nearly sickening aroma. The groceries in this store were probably spoiled. It was then that Will realized everyone had "reset". Some people were headed back towards their cars and others to the store, but altogether drone-like and inconsiderate of each other.

There was no more talking and no more laughing. He followed them into the store, which must have had the doors open when it lost power. The produce which should have been kept fresh with mist and refrigeration now decomposed on unmanaged shelves and hung the air with the stench of decay. The whole store was bustling with the commotion of what appeared to be an army of shelf stockers. All of the people who had been shoppers now worked diligently to put everything back where they found it. All the cans, bottles and packages were stocked back on the shelves by rote memorization. Will tried to move so that he wasn't in the way of all of these worker bees. Or perhaps "zombies" was a better term for them. The most anti-social zombies in the world with a mean streak for obsessive repetition.

Will watched until everyone had dutifully completed their seemingly God-given tasks. Then it was like everyone had hit play on the video of their lives again. They were coming into the store, grabbing hand carts and push carts and gathering the things they needed for the next cycle. They were talking again and laughing but the whole store came to life too. The cashiers beeped items through the checkouts and the whirring of refrigerators came online. There was just one issue. There was still no power. Will didn't think it possible that the refrigerators could start working again. If the produce was any sign, then the refrigerators weren't running at all. So, what was that sound? Will looked at the checkout lanes very intently for a few seconds, only to realize that the people playing cashier were making the beeping noises with their mouths. He looked to the refrigerated section and everyone who opened the door mimicked the whirring sound of a fridge purposefully as they took their undoubtedly spoiled prizes out.

It was starting to dawn on Will that these people were some other kind of crazy. Shopping at the end of the world was one thing. After all, that was what Will came to do, in a way. But replacing everything where you got it and then simulating the functions of the store itself? That was a step too far. People were even still inserting their debit cards and pressing on the keypad as a formality. But there was something else odd. Well, the whole damn thing was odd, sure. But this was something inconsistent with their whole scheme. If they were perfectly stuck going forward with their day and then reversing everything, why didn't they refund themselves? If they were going through all of the trouble of paying for it over and over and they wanted to simulate reality so badly then surely they would realize that they were running out of money, paying for groceries they were never actually getting.

They obviously thought they were getting real groceries, that's why they put them back before doing the whole cycle again. But didn't they ever consider they were spending real money and that they should therefore refund themselves? This observation puzzled Will until he thought that they weren't simply stuck in an automated loop. They were ignoring everything they conveniently could about the absurdity of their situation. They were ignoring everything that didn't fit the narrow focus of their occupation at the moment. They were certainly ignoring Will. They wouldn't even look at him. He felt like a ghost, invisible, even though he was taller than all of them with that new stature the Inferno gave him.

It seemed as though there were certain things they couldn't ignore. Reality must've hit them in the face before when they inevitably ran out of groceries to buy, which is why they restocked them now. It was just a way to make themselves happy. Maybe it was a way to ignore the fact that the world ended. Perhaps they were so desperate for a sense of normalcy that they ignored the very ground they walked on being covered with a lattice of vines and roots, the power being off, the perishable food being thoroughly perished, and the money in their banks not actually being transferred. Finally, they were ignoring him. Will decided to go about his business. All he needed was in the canned vegetable aisle. He would grab a few cans to last him a couple days and to finally get him away from those meal replacement bars with their grainy and powdery texture.

He made his way over cautiously, trying not to disturb the flow of things. Getting a better look at the people themselves, he didn't think they looked infected with a biological agent or fleeced with chemical burns. From the outside, they looked normal. That is, until he noticed the dried blood on their lips and around their mouths. It was nearly hidden with most people in the store. But one middle-aged woman had a very pronounced and rather fresh drop of it down the side of her mouth that was dutifully ignored by everyone else. Until it wasn't. Will fixated on the dried blood streak as she made her way to the checkout with a hand cart. The girl at the register finished with the couple before her and then, when she switched to greet the woman, gasped and froze in place.

The young girl, who couldn't have been older than sixteen, raised a very shaky and terrified little finger at the woman's chin. The young one held her mouth open, ready to scream, when the woman looked down with her eyes and frantically began wiping her face. She pried and clawed at the dried, flaky blood mark that still managed to stain and streak its way around the corner of her mouth. The cashier's breathing had become panicked, as if she was having some kind of attack. Then, with the magic of saliva and sleeves, the woman was cured of her visual disturbance and the girl stopped panicking. The woman shoved her groceries backwards on the belt before the till and went back with them to a place just before she caught the look of the girl.

She closed her eyes and took a deep breath. Her hands closed into fists of anxiety and rage with such a tightness that Will imagined her knuckles cracking. Or maybe he really did hear it? Then the girl at the register returned to a position as though she hit rewind. Then they suddenly resumed as if nothing had happened. They conversed about the weather in between the beeps the girl was simulating for the register. The girl complimented her hair, took her payment and sent her on her way, awaiting the next customer. As much as one could write several textbooks about the sociological nuances of a grocery store zombie cult, Will was becoming rather desperate to leave. He needed to get the canned veggies and potatoes. That's all he bloody wanted, and it didn't appear that anyone would try to stop him.

He went through an otherwise normal aisle which was partially blocked by two perusing customers, one on each side. Will went to squeeze through them and then as a completely automatic reflex he said, "I'm just gonna get by ya there." Both of them in the aisle froze up as if he had threatened them with a loaded gun. Granted, he did have a loaded gun on a sling over his abdomen. But they didn't look at him before he spoke. They froze up like that girl at the checkout did. The other three people who were down the aisle further also froze up. The people turned and looked at him for the first time since he got there. They pointed their shaky, scared fingers at him like he was an eldritch abomination. Admittedly, they had some reason for their fear. He was halfway to eldritch abomination thanks to the transformations the Inferno set upon him in New York.

Will was freaked out, but not panicked. He homed his focus in on the cans in the aisle, looking for his desired items. *I'm just here for the fucking vegetables*, he thought to himself. He found some green beans, corn, carrots, peas and finally canned mini potatoes for stew. He opened his bag and reached for the first can. When he grabbed the can, the whole store fell silent. Refrigerators stopped whirring, cashiers stopped beeping, and the lights turned off. Will hadn't even noticed that the lights were on, they were so dim. But the lights couldn't have been on. There was no power. But if the cashiers and the refrigerator people were making the sounds with their mouths, who was doing the lighting?

Will gulped down a pile of horror as he looked up slowly. The rafters in the ceiling were crawling with humans holding flashlights. He was horrified to know that these people had been watching him from above the whole time. The flashlight holding people scrambled themselves in the direction of the front door when Will saw them. Will looked back down to realize that he was alone in the aisle. Now was the time to panic. He grabbed as many cans as he could stuff into the sides and top of his pack and then sprinted for the door, where his worst nightmare was confirmed.

They were all standing in a line from one side of the windowed front of the store to the other. They were shoulder to shoulder and looked straight at attention, but not at Will. The voices came forward from three of them. They were just as shaky as Will expected. Their faces did not change and were completely expressionless besides a faint hint of desperate worry in their eyes.

One woman said, "Stephen? Please tell me that's you, hon. At this store."

One man in a green shirt said, "Daniel? Buddy... it's uh... been so long since I saw you here... at this store."

The third person, a man in blue from his T-shirt to his jeans, said, "Jesse! I was going to call you later! It's great seeing you here. At this store."

Will felt like throwing up. Were they trying to shoehorn him into their past experiences? There was no way, in his current state, that he looked like anyone they might recognize. He knew that he only had a short time to fix himself just like that woman from earlier with the blood on her lips. *And what the hell was that blood on her lips?* He decided it would be best if he went along with their lie. The woman said Stephen was a "hon" to her, so he would be difficult to impersonate. The man in green said Daniel was his long-time buddy, so that would result in the same problem. He decided to impersonate Jesse as there was some chance that he was a stranger or an associate or co-worker to the man in blue.

"Hey! Yeah, it's me, Jesse... at this store." Will decided

to add in the "at this store" part in case it was some kind of code.

Then a small, terrified voice squeaked its way from the checkout lane. "I can help you… over here. In this lane."

Now this was making a little more sense to Will. They probably thought he was stealing and were defending their store collectively. It was a hell of a defense, to give them credit. The "at this store" saying wasn't a specific code either. It was merely an affirmation. It was a way of speaking the store into reality. Just like this girl who said, "In this lane." She was affirming the existence of the lane and thus the store as a whole. It was a very interesting religion they had somehow created. *But what the hell was that blood on her lips?* Will moved over to the checkout and set only a few of the cans he took on the belt closer to the till so the girl could ring them in. She beeped the most frightened beeps Will had ever heard in his life. It sounded as if a microwave was terrified of someone approaching it for their food, but it knew it must beep because that was its function.

She finished scanning most of the cans and then hurriedly asked him, "H-how's that weather today? O-outside of this store?"

"Oh, yes, it's quite fine. A good day to go shopping. At this store," Will replied and added the affirmation part heavily.

He was terrified of his own words. He was careful to keep his opinions in check as though he was surrounded by judgmental family members at a wedding. But he nonetheless felt as though if he continued to talk like this, he would somehow find himself entranced and trapped into a lifetime of faithful repetition. At this store. She turned her face up at him for the first time with this desperate smile that wasn't so much a formality as it was a pleading "thank you". As if Will just saved her from some nightmare of her own.

"Will you be paying with debit or credit?" she said with an easier tone.

"Oh, uh, debit please," Will managed. She turned to hit a button on the cash register and turned back again.

"Whenever you're ready!" she proclaimed cautiously.

She was dangerously close to being happy with their transaction. Will felt now like an international spy who was pulling off his disguise incredibly well. But then he reached in his back pocket and, well... there was no wallet. Will searched his other pockets frantically and put a hand on his bag before realizing that for all the items he had prepared for the post-apocalypse world, he had forgotten his wallet. Yes, of course he did. The girl's smile dropped off her face lightening quick. He left his wallet in Ontario, Canada. *Because who uses their fucking wallet for anything after the world has ended!* Will saw that the girl's face had started twitching. Her breathing accelerated again while the corners of her mouth warped rapidly, on the verge of crying.

The man in blue spoke with a grave tone. "Jesse... you, uh... you would never forget your wallet, Jesse. At this store... Jesse."

His last words were conclusive, like a judge finding one guilty and bringing down the gavel. The girl screamed a short, panicked, and violent scream that hitched and echoed throughout the store. Will closed his eyes for just a second, absolutely furious with himself. Like a spy who had blown his cover by giving the wrong passcode. The middle-aged woman that had blood on her mouth earlier was among those lined up and suddenly said, "Thank the store for providing! I'm still hungry." Will turned to look over at her and she was baring her teeth. Her teeth were red with blood, and she looked at him hungrily.

They entire row of forty people snapped their necks towards Will in a dead stare of ill intent. They bared their teeth too and it was all red where there should have been white. That was the other thing Will never accounted for besides his wallet. It should have stood out to him immediately. The fact that this many people did this much shopping at a grocery store but returned everything afterwards. *What were they eating?* They couldn't eat the food in the store, or they wouldn't have anything left on the shelves. No, they couldn't eat from the pockets of their god. This store was their temple, and poor suckers like Will were their sacrifices. Sacrificing people's lives to maintain the appearance of order is a perfectly human thing to do. It's not particularly religious or cultural. It's just history. All of history. Eating the bodies after the fact is merely a utilitarian measure.

They converged on Will as a ravenous and unified mass of hysteria. Will stopped short of breaking that tree earlier that morning. But he was about to find out exactly how strong the Inferno made him. He shoved hard and six or seven people fell away like bowling pins. It wasn't difficult to do, so he did it again and again. He swung punches that cracked like a whip and collapsed whoever was unlucky enough to catch one. But there were too many. He had to make a break for the windows. He shoved hard again to make way and then ran himself into the window. It broke as easily as a potato chip, and he ran like the wind. The people followed him. Dozens of screaming feet upset at his defilement attempted pursuit, but the Inferno gave Will speed as well as strength. There was no chance to catch him. He could have turned around and shot them with the rifle he got from New York, but he was too scared to turn around.

Then, before he got too far away, he heard the rapid popping of something behind him. It wasn't a gun. He risked turning around briefly and found his pursuers cradling each other and screaming at a roll of firecrackers. More rolls were thrown from a group that Will now saw approaching the area. The grocery cult members retreated inside to avoid the chaos caused by the firecrackers, while one of the men approached Will. They were in plain clothes but looked highly coordinated. They had semi-automatic rifles and vests like the ones Will snatched from that Worshiper in New York. But there was a difference. They each had one grenade by their hips.

CHAPTER 19

"**H**EY, ARE YOU alright? Shit, boy, you can run—and you're lucky, too." The man's voice was gruff and southern. He was a stocky man who looked up at Will in disbelief at Will's height.

"Oh, yeah, I'm alright. Thanks." Will looked again at the store in amazement. "Who are you guys?"

"We're the Southern Rangers and I'm Jason. The other two guys are Cole and Dale." He gestured in their general direction as they approached.

"Well, it's a pleasure. I didn't think there was anyone sane left. You guys know how to handle these… people?"

"Yep, we're normally in the area to prevent people from going in, but we weren't able to be around all day today. We were just coming back from a scavenging run in the city," Jason said, shrugging under the weight of the pack he was carrying.

"So, what the hell is their deal in that place?" Will asked.

"Well, the way I figure it, they need that store to stay safe and they don't take too kindly to strangers. They are downright weird, though. We only found out that fireworks are effective because Dale wanted to screw with them a couple days ago on another run. I should really let Cole explain. He has a whole theory on that place."

"Ah, I see."

Dale looked over Will and whistled. "Holy moly, boy, you must a' been a basketball player or somethin' before shit hit the fan. And you're geared to Armageddon too, man. Just where the hell did you get all that?"

"Well, uh." That was going to take some explaining on Will's part. There was just no way he didn't come out of that explanation looking crazy either. "This stuff was mine, before the war."

"Nice prepping, then! Where are you from?" Dale said, clearly admiring Will's foresight.

"Oh, uh." That was going to take a heap of explanation too. And the man might get suspicious if Will said he was from Canada. There was just no way he got his hands on *that* rifle in *that* country. "I'm not from around here. I'm from up north a ways. I'm on a mission to find my wife in Florida."

"Ah, a noble man too. Hey, Cole! I think this one's useful!"

"Oh yeah?" Cole chimed in while already approaching them. "Well, when we get back, we can let her decide. What do you say, pal? You must've been in that grocery store for something, right? We cook fresh food back at base. We don't fuck around with that trail mix crap either." Will was wary of new people, and of straying too far from his goal, but he couldn't resist the opportunity for food and possibly information about the road ahead.

"Sure. Jason told me you guys were the Southern Rangers. Is it just you three, or…?"

"Oh, hell no," Cole quipped. "We're three out of twenty-three." Will followed them as they went north. "There's all of us Rangers and then there's the Baroness."

"Oh, hell yeah… the Baroness…" Dale said with an airy sense of forlorn love mixed with the heavy admission of desire.

"Shut the fuck up, Dale," Jason intervened with a jovial laugh. "You'll get your chance once you earn it. You'd do well to show some damn respect, boy."

"Get your chance?" Will inquired. Their remarks about her and how they hung with emotions made Will think that they saw her as some kind of idol or prize.

"Yessir," Jason answered. "She is something else."

"Yes… sir," Dale said with that same air of lustfulness.

Cole offered Will some explanation. "You see, the group got started when just six of us met up with her. She wrangled us up, more like. I'll spare you the details, but we all liked her already from… previous experiences. About a week ago, we realized we had to find her and make sure she was safe. It turned out she was more than safe and had plans. Big plans. The walls of her basement were covered in contingencies with maps of the region and targets of interest. She wanted to rebuild society from the basics up. She originally sent us out to find recruits who might not have been touched by the chemical. But now we do scouting for resources."

"Wait, what chemical?" Will asked.

"What do you mean what… say, just how far north are you from, boy?" Jason prodded.

"The northern states," Will said, hoping to excuse himself from this inquiry.

"Oh," Cole said. "So, you really are on a mission. That makes you useful. She would love to know what's been happening up north. But in the meantime, let me try to explain that store. It'll help explain the chemical. Basically, we believe that there was a chemical attack on the region (and as far as we can tell, the entire state). We don't know what the original plan was, but the outcome has been to prevent those affected from learning."

"More like prevented all new experiences from being recognized in the brain," Jason added to Cole's description. "I think the original, cruel intent was to prevent people from surviving in the post-apocalyptic world. Nuclear bombs can only kill so many of us, boy. We're tough. But if you made it impossible to learn how to adapt, for instance, the country would never bounce back. The United States would be extinct forever after everyone starves because they only knew how to source food at grocery stores that no longer have power. Cannibalism will keep them going for now. But there's a lot more hunger than there are people."

"So, you think it interfered with the creation of new experiences? New pathways?" Will asked.

"I don't fuckin know, man," Cole answered. "But if you thought that supermarket was tough, you ain't seen nothing yet. The inner parts of the city are brutal. That's why we're doing the scavenging runs and not the newbies we recruited yesterday."

"Good plan. It was so strange in there. Everyone ignored me until they couldn't anymore. First, they tried to cover up my presence by trying to make me someone from their past.

A few of them started acting like I was a long-lost friend. Then, when I failed to pay for the things I took, they said they were hungry and swarmed me."

"I said it once and I'll say it again. Boy, you are one lucky SOB," Jason reminded Will. "And I don't think I've ever seen someone run that fast." He chuckled.

"Alright, so, I gotta ask." Will was still puzzling over part of the chemical attack idea and also trying to avoid questions about his physical abilities. "What's the deal with all this overgrowth?"

"Probably a second chemical bombed into the country-side to accelerate growth," Cole guessed. "Why would they do it? As I said, I don't know. Maybe to erase the human impact and eliminate civilization from the area. Maybe it was to get at whatever survivors were hiding in the city. Hell, maybe it was to kill the country folk more reliably. Nobody knows. What we do know is that we've repurposed about half of the Rangers' efforts to scavenging the city. Because we give it about a month before it becomes impassable."

"Really?" Will said in amazement.

"Yes, oh, hell yes, really. We've already seen, what? Like, nine or maybe ten buildings fall due to shit growing up through the foundations. Once it reaches inner city, we'll have a serious risk of the skyscrapers collapsing in on them-selves. It's just too much. Concrete was never built for this much pressure and erosion."

"Holy shit." Will pondered for a moment. "So, how was the gas spread?"

"It wasn't gas," Cole said. "You wouldn't have this kind of effect if it was a gas. Gasses tend to distribute themselves over an area. The agent would be diluted over the sky and the wind. There would be no way to ensure everyone got the proper dose of air even if everyone went outside for the same amount of time every day. But everyone has to drink water."

"Ooh." Will let that sink in for a second. "But that wouldn't affect anyone who drank bottled water."

"You're only half right. On the one hand, everyone washes their hands and dishes using tap water. They cook using tap water. The food that they buy likely has water somewhere in its processing and that would have to be tap water, too."

"Fair point," Will conceded.

"On the other hand, I'm pretty sure bottled water is just tap water with a little processing. So, if they really wanted to compromise the ability for people to learn and adapt, the best place to do it would be the major water distributors a couple weeks before the war. Let it run through the supply chains."

"I don't know, man," Jason rebutted. "I think that water is quality assurance tested for chemicals leakin' into the supply."

"Yeah, but chemicals have to be tested specifically," Cole continued. "They probably didn't have the test kit for this agent. Hell, they probably don't test for anything that regulations don't force them to."

"So," Will interjected, "you think that those people in the store couldn't recognize new information or experiences. But I'm not so sure. People in there seem to be pretending. They do their whole dance and then seem to drop the act, restock the store and then do it again. They decide this collectively like a rehearsal."

"I'm definitely not the guy with all the answers." Cole chuckled. "You may have just got here, but we've only had a little less than a week to learn about it ourselves. It could be that what you said was right. Not everyone got the same dose. Maybe it only stopped certain parts of the brain from learning and everyone in there is just coping. Like, all half-conscious."

"So, how is it that you all weren't affected?" Will asked.

"That's a damn good question. We all had the runs for a week before the end. Everyone we recruit was on their own well water supply. So is the base."

"Alright, wait. If it prevents people from having new experiences, why are they eating people? Nobody has past experiences of being a cannibal."

"Hunger ain't a new experience, boy," Jason answered. "And hunger makes people do crazy things. You know what they say. We're only nine meals away from anarchy."

CHAPTER 20

WILL HAD NEVER heard anyone say that. However, he did hear about people going crazy after three days without food. The brain is very complicated, and it isn't easy to predict. There aren't really any nice and tidy ideas that don't include their ugliest extensions when people get desperate. They made their way back to the Southern Rangers' base of operations. It was a good distance northwest of Charlotte. It looked every bit like you would expect a place to look with only one week of work put in. There was a standard lawn fence which was reinforced and increased in height with random boards to make it look like a wall at a distance. A man sat on the top of a ladder holding a rifle just a little to the side of the main gate. That was their excuse for a guard. Will had to wonder what use people like this might have for a front gate guard. They were far enough from the city that random stragglers from there were not going to be likely to mount an assault. They just wouldn't need this unless they were expecting other enemies.

Will was excited for the food. It would be the first good

meal he would have had in nearly two weeks. The front yard of this white two-story house was littered with rusty things and the old stories that could be told from the objects scattered about. There was a car with no wheels which had the look of rust spreading over the paint like a fungus. There was an ancient lawnmower up against the house that was more at home in a 1990s home care catalog. One of those red and yellow plastic cars for kids had bleached pink and white and was left sideways. They were left long enough that the grass gave up on growing underneath. Even in a lawn which was unkempt for two weeks or more, the weeds by the rusted and sun-bleached objects were aggressive.

Will looked at the portion of the gate that was beside him. The wood was old and gray-looking and was pinned in with rusted nails. These Rangers didn't build this up. The house was like this already. Likely made up by someone who wanted more privacy from the neighbors or the road. The only new thing here was the ladder and the man on top of it who was eying Will with an uncomfortable pressure of suspicion. They moved inside the house and up the stairs and that's when Will met her.

She was a tall and shapely woman, which is to be expected for someone so casually referred to as "the Baroness". Aside from that, though, she didn't look like much to Will. She had almost standard-issue brown hair at standard length and volume with unremarkable facial features. She was simply bland to him. He really expected her to be something else, based on their reverence for her. It struck Will that she could have this kind of sway over them possibly because she was the only valid sexual option for these men. She held that over them like water in a desert. She beamed when she met Will, but he was mostly numb to it by now. Really, he was just hungry, and he had seen too much in this estranged reality to be swayed by this woman. Especially since he was hunting his own woman and was getting closer by the day. He figured that within two days, he would find Rachel.

But he was very tired, very malnourished, almost completely traumatized and halfway to being a monster thanks to that Inferno. When they found her in the master bedroom, she spoke to Will. Her voice was her one redeeming special quality. It was a deep, soft and smooth voice of reason and measure.

"Ah, is this a new guy, gentlemen?" She drew out the question as she looked him over.

"Well, I think he'd be useful." Jason repeated his earlier appraisal of Will.

"Really?" She seemed delighted about that. "Well, let's just see if that's the case, shall we? Take him to the tunnel we found. His mask will help him, and it'll serve as a test of worthiness... for me."

The Baroness tagged on that last part, and it hung with expectation. It was the kind of challenge that has been mass produced throughout all of history for men to go through some trial to impress a woman in courtship. She tagged it on in an attempt to place herself within his values as somebody worth impressing. Will wasn't taking the bait. He was too tired and too hungry. But she snapped her fingers and swung her hips and Will was being dragged out by the very same men who brought him here.

"Hey, what the hell?" Will protested.

"Sorry," Cole provided. "We have to keep up those kinds of appearances around her. We don't actually mean to throw you around. But look, if you do this, you'll get to sit at the table with us. It'll only take an hour. It's just that we have this tunnel that's nearby and we can't get through it because of the chemical gasses. But your respirator is rated for all kinds of things, right?"

"You're joking," Will accused. "They could be the same chemicals that turned everyone in the city insane!"

"No, no! It's not that. These are probably just some industrial chemicals or some shit. We had a few guys try it over the last week. There's a stinging of the eyes and nose that tells you it's toxic, but we haven't had anyone go crazy. Hell, you saw one of the guys when we came in. He was up on that ladder."

"Alright," Will took a moment to think. "And you need my filters because you don't have your own."

"Exactly. We're trying to scavenge for them, but they weren't very popular before the war. Now they're impossible to get."

They moved on through the woods which were gathered outside the back of the house. It was only a few minutes before they reached the entrance and Will could already smell something foul. It was certainly an industrial smell, but that could mean anything. He put his mask on begrudgingly. He didn't want to run some random errand just to prove himself to a woman he could not care less about. He wished he had just taken the food from the store and camped out somewhere else. But now it was too late in the day. He didn't want to be traveling out at night just in case there were still such things as coyotes, or worse, whatever it was that coyotes *became* because of this chemical.

"This is about all I can join you for," Cole warned. "You

got the mask, now just get in there and tell us what you find. A real quick search of like thirty minutes or so. Just get a good look. If you find anything surprising, then let us know up at the house."

And with that, he was off. Will put on the mask. The entrance to this supposed tunnel was actually a large pipe with an overgrowth masking the metal ribbing down the sides and a gaseous aroma coming from its depths. The whole of the area was difficult to see as light was becoming more and more scarce throughout the evening. Will took his flashlight and illuminated the first few yards of tunnel. It was nearly a jungle. It was still open enough to walk through, but the already faintly traced metal sides were quickly replaced by a very similar brown sprawl that had plagued the city.

Will pointed the light towards the ground and found that very same overgrowth had completely conquered the ground with its lattice of writhing roots. He found that the whole of the ground was covered. He must have gotten used to the lack of solid balance on his feet. He bent down for a closer examination of the roots and found that, yes, they were moving perceptibly. It was a slow thing at probably around one inch covered every minute, but that was incredibly fast compared to normal. What would normally take this ecosystem years to do was being accomplished in mere days.

Will sensed that the heart of the matter was inside of there. Or maybe it was one of many hearts. So, he went. The crunch of fresh growth underneath his feet echoed within the cylindrical confines of that tunnel. It was only absorbed slightly by the plant matter which harassed the inner circumference of the metal structure. He trudged along uneventfully for about ten minutes when he noticed an offshoot. He saw that the vines and roots which entered this area were thicker than the ones he had traversed thus far. They nearly pulsated with energy. He wasn't as nervous as he was curious now.

He turned down the offshoot pipe and didn't have to travel far before he found something so awful he had to close his eyes, brace himself against the wall and control his breathing very carefully. The vines were feeding. There were maybe fifteen or twenty bodies packed up in this dead end. The vines had worked themselves into various orifices and jutted out from one body to the next randomly. They were decayed, not by time, but because the plants needed their nutrients to spur growth and were sucking them dry. Whatever the gas was in this region, it was even making the plants carnivorous.

Will composed himself outside of the offshoot and back into the relative safety of the main tunnel. This just about turned the whole experience upside down for him. If this was just a simple exploration mission, why were there so many bodies here? And now that he had asked that question, he had to examine the whole thing. Why did the gate guard really look at him like that? Was it really suspicion or was it more of a hungry look? Why was the Baroness so keen on sending him here instead of hearing what Will had to say for himself? Why had she been so matter of fact about it? It was as if she was talking about a raw resource that needed to be moved from one place to another when she told them to take Will to the tunnel. Finally, why did Cole ask him to report anything surprising? This just wasn't making any sense.

Still, Will decided to brush aside all of the smaller details. There were only three observations that really counted. First, there would be very little chance for all these bodies to get here themselves and die in the same spot. Second, it would take many people to move this many bodies all to the same spot through these kinds of woods. Third, these "Rangers" had been here for a week. This is their literal back yard. The only reasonable option was to assume the Rangers had been feeding the vines these poor souls. But that left out a major conundrum. What the hell was Will doing there?

He had to think about this for some time before the store flashed back into his mind. The store cannibals had a trial for him, too. He just had to buy something so they could ensure he was part of their identity. His undoing was that he forgot his wallet. He broke their spell and they decided that he was better off as food since he couldn't make the ranks.

Will decided that this was it. The Rangers were checking if he could notice anything wrong. If he did notice something, he'd end up like the bodies here. If he came out learning nothing "surprising", then he could be counted on to not disturb their order. It was a long shot, but Will thought it was his best chance if he was caught leaving. Otherwise, he was sneaking out. It was better to avoid it all together. He made his way back to the entrance and was almost there when he stepped forward and tripped on a root. He fell sideways, hit his head on the side wall of metal and vegetation and all went dark.

CHAPTER 21

WHEN HE *THOUGHT* he woke up, it was due to a tickling sensation on his neck. He didn't wake up, but he would find that out later. The daze of being lost was quickly replaced by the realization that he couldn't turn his own body on the ground. He couldn't move his arms or legs much at all. Then all of that was rushed away by the horror and panic of what he was restrained by. When he focused his vision on the rootstocks slowly slithering like worms around the edges of his mask visor, he knew. The vines had got him now. The growths were trying to find a way into his mask inch by inch. He reached for the kukri on his left hip. His right arm was entirely restrained as it was pinned to the ground by the weight of his body and the dozens of rope-like appendages subsuming him into the bed of this conscious forest.

His left arm barely budged under the python grip of the root. He thrashed wildly to hopefully gain some room. The fabric of the forest floor fought him at every step. He was only barely able to reach the button snap that secured the machete in its sheath and clicked it open. He levered and tried to wrangle the blade from its secure sheath. Ironically, this was one of the few times the safety of the thing was deathly detrimental to him. It was a very secure and well-made sheath and so it was impossible to pull the blade out improperly or by some loose accident. Will was surprised that he was struggling this much, given the strength he received after the events in New York. He felt as though he was much weaker somehow.

He hunched his shoulders forward as far as they would go in an intense effort to stretch the forest cables far enough to let his arm move the blade. The vines gripped and cut circulation as he moved, but when he returned to his original position, he found he had enough room to pull it forward by a few inches. He then had the idea to grab the spine of the blade, now partially exposed, and inch it forward until he had the machete near the tip, and it was out of the sheath. He repeated the process in reverse to bring the butt of the blade back towards his hand. He bent his wrist, positioning the blade's spine beside his arm and beneath the vines, ensuring the blade faced up and away from him. He wanted to cut out the vines like opening a letter. He needed to use the blade to cut his own arm free first, before anything else could happen.

Upon grabbing it as firmly as he could, he shimmied his arm up and down while providing outward pressure against the vines with the edge of the blade. He was trying to saw the vines apart, but he experienced the same problem that he did with the seatbelt when trying to remove the girl's skeleton from the car some time ago. Kukri typically are not made with a toothy edge that will give the kind of cutting

power expected by dragging any knife edge against a rope or a string. Kukri are made with a polished and smooth edge to help with chopping tasks to prevent rolling or chipping the edge on impact. They are designed for chopping, not for draw cuts. So, Will's plan wasn't working. He couldn't tell if he was failing to cut open anything on these rapidly growing vines or if they were healing it all back together faster than he was working. Regardless, he needed a new tactic. The vines were continuing to gain ground on the rest of him.

He shimmied the blade over to his elbow to attempt to use his arm as a lever and push the blade through this carnivorous, tangled net. His right shoulder was now completely immovable on the ground. He noticed that even with his temporary win, which gained him enough room to move his hand, his overall freedom of movement was being tied up fast. His trap was starting to feel a lot more like a spider wrapping its prey in webs. Aligning the blade's spine with his forearm, he flexed his elbow outward. Finally, the vines snapped apart all along the length of his lower arm. From there, he was able to lay the blade on his leg and grab and tear the rest off his upper arm until it was completely free.

It's amazing what can be done with one free arm if one is desperate, but calm. He was able to work the blade up the space between his torso and his right arm. He pried off the cords of death in small bundles until his torso was largely free. His right arm could help his left in breaking his legs out. His right arm was numb, and Will had to sit up in an odd angle forced by how his legs were bound one on top of the other. He ran the blade between his legs, prying like a crowbar to split the vines, and got everything free at last. He watched his step this time and carefully traversed the tunnel, moving towards the exit. He noticed that the available space in the tunnel had shrunk considerably since he last tried to traverse it. It was darker with terrible greens and browns. It became a constricted and oppressive place. To make matters worse, he was not alone.

He heard crawling and booked it. He didn't care to look behind him and face his fears one bit. The tunnel was different to how it was before. It was more gnarly and some of the roots that had previously grown as wide as Will's thumb now had the diameter of small trees. It was as if a mad scientist had experimented to find the limits of what plant life could do. For all he knew, a mad scientist did experiment on this country. Whatever this chemical attack on the Charlotte area was, it commanded nature itself to become more aggressive and much larger. Maybe the fact that people lost the ability to learn and adapt to the new world was merely a side effect. After all, if castles and civilizations can be buried by time slowly, imagine what could happen if you sped up time? If their goal was to bury America, imagine what five years of *this* could do? It was the perfect weapon, and it only needed a little encouragement.

Whatever was behind Will was closing the distance. He burst through the opening of the tunnel, which was narrowing even more. He emerged from the exit, moved to the side and stared at the entrance, machete in hand. He had his rifle strapped to the side of his bag on his back but didn't consider pulling it up under the panic. Again, having a weapon and knowing how to use it when under pressure are very different things. What burst from the tunnel afterwards were ants the size of his palm. He froze over with fear and the knowledge that all of nature was growing exponentially. Will got control of himself for the first time since exiting the tunnel and finally got his legs to agree with his brain. Now was the time to leave.

He ran as fast as his legs would allow, striving for stability on the ever-changing terrain. The forest he remembered had become a jungle, practically. Everywhere it was possible something could grow, there was a new competition among the species. It started with the vines and then the ants but as Will ran, he could feel the land humming with expressions of life in every form. The extraordinary growth had toxified the air with an aroma of pure oxygen and genesis. New things came in place of old even now as he ran up a small incline back to where he thought the house was. There was no such house anymore. The land had not only reclaimed it but had repurposed it. The only recognizable remnants were the occasional white panel of paint hiding the strangeness of the growths. The fence which used to be tied up with boards as a makeshift wall was now tied up in a different way. It was smashed and gnarled into a spikey barbed wire which the plants could use to climb to otherwise unachievable places. The yard was now a garden of the absurd. Will wondered if he was dreaming or if this was real. His perception of reality did not suffer well in this world. The impossible became the new trend here. He brushed the question away like a cobweb. It just wasn't that useful to be thinking like that. It certainly felt real to him.

Will ran out past the house in the only direction which was familiar to him. He was heading for Charlotte and the car he'd parked on the outskirts when he first arrived. He could not see the sky except in the rare opening where life had nothing to grab onto to close the heavens. Will caught a glimpse of the available daylight as he ran through. The sky was an odd indigo with patches of dark gray clouds turning black in the east as the sun retreated off the face of the Earth in the west. It was dark enough with everything going on and now it was soon to be night. He stopped when an interesting rock was blocking his path, however. It covered his whole way forward for the moment, so he didn't have a choice but to observe it. This rock was something of a kind that Will had never seen before.

It was beautiful. It was a remarkably rounded and dome-shaped structure which was much wider in all directions than it was tall. It reminded him of an upside-down bowl. It was black... for lack of a better word. It was really almost like an oil slick where colors of refracted light abounded across the surface in an uncertain shimmer of artistic flux. But it didn't possess the same feeling of being as dirty and soiled as an oil slick. It was magnificent and solid. Will got closer, forgetting the troubles of the forest around him for a moment. He saw angular flakes of gold in this round rock that were evenly distributed along the surface. They were cut at regulated, pointed angles and all of them were cut the same. They each shone against the dark as Will noticed them, even though there was no light source to reflect.

The rock was about ten feet across and looked as though it went much deeper under the surface. Will stepped forward to touch it. The rock had lumps of a smooth, flattened curvature all over. Each of the shallow lumps were more than twice the size of Will's hand and they were longer than they were wide. They were all oriented in such a way as to be swept back from right to left and layered over each other, not unlike the scales of a fish. On the edge of the long side of each one sat the golden angles. Will saw his reflection in the oil-black lumps while the gold seemed to illuminate him. Then his reflection was contorted and twisted as the rock came to life. It turned over clockwise like a wheel with a thunderous quaking in the Earth. The rock narrowed as it pulsed itself forward into the ground. It tapered into a tail as Will realized that this wasn't a rock and it wasn't rotating, it was burrowing. It was moving so much earth underground that dirt was spilling over onto the surface as it was displaced from the size of whatever *thing* was underneath. He heard wood buckle and break as the forest tried to accommodate the new contortions of earth. He gazed into the tunnel that was left behind. He was left with the sickening feeling that he had just awoken a colossal serpent of an unknown length, ten feet across, whose individual scales were twice the size of his hands.

Will couldn't fathom the feeling that came over him. It was a very specific disorientation that made his knees feel weak and he suddenly became uncertain about continuing in the direction he knew he had to go. That was where the serpent was going. But when he realized that the snake would need to eat at some point, he decided it would be wise to find the car he was driving at the edge of the city. He carried on through the most aggressive forestation in the history of the world with the help of his machete and, to his surprise, emerged from it eventually. Then he saw Charlotte.

It was a very strange oasis of openness in the middle of the suffocating forest around it. He approached the space carefully. He was conscious of the feeling that the woods were watching him from beyond the veil of darkness. The vines still slowly slithered their way across the ground just like when Will was in Charlotte earlier. But they had grown bigger. Now, Will could not see the cement of the streets or sidewalks at all. The colors of individual buildings were muted beneath the oppressive greens and browns of plant matter. But he recognized a tall building of about seven stories that he remembered parking near when he first got to Charlotte. Then he felt the Earth shake.

The ground swelled before him, and an eruption of dirt introduced an awe-inspiring sight. The serpent burst forth from the earth and constricted the seven-story building in a maddening display of power. The concrete was crippled under the constriction of that terrible being. Balconies sloughed off the sides of the building. Windows shattered under the structural pressure. The serpent had wrapped himself around it three times and he looked right at Will. Will was struck by something other than simple fear. He was also enamored by his beauty. The gold edges of his scales created waves of shimmering illusion. The oily black scales reflected more than just Will, now. The sky had opened up over the serpent and the stars themselves seemed to volunteer for the artwork on each and every scale.

Will felt something more ancient than fear of snakes and far older than the horror of abominations. It was the same feeling one gets when one stares into a dark place without knowing what's there. The very same feeling when you go swimming in the ocean and dare to look down. You cannot see the depths and, for that, be grateful. Be grateful and remain merely afraid. For Will, it was both the fear of darkness and the fear of heights. It was the feeling of powerless rapture without destination.

CHAPTER 22

THE EYES OF the serpent were a piercing silver which stood out like the moon on the midnight-oil hues of his scaly head. Then the voice came forward. It was buttery smooth with a hint of masculine grumble supporting the weight of his words. The voice was startling and paralyzing. It came from the mouth of that serpent, but it felt like it started in Will's spine. The serpent spoke the following:

"You think I am new, don't you? Some abomination of *radiation* or the chemicals that your kind *burned* into the soil. You people *always* think that way. But the truth is that I am old enough to remember all the civilizations before you and the ones *underneath* you. I was old when the Earth was *young*."

The voice was nearly dripping on every word. It wasn't a wet sound, however. It was remarkably dry and clear, but it was also clear that he savored every word. Will squeaked out, "How—"

"How can a serpent speak? Really? You gaze upon me and *that* is what you ask? Come closer, boy. Look at my scales *intently*."

Will's legs moved awkwardly as though by remote control. He approached and saw that the shiny things glimmering within the scales of the serpent were not stars, but spiral galaxies and nebulas of gas. The longer he stared into the scale, the more of these things he saw. Just one scale showed him all of this. The others showed different places of the universe. Will was now sure he must be dreaming, but he also knew he was suffering from denial.

Will squeaked again, this time with more volume, "Who—"

"The ones before you have called me many *useless* names. You may call me *Death*."

Something about the voice was deeply familiar, like a mother's heartbeat is familiar to her infant. It was just as disarming as it was threatening, but Will had been threatened plenty at this point. He wasn't as fearful as he should have been. He began again with more confidence. "Death? Right. So, y-you've come for me then?" Will suffered a flash of anger and heat. "This is how it happens? What am I dreaming? Am I dying in my sleep?"

"No… You are not *dreaming*. I am here because you have *broken* The Veil of your world. I have slumbered for thousands of years, *satiated* by the millions of corpses your history has brought to me. But now it is different. Several billion screams *woke* me from my slumber. The souls of many billions flowed into my domain. I am the *death* at the end and the *birth* of the beginning."

Will stuttered out more, "What do you mean by 'broken The Veil' of the world? You mean what James said? The Veil of protection?"

"Your world was so *secure*. Some of the time, horrors

would creep into your lives, but the *brutality* of the universe was kept out. You *brought* that here. You took the violence of the universe for *granted*. You thought you could handle your *limited* understanding of it all. You could not. Yet I have the sense that you aren't very *afraid* of me. You've seen what a few trillion atoms in those bombs can do to your world. Care to see what the rest of the *universe* can do?"

The serpent flared its neck out like a King Cobra. In this flare, Will could see the early solar system. That famous collision between early Earth and Theia which supposedly formed the moon. He was astounded at how the solid, rocky planets looked like they turned to liquid on impact. With that much energy, anything is possible. Will stumbled over the idea that this serpent could read his mind so easily. It could finish his sentences and guess his dispositions. It was starting to wear down the temporary confidence Will had summoned to look Death in the face. Will felt suddenly like this serpent was sizing him up. He had already mentioned devouring corpses and souls. Will did not get to finish clarifying his suspicions when the serpent pounced.

It definitely crushed the building it was using to hold itself up and loomed over him in a dramatic arc. Will immediately sprinted past the serpent as it struck the ground with a heavy impact.

"Where are you *going*?" the serpent asked, venomously.

The voice boomed like thunder across the sky. Then, with a shout, the snake burrowed below the ground. Will ran as fast as he could, but the serpent must have been faster. The ground buckled under Will's feet and soil rose in a line following the serpent's underground movements. The car was nowhere to be found and neither was the rest of the outer city at this point. Still running for his life, Will found himself in front of a sea of hills where there used to be flat land just moments before. The hills were moving and rolling like waves without crests and the whole Earth seemed to destabilize under the pressure exerted by the serpent.

Will turned back in an attempt to keep moving but everything around him was performing that same chaotic shuffle. Will was standing on the only solid ground left. It was one small island of peace in a storm of undulating hills and crumbling rocks. Will gazed around and realized that he couldn't account for how long the serpent went on for. It could have been five hundred or a thousand feet long or maybe more. For the snake to move all that earth was unbelievable. Unless there were more serpents than just the one Will met.

Still, he was completely encircled by Death the Serpent and the serpent knew it. Death burst out from the ground several meters away and shot his gaze at Will, hoping to turn the young man into stone. Finally, the serpent dashed for its prey. Then Will did the unthinkable. He ran away. He was completely encircled, and he simply picked a direction and ran that way. The instant of decisiveness saved his life as the snake slammed his heavy head into the ground, eating nothing but dirt.

Will ran towards nothing in particular without looking back. He was racking his brain for ideas when he glimpsed a great tall tree in the distance. It was much taller than everything else around it and it was very out of place. Will caught sight of a glowing yellow orb which illuminated a slightly square profile at the very top of the highly unorthodox tree. Seeing nothing but Death behind him and endlessly overgrown forests everywhere else, he decided to make that landmark his goal. He felt, for some reason, that it was a sanctum.

He was almost to the base of the tree. It wasn't lost on Will that, even though he was faster thanks to the mutations he suffered in New York, the fact that the snake couldn't catch him was astounding. It was never far behind, but there should never be any possibility that a snake like that was only as fast as Will. Not only that, but the serpent let Will reach the tree rather than cutting him off like he did before.

Reaching the base of the tree, Will looked up. This tree was completely unlike anything he had seen before. The trunk had a solid core to it, but the outer parts of the trunk made a corkscrew spiral about two feet deep into the gargantuan tree. It seemed like the depressions were squeezed in towards the core rather than cut. Regardless of design choices, the tree must have been twenty feet across and the depressions which were part of the corkscrew shape ended up serving as a spiral ramp which promised to bring Will to the top.

The depressed parts of the tree gave Will a couple feet of footing to make his way up. He stepped into the deep grooves of the tree and proceeded upwards. He went around twice without daring to look down. He would have to move around the tree maybe twenty or thirty times to make it all the way to the top of this screw-tree. The wind was heavier, unrestricted by the newly growing forestry near the ground.

Will looked down and nearly lost himself over the edge. The grooves which he used for footing were becoming more and more shallow as he went up. He was now hugging the tree. He didn't have a grip on anything exactly, but he had hoped that the added friction would keep him from going over the side. So, he clung onto it. Then, he suddenly reached a door.

It was a narrow door at the top of the tree. Will's eyes were right about it from a way off. The top of the tree was not only square, but it was also a house! A small, square tree house. Will opened the door for dear life and stumbled in to find a rather non-threatening man sitting in a chair by a small, slow fire.

"Close the door, please. You'll let the chaos follow you," said the man. He was dressed in the same colors as the tree. His sweater was a deep, leafy green. His pants were a khaki, bark brown. He had a calm and matter-of-fact demeanor. Will closed the door in defiance of the wind, which had become curious about the calmness inside the house. Will went to speak and was silenced by the man's hand coming up to halt him.

"Let me answer your questions straight away," the man started. "No. This isn't really happening to the world. Yes, this is really happening to you. No, you are not dreaming. You are dying and this is your brain's last hurrah."

"What?!" Will demanded. "Dying how?"

"In some gutter in North Carolina," the man flatly responded.

"What?!" Will felt like he couldn't see straight even though there was nothing wrong with his vision. Vertigo and confusion will tend to have that effect.

"Here, sit down," the man invited, and the chair obeyed, pulling out just enough for Will to plop down and try to center himself again.

"You said I'm dying in a gutter. How? Has this all been a dream?"

"Jesus, boy. I know I say this kind of thing a lot, but nobody listens to me. I just told you that you weren't dreaming."

"Oh, right." Will began to massage his neck and temples.

"The wonderland you find yourself in isn't happening to the real world, but it is certainly happening to every part of the real world that has anything to do with you. Everything you're seeing and sensing is the brain trying to anchor itself to real ideas and failing because of the toxins that are killing you."

"Oh, that's fucking great," Will snapped sarcastically. He knew the man was telling the truth. "Hold on. Who actually are you?"

"I'm going to let you guess. You've already met Fear. You will certainly meet Death in the near future. You might meet Anger depending on how you respond to your situation. You'll have to conclude one other emotion on your own. But what am I?"

Will gazed around the room and noticed several things. The table he was sitting at was an unfinished and asymmetric wooden slab that was flattened for all necessary table purposes. The chair he was sitting in was crafted out of branches of different sizes and thatched together with either old vines or some straw. The fireplace was open fairly wide for the fire to heat the room, yet the fire was far enough back to have all of the smoke go up the chimney instead of in the room. The man himself was a calm figure with an upright but relaxed posture.

"You're Peace."

"Close. But not quite."

"Serenity."

"Close. But not quite."

Will thought for a moment about the tree and specifically about how it loomed over everything. "You're Vigilance."

"Close. But not quite."

"Damn it, I don't have time for this! I'm literally dying as we speak!" Will shouted as he got up from the surprisingly comfortable chair.

"I didn't realize you had somewhere to be inside your own head," the man calmly refuted.

Will sat down to process that statement. He was beginning to realize that he was pretty thankful to be there. The warm fire and quiet cabin were wonderful juxtapositions to what he'd been through in the past few days. Even if it wasn't *real*... whatever that means. So, he decided to play the game.

"Wait, *time*. You're Father Time. That's why we're sitting here waiting. You're trying to trap me just like the serpent tried to!" Will stood up again, feeling confident about his chances against the old man, who simply leaned back and laughed.

"Holy shit, boy. How old do you think I am? Remember that we're all part of you. Look, I'll give you a hint. People normally spend much longer than you did running away from Fear. Some people spend their whole lives running from him and only near the end do they find me, if at all."

"You're Regret."

"No, but I can be if I'm not used early enough. It's impressive that you've almost perfectly circumscribed me without naming me. Usually, people can name me easily enough, but finding out what I actually entail is the hard part. It seems you've done that first."

"Wisdom," Will concluded.

"Yeah, we'll settle for that," said the man.

"You don't seem like Wisdom."

"I rarely do."

CHAPTER 23

"So..." WILL SAID after a pause, "you said the serpent was Fear. He told me he was called Death."

"Fear masquerades as Death from time to time. Sometimes the fear we have of something tricks us into thinking it's deadly in some way. Either that our reputation will die, or our confidence or character will. It paints everything as a death or an ending because that's its job."

"But he told me he was also responsible for everything new that was born."

"He's not entirely wrong. You feared for Rachel. That's what started your journey. Hell, kid. You saved the world because you feared for her well-being if the Inferno was to expand past its weaknesses. You killed a god of the dead while being completely terrified of everything constantly."

"Huh. So, what's Fear's deal then? Why did he try to kill me?"

"He didn't. A snake like that wouldn't have any trouble doing it if he wanted. The truth is, Fear is there to protect you to the death. He probably sensed you wanted to continue your journey and deemed it reasonable to stop you in your tracks."

"And when I decided to run past his guard anyway, he failed and realized he couldn't keep up. He couldn't stop me again just then because I wasn't as afraid as I should have been."

"Exactly."

"He was talking about devouring souls and screams waking him up. I get the screams part, but what did he mean by souls?"

"Don't be surprised that Fear can exaggerate things. He can outright lie, too. Despite being a massive part of your existence, he's been around far longer than you and I. He's bound to have picked up some tricks while pent up in that DNA of yours."

"Yeah, he did say he was ancient."

"Yes, Fear is far older than we can imagine. It would be wise to respect such a being even though he is troublesome and aggressive. This universe is a place where ideas that don't work die young and are outcompeted by stronger ones. He's outlived and outcompeted just about everything. He'll out-live us, too."

"Why does he look like that? I'm assuming you've seen him."

"Yes, magnificent, right? Fear can be mesmerizing, impressive and awe-inspiring all at the same time. In my opinion, his appearance reflects this."

"It reflects a lot more, too," Will remembered.

"I don't know why that is," Wisdom said. "Did you real-ize that those were galaxies, not stars?"

"Of course I did. You should know what I saw. On top of

that, you're telling me that you don't fully understand Fear. I thought you were Wisdom?" Will prodded.

"You and I aren't always on the same page if you haven't noticed. Additionally, Wisdom and knowledge are two totally different things. It is always wise to admit what you don't know," Wisdom parried.

"You said he masquerades as Death. Is there a purpose to that? Or is that just because death is what we fear the most?"

"Good questions. I find that there are two deaths one can have in their lifetime. There's the death of the soul, firstly, and then the death of the body, finally. Fear is the first death. When we are too afraid to do something because we fear some kind of embarrassment or risk, then that's it. If you never remedy that fear of the world, that risk, then the rest of your life is spent waiting in line to die your last death."

After a pause, Will started to feel a strange pressure. It was as if the conversation was leading to something he did not want to face. He decided to move things along. "So, you said I'll meet Anger depending on how I process things. How do I beat it? I assume it's a more aggressive and destructive monster than that serpent."

"Anger is very difficult to judge. I am unsure of how aggressive it really is. Certainly, Fear is aggressive. You climbed this tree using the imprints he made while trying to get to me."

"How'd you stop him?" Will inquired as he was hoping to gain some insight for his own use.

"I didn't really. Not on purpose, anyway. I am always an option. You cannot kill me unless you were to choose to abandon me. The world could throw its weight against me, but there is no law saying that I must move under that pressure. I am planted, like this tree which even Fear could not break."

"How do I stop Anger, then?"

"Well, the idea is to not get angry. But you have to realize that Anger, like Fear, is not always bad. It has its uses. It is one of those ancient and primordial feelings like Fear that are present in every creature. Sometimes Anger can give you purpose where hopelessness prevails. It can give you the attitude necessary to take risks that look untenable or scary. It can do a lot of good. It would be foolish to advise you to avoid Anger on your way to meeting Death. It's only natural."

Just then, a voice boomed from the sky. It was a voice that was familiar to Will, and it said, "Will? Buddy? You doing okay in there? You've been at it for quite some time…" The voice sounded like it was at the entrance to a cave—or a tunnel.

"Holy shit, I think that's one of those 'Ranger' guys. Are they looking for me?"

"Possibly. I don't know how long you've been out for. But my world is showing me that you're dying. The sky, the forest, the ground, they all show me you're in danger of it. That chemical in the cave is probably what's getting to you. You must have cracked your mask when you fell."

Will was silent for some time. It had been a long time since he had been able to talk about how he really felt about all this. "Can I be honest with you?" Will asked.

"Well, you should hope so. I'm Wisdom, after all."

"I feel like I've lost my only dream. The only thing I care about. The world was going so well before it ended abruptly. I've gone through hell in my life before the end of the world happened too, you know that. When I met Rachel… actually, not when I met her. When I got to know her and we were together for a while, I thought that the struggle was over. That I had been accepted. That life would be good now. God damn it, then hell had to boil up from the underworld and vaporize that dream. I've been through… whatever the hell all that was in New York, and I want to show something for it. Not a vast wealth of earthly possessions, not even some easy way to fix the world. I want a fucking hug, honestly. From the arms that I love." Will looked down in sadness.

"Can I be honest with you?" Wisdom asked, earnestly.

"Well, I should hope so. You're Wisdom, after all."

Wisdom appreciated that gesture with a smile and a brief chuckle. Then he looked down in a sullen pose. "I miss her too. She is one of the reasons that I'm here. You know what we were like before her." Will chuckled and then Wisdom continued. "We had so many opinions. Still do, really. But the fact is that we're accountable now. We're accountable to her and to ourselves. The actions we take no longer affect just us. We're forced, in the best way possible, to care about what happens to us in a way that we couldn't be without some oversight. You've lost some of that as your confidence in her survival has waned."

"I'm sorry?" Will asked with a confused tilt.

"You should know. You're not bothering to check the radiation of the places you're going, to start. You were so detailed about everything you did at the beginning. You cared about where you camped out and how much you ate. You cared about wearing your mask whenever you could. You not only wanted the best chances of finding her quickly, but also the chance to get there in good health. Now you don't."

"Pardon?" Will demanded in disbelief. "You think it was my choice to go to New York? I'm pretty sure I was kidnapped by a galactic alien or some shit. I killed in self-defense. I had my mind completely opened by some psychic god-fireball-thing and had my family used against me like the Sirens of ancient Greece, calling me to my doom. I only persevered through that *because* I cared."

"Will, you died because you wanted potatoes," Wisdom said frankly.

"What?"

"You died because one more day of those grainy granola bars was so terrible that you decided to raid a supermarket, got chased out by cannibal-zombies and then decided to follow these 'Ranger' fellows back to their base instead of continuing on your way. I know you haven't listened to me since New York but come on, man. It's the end of the world and you're out here sightseeing like the end never came. They used you, Will. They used you because you weren't one of them. Now you're dead."

"Oh," Will said flatly.

"You were out of control," Wisdom said, rubbing his hair.

"Were?" Will inquired.

Then a masked voice broke the sky again and rained down from what seemed like the heavens: "Holy shit. Here, let's get you out of here." Then another voice was heard: "Ah, shit. He's dead." The first voice calmly said, "You don't know that."

Second Voice: "Yeah, I do. He's been down here for like fifteen minutes. Earl went mad after less than a minute's exposure to this stuff. Let's just leave him. He was obviously not worthy of the favor of the forest. It saw him as a sacrifice."

First Voice: "No, look. The vines have sealed up his mask. It's cracked, but it will have held together. Yep, he's breathing. The forest grants that he's worthy."

Second Voice: "Well, let's take him back then. See if we can resuscitate him. If we can't then he was too weak."

First Voice: "Agreed."

"See?" Wisdom said. "I told you they were using you. They see you as either a recruit for their little militia or a cult sacrifice for their forest. They tricked you into undergoing this trial."

"Oh yeah? And where were you to tell me I was being tricked?"

"I'm an option. You don't have to take it. I'm not some angel who can just poof myself onto your shoulder and tell you right from wrong. A good voice needs a good listener, or it might as well be silent. You weren't in the cautious mood. I'm never there by default, but I can appear anywhere if you focus on me."

"Hmm," Will expressed skeptically.

Will spent a few seconds trying to remember what his attitude was like in the last few days and found he could not remember. In a way, that proved Wisdom's point. Will had been so mindless about his self-care that he didn't even remember what he felt or what he wanted from all this before he went unconscious. He did remember the potatoes, which proved even further that he had been absently single-minded about his stomach's needs. But would he really have died because of that? He turned down the wrong street and set a series of events in motion which led to his unfortunate fate.

He decided it couldn't be. That to the best of his ability, he would have to live. If not for himself, then for her.

"Good call," Wisdom interrupted.

Will didn't know what he meant immediately. "What?"

"What, you think you can hide your thoughts in this place? In your brain? I'll tell you the answer to the question I'm surprised you haven't asked yet. How are you going to beat Death?"

"I haven't asked that question yet because, until now, I wasn't convinced that one could."

"Well, hear me out one last time before you leave. Because I believe now you have some chance of living through this. There is a way to beat Death in a very roundabout way. Death can only wait for you. It can't kill you, at least not directly. I mentioned two deaths that happen to the soul and the body. You cannot help the body if its time has truly come. But the soul is immortal, at least as long as you live with it."

"Really? You think it lasts forever? That's a bold statement." Will said.

"I don't know about forever. That's a different question. I mean 'immortal' in one, very specific sense. Your soul is the only part of you which does not have to age. Eventually your body is forced to ache, and your muscles become weak. Maybe your heart stops. But the soul, your attitude, feelings, memories, love of the world, your will to learn, etcetera is not bound by the same obvious constraints. It doesn't have to become weaker or grow dimmer. That's the great secret. All the time that you live, and all the toll it takes on your body is evidence that you will eventually perish. Your soul has no such evidence."

"Okay, I see that. But where are you going with this?"

"Straightforwardly, you must beat Death the only way your existence allows you to. You must want to live. You must regain your focus, shed your fear and live a life that's worth continuing. Don't let your soul flicker. Even now, your body is being damaged by the chemical. But your best chance at living is simply not giving up on Rachel, or yourself."

"Right, yeah." Will paused for several moments. "It seems like time has slowed down for us in here."

"It's your perception of it. Even so—" Wisdom got up from his chair. "—it's time for you to go."

"Yeah. But one more thing: Do you think the gas will affect me like it has the others? Turning them into mindless zombies who cannot learn and cannot live in this new world?"

"Are you human?"

"Well, yeah."

"Did you inhale the gas?"

"I suppose so."

"Then, yes, Will. You saw how your body changed from New York. You were very nearly turned into a man-thing. You're not immune to these forces. If you survive this at all, then the evidence we've seen says you will become like the others."

"Yikes," was all Will could reply to that.

"There are other options, of course. We can speculate. We aren't positive that the gas you've inhaled is necessarily the same compound as the one which triggered the madness you've seen so far. We aren't sure if the dosage was right for that kind of dramatic change either. Perhaps the chemical got weaker over time. Maybe genetics will help you overcome what would otherwise be a bad chemical interaction for others."

"Yeah," Will concluded without energy or hope.

Will agreed to disagree. He knew he had to live through this, if possible. But he could already feel the changes. Either that or he was growing tired. He decided time would tell. Really, though, he just wanted this to be over with. He was not certain he had the strength to face Death and come out victorious. This whole trip had been a destructive grind against his resolve. Somewhere, deep in the pit of self-actualization, Will didn't want to do it anymore. He wanted to huddle up in a ball and never see another giant universal serpent or another fireball god or another zombie-thing ever again. He just wanted to see Rachel and be done with the rest of this world which used to be so beautiful and normal.

Humanity's worship of the violence of nature mired and marked the landscape. It turned cities into crags of helpless ghosts and twisted steel. It turned fields into unbearable jungles of ravenous plants. The only thing unchanged by this would be Rachel's face. The face that he looked forward to seeing every day before the war. He remembered her face. He was desperate and hated himself for bringing seemingly everything but a picture. He found it ironic, and terribly so, that all the prepping things he brought with him didn't save his life. But the picture might have saved him now.

Will and his Wisdom did not say goodbye. It's not like they were leaving each other. They both knew what had to happen now. He made his way out of the door to the cabin and onto the grass of the open expanse before him. Then, Will realized that he could cook up the cans in his bag. This hallucination of his seemed realistic enough. Maybe he would be more confident with a full stomach. He turned around to find the base of the tree that he had climbed earlier to get to the cabin. He looked up to see the cabin at the very top, then realized he did not have to take the spirals of the tree all the way down. He simply stepped out of the cabin. Thus was Wisdom's final point. He was difficult to get to, and very easy to leave behind.

CHAPTER 24

WILL BECAME FRUSTRATED with himself for his lack of foresight. If these damn cans of potatoes and vegetables were going to get him killed, he was at least going to eat them. He trod forward for a bit before feeling a sudden rush of cold. He didn't know when Death was supposed to find him, but he knew that it would eventually. As Wisdom suggested, Will wasn't under pressure to cross any kind of distance in this place. He was passing time, not space. So, he decided to set up a little camp for himself. He gathered some sticks that were dead and dry and started a fire with a ferrocerium rod and a striker.

He set up a crisscross of sticks over the fire and hung a couple of the cans on it after opening them. He made up a little lean-to tent with the tarp and the same paracord he had used earlier in his adventure and decided to check on the cans to see how they were heating up. But as he turned around to check on them, he saw a genuine monster of a rodent.

It wasn't actually that large in total. It was maybe the size of a capybara or a large beaver. But it was hideous and was a very messy being, like a possum. Its solid black eyes must have been larger than its brain, however, and covered most of its face, like a fly. It was the very image of death, Will thought. Most importantly, it was plopped down on its backside, rear legs spread wide, sitting straight up, and eating Will's fucking potatoes. Will went into a frenzy. He ripped the machete from his hip and slashed at the ugly beast. The rodent scampered loudly around the campsite. Will slashed towards it near the fire and hit the sticks instead. He slashed through his tarp when the rodent went under it to hide. Will checked to see if he got it. But it was gone. Will looked around at his campsite, which was now destroyed. He saw the empty cans by the fire, the contents of which were spilled all over the ground.

Will stormed off, shaking with fury and frustration, in the direction he determined to be south. He refused to be starved by Death's assault on his food and his sanity. He was quickly met with a wall of trees. The sign in front of them read "Welcome to Florida!" Will approached the wall, expecting to squeeze his way through, but he couldn't. Every tree was as close to each other as they could be. He couldn't even get an arm through. He backed off and tried to look for a way around and there was none. The forest wall went on forever in both directions. Then Will thought to climb up, but there were no branches on the trees and no room to get his limbs around the trunk. He looked again down each side of the wall and noticed now the wall did not go on forever. It ended where a new wall began, and he realized he was in a box with the sky as its lid. Then the box got smaller.

Then a voice came down from the sky, this time quieter and more distant than the last.

"He's not going to make it."

"Let's get him in that bed there."

"I think he went into shock earlier."

"Oh well, we'll have meat tonight."

"We were going to have it anyway. Remember that family down the trail?"

"Ah, yes. The nice ones taste better. Less cortisol in the meat and likelier to be healthy."

"I wanted him to be one of us."

"Me too."

It was then that Will broke. He made some noise between a scream and a roar which was primal all the same. Then he yelled at the forest.

"This is not it! What do you want? You want me to bargain for my life? Huh? Sell you my soul for a few precious years? Too fucking bad! I faced down a horde of zombified mutants *twice*! I killed a fireball god to get here! Even in my dreams I stared down Fear, found my Wisdom and chased away that little rodent you call Death! I want my wife and I'll be damned if *you're* going to stand in my way!"

Then, the forest hissed as if telling him to *shush*, and the treeline broke. The ground quaked and the trees combined themselves out of the way in order to make a path through the wood. Will was about to step through it when he saw something hanging from the branches of the trees further in. Several things hung there, just barely visible. The objects required so much focus to materialize in Will's vision. But when he saw it, one shape filled in after another and he realized that the path in the woods was not meant for him.

Eight deep black spheres shimmered in the midst of the trees. The two in the center were the largest, at least six feet across. They were like big round windows of nothing, and the six peripheral eyes were smaller. He realized that the tufts which tapered down towards the ground in the middle of all this were not bushes, but fangs. The canopy above the eyes was nothing more than the green, brown and black hair on this great arachnid's back. It moved forward, and when it did, Will heard the trees cracking as though they were being broken. Caught now in a wave of panic, Will saw some of the trees in this forest were not trees at all, but legs. Eight bark-covered legs broke from the treeline suddenly at odd elbows and shifted the heavy body of this terrible being forward with a labored stagger. The groaning of strained wood brought with it the suffering of the damned who had dared to toy with her. Then Will realized that the rodent from before was not Death. Based on how he felt helpless and paralyzed here, *this* must be Death.

The two-story-tall spider glanced over in the direction of Will's former campsite, seeing clearly beyond the range that Will could at that time of night. Then the voice came forward. It was a voice of age and the inevitable. The sound felt like beetles scratching to enter his ear canal. It was also feminine and dominant. The only thing you could hear, or feel, was this voice rattling your bones and slowly separating you from your body.

"I see you've met Anger," she said calmly about the wreckage of Will's camp.

Will could not respond. The rest of the scenery around her seemed to fall from Will's vision temporarily. Then it was just the two of them and Will could not tell whether he was standing or falling.

"Since time began, I have never needed an introduction.

You feel who I am and that's good. It's good to pass with acceptance."

Will felt like he was upside down suddenly and that his stomach was trying to pull him back up. Every bit of it felt wrong, like he didn't belong here. Or perhaps that *here* didn't belong with him.

Death continued: "Paralysis is the natural reaction to my presence."

When Will did not respond, her face softened, if that was even possible for a spider.

"It was quite the speech you gave just now. You really have been through a lot, Will. I think you've lived quite a life so far."

"—will continue to live," Will interjected. He didn't like how final she was being about his life. She spoke of it in the past tense. His bluster and discoordination made his interjection slightly nonsensical. He hated not making sense, so he closed his eyes and focused.

"I want to continue. I want to see Rachel. I'm not done yet," Will confidently said.

"I'm listening," said the spider. This confused Will.

"What? I-I just said it," he said, questioning himself.

"You intend to make an argument for why you should live. I want to hear it."

"Uh…" Will stammered. It was clear his mind wasn't in the right place for all this. It was like Death was reaching into his brain every second they spoke and sabotaging his connections to the world. She was taking him away as they talked. Separating him from that which tethered him to the physical. He had to resist.

Death waited patiently. Her wooden legs were slightly

creaking over the strain of carrying her body, which she didn't seem to mind. She observed that time was on her side. Will collected himself. He put himself in the same position that he was in when the Inferno in New York tried to trick him with memories of his family. He tried to focus on what was real, that which existed beyond what his eyes saw and that which was beyond whomever was speaking to him.

"You probably get a lot of arguments that pertain to being too young to die or having too much to live for."

"I never get tired of hearing what people value," she said encouragingly.

"Well, I started on this journey for one reason and one reason only. It wasn't for the adventure. It was for Rachel. I told her before the world ended that I would find her."

"And you recognize that she could be dead by now. It has been a few days since you were told otherwise..." the arachnid protested.

"I'm good and ready to die if I find her like that. I have thought about that many times along the way. Whether it was even worth continuing because she was probably dead. Sure, an alien told me otherwise, but he lied to me before. I've seen the condition of this world and I know basically nobody survived it. Here's the thing. If she is alive, then it is the only thing worth doing with myself. If she is dead, then that is even more true. The thought of going back on that promise, especially when those may have been the last words I ever said to her, is unacceptable. So, this was a risk I was willing to take."

"Interesting," the spider brooded. "It's fascinating how people are always convinced that things matter once I've taken over. Your promise to your loved one is only one of many. Billions, even. When people come to me, their second question is often the same as yours," she said as if leading him to ask it.

"Is Rachel alive? Have you seen her yet?" Will asked involuntarily.

"That's the one."

"Is she, though?" Will asked this time voluntarily.

"I have been forbidden to tell you whether she is or is not," she said flatly.

"Forbidden? Who forbade *you*?" Will pondered.

"Now, if I cannot tell you about your loved one, what makes you think I could reveal that?"

Will thought for a moment and decided to get clever. "Is it important that I do not know?" he investigated. He already thought he knew the culprit.

"It is. But don't try to be clever. I have been around far longer than nearly everything else. Almost every lawyer and salesman who has ever lived has passed through my realm and bargained in their way. It is important that you don't know because it could influence your next actions."

"And that's what's forbidden, hm?" Will concluded. "The only reason why the independence of my choices matter is if someone is conducting a controlled study. Am I being watched?" Will accused as much as he asked.

He knew that James or "Number One" was the one forbidding this. But that begged the question: Was he responsible for these visions? Or were they really part of Will's mind? Will decided it was more likely that the visions were not caused by James. It would have violated his precious policy of not interfering with the normal course. However, this issue wasn't settled. Not even close. If these images before Will were due to Will's brain dying, and they came from Will's brain alone, then how would James have any influence on the arachnid of Death? Moreso, why would he forbid that kind of information? If Will was dying, then it shouldn't matter what he was told. However, if he wasn't actually dying... If the outcome of his survival was already known, then...

"How interesting," Death said, intercepting his thoughts. "My web has been weaved between the galaxies. Everything ever to live has been ensnared in it. It has no strands, no silk, only laws. You cannot break the bounds of it because the very parts that make you possible are part of it. That is all I can say."

Will wasn't sure how that was at all relevant to what he was thinking. Was she trying to say that he couldn't escape the physical consequences of this situation? Wisdom told him that. That wasn't new information. However, maybe she was answering the question he had about her origin. Whether she was caused by James or by his own dying brain. Before he could think more about it, he suddenly felt very tired. His brain function was now being critically hindered by his exposure to the gas in the real world. He thought he might not be breathing out there.

"Umm..." he started after several moments, trying to find his memories of the English language.

"There's not much time left. Make your argument," she prodded.

"Now... you can't control my voice if you... expect me to make an argument," Will claimed in protest of his forced question earlier. James was right. The human mouth is very... clumsy.

"I can't control anything. If you felt forced to say

something then it's because you are entering my realm as we speak and losing control of yourself as a result. Your brain cannot hold itself together forever."

Will shivered. "I need… to live to see this… through," he said.

The arachnid was silent for some seconds. "Tell you what. I'll help you. I cannot control whether you live or die in actuality, but I can help you focus. This is always a more pleasant experience for me when someone is good and ready to die. At least they don't blame me, then. You see me as some spider, yes?"

Will did not complain about her sudden change of attitude, though he found it odd. "Yes… a giant forest spider… actually."

"Typical. That explains the trepidation. I can take the form of anything, actually. Nearer to someone's peaceful death I can take the form of a family member. It's usually someone's parents or spouse but there have been a few cases where I've acted as their long-lost family pet. The oppressive trees here before you become a flowering field for some others. This usually is where they spend their last moments. It really reflects how someone feels and where their frame of mind is at."

"How… does that help… me?"

"I cannot direct you in that way. Think about what you really need right now, focus."

Will tried to throw away his confusion and focus. He conjured up the only image that mattered to him and opened his eyes. Rachel stood before him, the forest was no more, and they were back at their apartment. But Will was not convinced. If the very real sensation of her did not fool him in New York, it wouldn't fool him now. That doubt shattered that comfortable image, and he was back in front of the spider.

"Be clever," the spider said. "Focus and be clever. What do you need to get to her?"

"Well... I need to live," Will said.

"Obviously. So, think really hard."

"I don't... get it," Will said, dismayed. He could feel his grip on things slipping. Not just some things, though. Everything.

"Miracles happen all the time," Death said to Will's surprise. "I don't believe in them, but for some, they happen. The brain can do a lot more than people realize. It runs everything. It decides which organs work and when. Impulses from your brain electrically stimulate your heart, for example. Without those impulses, you're dead before you can realize it. We are in your mind, right now. Do the math."

Will concluded that he had to be that impulse, otherwise she wouldn't have told him that. However, he didn't know what was specifically wrong with him. He eventually, through struggling episodes of unfocused thinking, reasoned that he needed to breathe. Then his brain could at least function somewhat. If he didn't do that, then the only thing left would be darkness. Not even Death would be there to talk to him. Soon after that, there would no longer be a Will to talk to. There was just one problem. He had no idea how to do that. He focused on his diaphragm and there it appeared, in front of him and in place of the spider. He saw that it wasn't moving. He then decided to do the only thing he could think of. As hard as he could, he pushed on it.

CHAPTER 25

WITH A GASP of breath, Will woke up with just about the worst headache he ever had. The Ranger, who was by the bed, stared at him with a combination of disbelief and wonder. He whispered to himself, "The forest... it did..." Then he scampered off to call attention to Will's apparent resurrection. A crew of six people flooded in, with the Baroness positioning herself by the door. She was smiling, as was everybody. They congratulated Will on his recovery, each making various claims about his survival, but Will was not yet aware enough to know who said them. One claimed that they never doubted the outcome. Another said they were happy to see him alive. Yet another seemed to be giving thanks religiously.

Will knew the truth. He was sent into that tunnel as a guinea pig. An involuntary initiate into their monstrous club. It was his job to go into the tunnel, breathe the gas and either convert to their insanity or be sacrificed for his weakness. He presumed that they knew what the gas was and what it did. The more potent version was probably to blame for the cannibals at the supermarket. This lighter version might have been the cause of the mental state of these "Southern Rangers". It would explain how they knew about the existence of it. After all, if they were completely incapable of learning new things, they wouldn't have adapted at all. They must have received a lower dose. Enough to be crazy *and* continue learning about the world they lived in.

Will thought, now, about what he hadn't noticed before. It was no coincidence that they decided to set up base right beside this leaking tunnel. It was no coincidence that there were bodies there. These people had a system of information between them. Just like the cannibals in the supermarket, whose entire world was those shelves, cash registers, and parking lot. The world of these Rangers was in the forest. They were just as willing to make sacrifices for their understanding of the world as the other cannibals were for theirs. Except that these Rangers had considerably higher social functionality.

Despite the fact that he knew he was being lied to by people whose humanity had long expired, he remembered his mistakes at the supermarket. He let himself get dragged in and trapped. He couldn't play the part of fitting into their storefront delusions when it came time and nearly got devoured for it. He knew he had to play this very carefully. He was weakened now because of the gas, and he wouldn't be able to rely on his strength this time. He saw now that this was completely similar to the supermarket. But these guys had guns. Yet, despite the imperative to fit in and not arouse suspicion, he knew he was given new life. He was not going to remain passive or afraid. For them it had been thirty minutes, but for Will, a lifetime of changes had happened.

After coming to his senses and brushing away the various congratulatory phrases that were hung on him ceremoniously, he was taken to the dining area of the house. There was going to be a dinner which was even now being prepared in the kitchen. A nice family, Will remembered, was going to be a feast for these twenty-three Rangers plus the Baroness herself. To get to the dining room of this two-story house, he went down a hallway. He thought of Death, the two-story spider, and shivered. He imagined the walls to be the arachnid's body. She really was that enormous. He passed by a closet with an open door which apparently held the weapons and equipment for the whole crew.

It was a large closet, but it was essentially bristling full of firepower. There were grenades of the same variety that he had seen on Cole, Dale and Jason right after his encounter at the supermarket. Thinking and remembering along those lines, Will also remembered that those three, who initially introduced him to the idea of the Southern Rangers, claimed to be returning from a supply run. None of the three of them were carrying any supplies. Will had to assume it wasn't food they were after, then. They might have been after something that was more compact, like ammunition for this vast arsenal or perhaps the location of new victims.

Regardless of their actual intentions, Will thought more about whether these Southern Rangers were under the chemical attack or above it. Those three Rangers outside the store knew about the chemical. They were able to learn things about it after clearly being exposed to it. The people of the supermarket didn't seem to understand that anything at all existed outside the store. They certainly didn't realize that there was a rogue chemical agent sabotaging people's ability to learn. If the chemical affected a person sufficiently, then they couldn't possibly know about it, which was a concerning paradox.

Will remembered what Wisdom said. There was the distinct possibility that the chemical that Will experienced, the one nearest to this house, was different to the chemical dropped on Charlotte itself. By extension, it remained possible that the Rangers were not as affected by the same chemical as the city people either. They told him that they were originally from this area in the outer regions, away from the city center. Their ranks swelled by recruitment from this area as well. Will considered two options as he waited in the living area on the assurances that "dinner" would be ready soon.

The first option was that there were two different chemicals that were dropped on the area with the one near the outskirts being for some reason much less potent than the one in the city. This seemed a little unreasonable. If both chemicals were manmade, then why would they drop one that was decidedly less severe than the one they dropped on the city? Why would they purposefully drop a weaker weapon in an all-out war? There was the possibility that they wanted to create cannibal terrorists like these Rangers happened to be. The way they snatched up stragglers from the countryside was far more efficient than what any bomb could cover. Perhaps they were useful.

The second option hit very hard when Will thought of it. There was the possibility that the potent chemical was actually dropped everywhere, but something about the forest was changing that chemical. Perhaps absorbing it and re-emitting a new chemical as a by-product. Perhaps it had some use to the fungus. Maybe the chemical just didn't mix well with the soil. Whatever the case, the forest might have made the chemical attack less potent for those in the area. The reason this hit Will so hard was because he realized it may not be a coincidence that these people were worshiping the forest as some kind of intelligent entity. After all, if the forest did interfere with the effectiveness of the chemical weapon, then it saved everyone's lives in the area. At least, that's what it would look like to the Rangers.

It was then that the Baroness came to speak to Will in the dining area, just outside the door to the kitchen. Will was still trying to recover from his unconsciousness and suffocation, but he woke up right away when she spoke.

"I'm so glad you passed the test," she said, glowing. "I'm sorry that we tricked you, but we have to ensure the mission is not endangered by the weak. Now that we know, now that *I know*, you're strong, welcome to the team." She proceeded to gaze over him like quality meat at a butcher shop. Or perhaps like something more.

"Thank you," Will said, weakly. He wanted to feign a difficult recovery so that he did not have to show too much enthusiasm for their group, or her.

"I know. It'll take a while to get your bearings. You just woke up. From what they told me, you were about as close to death as anyone had ever seen."

"Tell me about it," Will said, not at all kidding.

She giggled. "I like you, Will. I really, really like you. You said you were heading to Florida, yes? For... someone?"

Will's brain caught on with such precision. She was testing him in two ways. She was testing his memory, and his commitment. She knew damn well who he was after. "Yes," he claimed without further elaboration. He rubbed his forehead in an attempt to fool her into thinking he had a hard time remembering.

"Yes," she mimicked. "But you don't remember who, right?"

"I'd have to think on it," he said.

She cranked her head to the side, still smiling. But something about that smile changed. It was curious, or jealous. She looked at the ground like she'd been struck and raised her head back up a little higher than it used to be. She looked at Will when she gathered herself up. Will could feel an accusation was looming.

"Tell me about Florida," she demanded, calmly. "You seemed to be very confident that humans had survived down there." She rubbed the cut of his jaw with the tips of her fingers. Will could not puzzle why.

"Uh, yes. I did believe that. I'm not so sure now. I haven't seen many people anywhere." Will was trying to disarm her interest in Florida. He didn't want them anywhere near there. Their nature already threatened the people of this area. Will was not about to let them threaten Rachel.

"Tell me about the rest of the east coast, then. Jason said you were from the northern states," she pried.

"Well... um..." Will started or tried to start.

He really didn't know where to begin. This world was not a place you could describe in a conversation without appearing like a complete lunatic. The Veil was gone. The world had lost its innocence with the nuclear and other experimental bombs humanity leveled at each other. The terrors of the universe had crawled their way in. They had come from the center of the Earth or perhaps other planets entirely. Maybe these things that Will saw weren't alien, however. Maybe they were here all along and guilt set them free. Like Fear the serpent implied. The billions of screams called them here.

Whatever the case, there wasn't a single bit of it that he could tell this woman. With the condition that these people were in, they wouldn't accept such delirious descriptions. What was he supposed to say, anyway? That the energy from the bombs shattered The Veil between fact and fiction and now horrors beyond our imagination were invading the Earth for whatever scraps remain? Or how about the description that the screams of nearly the whole human race meant that we forfeited whatever protections were promised to us at the dawn of time?

"There's nobody left up there," Will finally but mindlessly admitted. "I drove quite a way and I didn't see any evidence of the survival of large enclaves or otherwise," he said, attempting to signal that it was unlikely there were survivors in Florida. He was trying to give her a way out of this.

"See?" She shone with victory and malice. "Then we have to go to Florida."

Will searched her face for answers. He wondered just how the hell she came up with that solution. She continued, "You just said there was no one up north. That means, if there's even a chance that there's people down south, then we have to go."

Will saw his mistake. He wasn't downplaying the possibility of life in Florida. He was amplifying it in her mind. He grimaced and attempted damage control. "I would assume the opposite," he said. "With no one up north, there are grocery stores that have good things on the shelves still untouched."

She gave him the kind of smile a woman might offer to a child who doesn't grasp what he's saying. She cherished his ignorance. His innocence. She lived for precisely the moment where she made the full decision to take it all away. This much could be read from her face and the way she looked at him. Her body shifted side to side and her dress twirled a little. Her shoulders bunched up a bit higher and her smile turned with her as she thought of what to say.

"My dear," she started. Her voice took on a new shape. "After tonight's dinner, darling, I think you'll be convinced why we aren't after groceries."

CHAPTER 26

THE BARONESS GRABBED his shoulders in her surprisingly strong hands and looked him up and down like a whole buffet. She didn't intend to eat him, however. If she did, she would have killed him when he was helpless. No, she looked at him and wanted something rarer. She twirled away in excitement to the kitchen to see how long the food would be, turning back to look at him again with a sly smile before passing through the doorway. Will was incredulous. He just got done telling Death to her face that he wouldn't be caught dead breaking promises to his potentially dead wife. If this woman thought for a moment that he would be cheating on the memory of Rachel with her, then as the saying goes, Will thought it would be over his dead body. Or hers, for that matter.

He took the time to examine the living room as he waited. He really did not want to see who they were preparing for dinner. He had seen enough leftover giblets of people in New York. He figured he might as well get a layout of the room memorized because he certainly had no plans to eat their "meal". There was a large oval of a dinner table that had plenty of room for twenty-three guests. Twenty-four now with Will. It had a white cloth. There was a chair on one of the two commanding sides of the oval table. The chair was painted a deep red and though there were chairs all around the table, the place left opposite the red chair was deliberately empty. Will guessed it was because no one wanted to be the one to sit farthest away from the Baroness. He assumed the red chair was hers. He also assumed that he was to be invited to sit beside her as she tried to bring him into the fold.

If the proverbial dinner bell did ring, Will didn't hear it. He was surprised as he watched a parade of Southern Rangers march out from the kitchen suddenly with the look of disastrous desire. They formed a line behind the Baroness as she brightly led everyone to the table. She was like a homing beacon. Will didn't know where they were previously. But through many directions of doors and stairs there emerged the twenty-three Southern Rangers. They all converged on the table with a feeling of ceremony. Then all eyes fell on her. She twirled at the end of the table as two men grabbed the red chair and pulled it out for her. She sat down, ladylike, and scratched the chin of the man on her left as you would a good dog.

To Will, she looked and said, "Will, baby. You can sit beside me tonight as my right hand." Her face filled with a very specific joy. It was the joy of being in power, yes. But as Will examined her, he thought she really just enjoyed being treated as beautiful and the center of attention. Isn't that something everyone wants at some point? It may seem like such an adolescent vision, but it is really important to realize that the dream is still there. There are only a couple of times this vision can be realized in one's life. Prom, perhaps, or one's wedding. But it is incredibly important, no matter what. It is difficult to say exactly how this is important. It is all too easy sometimes to reduce everything to some abstraction of a biological courtship.

This, however, Will did know: It could not be healthy for someone to essentially bathe and breathe that attention for as long as the Baroness had. This is the kind of thing that spoils people. Once or twice makes good memories but a lifetime will make a monster. He approached his seat on her right side as an odd objection came through from the man on her right already. The man who did not get scratched on the chin.

"I thought that was my seat," the man protested with a disappointed smile.

"Greg," she nearly snapped at him.

She whipped her head and looked to the ground at his feet instead of at him. "Would you do me the honor of bringing in the food?" she commanded and then looked up at him. Her face was cold, but still held the promise of warmth and pride if he was to complete his assigned task. He looked at her sorrowfully and then glared something fierce at Will before doing as he was told. Will approached the seat carefully and sat in it. Everyone else sat down and postured up in unison and bowed their heads for grace as Greg came in with two arms full of platters.

The Baroness was about to begin the prayer when Will gasped. He glanced for just a moment outside one of the two dining room windows and there hung the eight black eyes of Death herself. The very same arachnid that he thought he left behind in the land of make-believe. When Will gasped, everyone looked towards the same window that Will was looking out of.

"Will, what did you see?" the Baroness asked.

"Uh…" Will stammered. He couldn't believe that they couldn't see it. It was so visible. The shape of Death's face wasn't obfuscated by the dark whatsoever, even though one would think it would be.

"I'll go check it out, miss," Greg proudly volunteered. He left through the back door once all the food was on the table.

"Alright, let's begin grace then," the Baroness called. She pontificated both hands in the air as the rest bowed their heads. "Oh, forest of our elders, we thank you for another night of deliverance from the plague. We know that you are happy with our mission, as you have seen fit to spare the life of young Will and deliver him to our care. Our numbers continue to grow and soon we will undertake a pilgrimage to Florida, for sustenance and to ensure your spread across the whole of the world. We thank you for this day and this dinner in the names of the land. Thank you."

"Thank you," the rest echoed.

"Will, is there anything you would like to add?" the Baroness invited.

Will thought for a moment and decided blending in was more important than his personal reservations about religious prayer. "Yes, and dear forest, please forgive us for those things which are necessary to complete our mission. Thank you."

"Thank you," the rest echoed.

Everyone raised their heads and began to pass around plates of various designs. "That was really nice, Will," the Baroness mentioned. "Bill, would you like to tell Will what we have here today?"

"Right," Bill immediately began. Then the heavy man elaborated the different platters with technical efficiency and professional speed. "We have here three primary trays. Each one represents a certain flavor. The one closest to you is the 'I'm sorry' flavor. The one in the middle is 'Please, no' and the one on the far end of the table is the 'I'll do anything you ask' flavor. We generally name them after the capture's dying words."

The man continued. "The 'I'm sorry' flavor in front of you is a special one. We often get the other two when the capture is begging. 'Please, no' is generally more sour and bitter than the 'I'll do anything you ask' flavor, which tends to be sweeter and tangier. I infuse the meat by squeezing the heart of the captured all over the meat as it cooks, which is how we get the distinctions in the first place. Which reminds me, I'll be right back."

The man excused himself. When he came back, and before he sat down, he was carrying a plate and said the following: "We don't really know what the 'I'm sorry' flavor will be like. The capture's exact words were 'I'm so sorry, Deloria' and I'm not quite sure what he meant. I would recommend the new flavor, seeing as I have a surprise for you." He leaned down and took some meat from the "I'm sorry" platter and put a heaping serving on the plate before passing it through to Will.

"The surprise is this, and I hope you don't mind, but I took the liberty of cooking up those canned potatoes and vegetables you had with you. This is an important day for you, and I figured those were important as they were in your bag. I took the heart of the 'I'm sorry' guy and gave you a little extra over the potatoes as well, like a premium gravy. I hope you enjoy it." He finished off with a sincere smile spreading across his round face like a proud chef.

Those fucking potatoes, Will thought. He nearly had a seizure when he saw them on the plate. The same potatoes that had gotten him into that mess at the grocery store with those cannibals and which he had tried to heat up at a camp in his dream with a disastrous outcome. They had now been placed before him, cooked well enough, but absolutely ruined with the juiced heart of a dead man who apologized in absentia to his likely wife or daughter because he wouldn't be coming home ever again. The plate in front of Will proved that Deloria would have to make it in this world on her own. God help her if she tried to follow this man's tracks.

The potatoes being ruined by the blood of a man was an emotion Will did not know he could have. That's what really started the series of events to come next. Death, the spider, was now much closer to the window. Will glanced at Death through the window and although he didn't know it, he had the same blank, cold, inevitable stare as she did.

"Dig in, Will. Let me know what you think," the Baroness said with an excited inflection. "Once we handle business in Florida, you'll be right at home here among us," she said.

Will reluctantly picked up the fork and knife. The knife was a chef's knife, rather than a simple steak knife. It was quite large and extremely sharp. Will decided to cut through the meat to feign interest in it. The time that he could continue faking it was coming down to seconds. If he didn't eat, they wouldn't like it. The knife passed through the tender meat and the Baroness's eyes were on Will like a spotlight. Will abhorred the way the meat fell apart and the fact that he was in a dining room with all those cannibals. He felt something else peculiar.

There is this feeling one has as a child which is quite

unique: When one is sat down at a table and forced to eat something one hates. The feeling of wanting to pout and cry about it, knowing that it would be futile, and ultimately feeling the pressure of your parents' passing gaze while wondering to yourself if they've noticed that you haven't eaten anything and only moved the food around the plate. Now, add in the adult problems. It wasn't something Will didn't like. It was something that was wrong to eat. It wouldn't simply be futile to complain about it. It would be a deadly mistake. And it wasn't just his parents watching, but two dozen practiced killers.

Then, one must account for the emotional context. Will was nearly dead just a couple hours ago. He had endured suffering and confusion the likes of which could never be imagined before the end of the world shattered the innocence of Earth. He had been held to wonder whether the woman that he did all of this for was still alive. Now, he was so close to his destination. He would only have a little farther to go and then enter Florida, head to the east coast and reach whatever was left of Daytona Beach. Recounting all of this is important to understanding Will's next set of actions. It's amazing how one can commit an action, but not be in control of what happens after.

Death was now so close to the windows that she threatened to come through the wall entirely. Will knew what she was telling him to do. He didn't know if he had the strength or the actual ability. Then he remembered the supermarket. He remembered that when something was amiss in the store, the people froze up. These Rangers were certainly not as basic as the store people, but if it was something dramatic enough, it might freeze all of them in place while they had a mental breakdown. He might also feel the greasy hands of these psychos clasp around him and twist his neck until his life ended with a crunch. It all hinged on this one assumption. The assumption that the store people worshiped the store and were thereby frozen when something threatened its continued operation.

The assumption that these men didn't worship the forest. They really only worshiped the Baroness.

CHAPTER 27

THEN SHE PUT her hand on Will's shoulder, pulled herself in close and said, "Will, once you finish this meal, I want you tonight. Upstairs in the very same bedroom where your... strength... warded off your death."

That was the last straw. Will turned to her with a manic expression. The anxiety twisted the muscles in his face. His smile nearly reached his ears and he said, "I'm so sorry. But thank you for your hospitality."

Will grabbed the chef's knife and thrust it into her chest so deep that the tip stuck out of her back. She took a deep gasp that was cut short by a retching hack. She looked into his eyes as fast tears streaked down her face. Forty-six utensils clanged against the plates on the table as the Rangers realized what had happened. Will yanked the knife out again and the Baroness wailed, looked at the wound, and held her mouth open silently while she tried to use her hands to catch the unstoppable flow of blood.

She looked back up at Will, now, with finality in her eyes. "What was it?" she whimpered. Her voice was not the same confident leader of a pack of wolves like before. It was a trembling, hoarse whisper.

"Wasn't I pretty enough?" she said, shaking her head apologetically. Will's satisfaction dropped along with his soul. Just then, he felt something leave his body that would never come back. For those few seconds, there was no one else, just the two of them.

"I can do my makeup again… if it's not to your liking." She paused for a few seconds that she couldn't afford to spare. "I have more…" Her lips trembled under the weight of confusion, emotion and pain.

"Will, darling?" She smiled, begging his forgiveness. Begging him to fix this. To bring it all back to normal.

She reached out one bloodied, shaky hand to Will's face. He held it off at the wrist, looking at the blood on her hand. She tried to push her hand through anyway, but it was far too weak. The color drained from her face and her head landed on the table with a thud that ended the exchange and her life. Will was stuck. Even if he wanted to move, in this moment, he couldn't. He thought about what the hell he just did. He fully expected that he would kill the leader of a predatory cannibal cult. Instead, he felt as though he had killed a young girl who was just trying to live in her own private beauty pageant where she was always the winner.

The Rangers were all frozen, no one moved a beat. They all simply sat there, agape with their minds quickly rotting away from the dissonance of this apocalyptic terror. Will had all the time he needed to escape, but the Baroness's haunting words tethered him in place. It was a few soft, whimpering sentences that would punish Will for the rest of his life. His eyes were wide open, and he was hyperventilating without knowing it. The emotional toll that that took was too high. It bankrupted him. He noticed one thing that snapped him out of the moment, however. Her seat was painted the same color as the blood down her white dress. Same shade, too. It wasn't paint on that chair that made it red. It was the blood of her victims.

When Will came back to his senses, briefly, he realized that he needed to leave before the Rangers broke from their collective crisis. A couple of them whined a bit. Some of them whispered the word "no" on repeat. Still others were shaking their heads violently and flapping their gums like dogs trying to shake themselves off after a swim. It was a stuttering room of coping mechanisms. Will sprang up and walked quickly to the closet, now fearing for his life. He grabbed three of the fragmentation grenades he saw in the closet just inside the hallway. He pulled the pins on all three and bowled them into the room. They rolled until they were roughly equidistant and all under the table and beside the feet of all the Rangers.

Will ran as hard as he could for the entrance. He didn't know how long the fuse was or how long he was holding them before he rolled them into the room. He found out the hard way. He was almost to the entrance of the house when he was forced through the outer wall. The explosion was ear splitting and hotter than hell. But as Will lay on the ground, he was surprised that he wasn't dead. He looked at the wall he went through and there were wood splinters that exploded through drywall and paneling. The house was a disaster. Will lay there for a few moments, shaking uncontrollably and holding on to his ears as though they would fall off at any moment.

It was when he tried to sit up that he felt stings all over his body from shrapnel of various sorts. The only thing breaking up the tinnitus was his labored heartbeat. He looked at himself and he wasn't bleeding very much. The back side of him was covered in wood and glass splinters, which explained the stinging. The other side of him might have had muscle sprains or bruises from the impact. Perhaps fractures too. But largely, and miraculously, he was sort of alright. So, he sat there, cross-legged, for some time. He decided that this was the last horror he could stomach. He had seen a lot since leaving that apartment building in Canada. This was too much. Horrors of a strange nature he could accept. He hated it, but he made it this far. Killing over twenty people in cold blood after they tried to bring him into their cult was a different kind of horror that he couldn't handle.

That put him on a list as one of the deadliest mass murderers in world history. It was the words, mainly, that did it. Instead of cursing him or panicking, the Baroness offered to change her makeup. She thought Will killed her because he disapproved of her physical appearance, which was everything to her. And instead of calling him a psychopath for it, she offered to change it to be more to his liking. The saddest irony Will had ever imagined just played out before his eyes. It was at his hands. There was no way to take back that action, yet she offered it anyway. She begged for the impossible, like a child who doesn't understand what's happening or why. He couldn't bear to think about this anymore. He didn't want this anymore. That was when he decided to end things.

He raised the blade of the chef's knife that he forgot to let go of so that the edge rested against his neck. He closed his eyes, breathed in one final, determined breath. Then the land exploded in front of him. The ground burst up in a cloud of dirt and rock, some of which splashed against Will's face. Fear the serpent looked Will in the eye and paralyzed him for the time being and with his smooth voice said, "Calm down. You *don't* want to do this."

Will realized that he froze that instant when he tried to move. "I made a mistake!" Will confessed, panicking.

"No, you *didn't*," Fear said.

"I made a mistake. They weren't really cannibals. It was in my head!"

"That's not right. They told you *where* that food came from. The different *flavors* of it. You saw the color of that *chair*. Just calm down," Fear reassured.

"I must have made some mistake…" Will was now crying full force. "My mistake was coming here. Wisdom was right. I was careless."

Wisdom walked through the front gate of the fence in front of the house. "I only meant that in that one decision. That doesn't mean that every consequence thereafter is your fault."

Will breathed normally for the first time in a couple minutes with tears drying on his cheeks.

Then Death, the great spider, crawled around the corner of the house and said, with a voice that he felt more in his spine than heard in his ears, "You just finished telling me that you want to live. That you would do anything necessary. That was necessary, don't be foolish."

"Was it?" Will protested. "I could've run!"

"They would have *shot* you," Fear pointed out.

"Then why the woman, hmm? Why did she say what she said?"

Wisdom answered. "People can be horrible and childish at the same time. You feel like she was somehow more genuine just because she said something near her death? Look at how she lived her life, Will!"

"I don't know anything about anyone here! I killed two dozen people who have never so much as pointed a gun at me!"

"Will, you know what you *heard*," Fear pressed.

"Yeah, what I heard was someone begging me to let her change her makeup as she was bleeding out at my hands!"

Wisdom approached Will and clasped him hard, as if to wake him up. "Her chair was painted with blood! She was supporting the man who described the flavors of human meat *by the way they begged for their life!*"

At that, Wisdom lowered the knife a little from Will's neck. Will had no response for some time.

"Why is everything awful?" he asked them all with a choke in his voice.

They looked at each other for a few seconds. Will expected Wisdom to shed some light on it, but this was an area of knowledge where he could not venture. Instead, it was up to the ancients, Fear and Death, to try to explain things.

"There is a… *barrier*," Fear started.

"It's not a physical barrier, but one of understanding," Death continued.

"Your *brain* has grown philosophically, emotionally and even physically *dependent* on your circumstances before the war," Fear stated.

"Where and when you are alive almost entirely determines what kind of things your brain can accept as possible," Death said.

"Think about it like *this*," Fear introduced. "It is perfectly *normal* and *rational* to you that galaxies exist. You know what they *are*, and it isn't that difficult to figure out how they *formed* if you don't know that already. But imagine you had told all of this to *anyone* from the past, before the *invention* of the telescope certainly, in a time when *religion* and *philosophy* were the only ways to determine what was real and possible. You can *imagine* how that would go."

"Well, yeah," Will admitted. "But we didn't invent a new technology. We ended the world. I don't see your point."

Death tried to explain. "And with the end came the end of everything you understood. Your psychology. Your perception was based on and developed within a world where these things weren't possible. The Earth had a certain level of stability. It was very rare among planets. It had a stable and replenishable ecology which most habitable planets either do not achieve or cannot maintain. With the bombs, certain things which used to be normal became invasive. Like the forest consuming Charlotte."

"The Veil," Will said, remembering what James told him.

"That isn't really possible to explain here and now," Death answered. "Let's just say that not everything which is possible is conceivable."

"Yes," Fear echoed. "It is up to you to *decide* if you learn from what you've been through or if you *deny* its possibility entirely. There is no *precedent* for this. You're human."

"You're saying the whole world has changed in some fundamental way. Then how can I rely on the idea that there's something worth living for at the end of all this? When I get to Daytona Beach in Florida?" Will tensed up again.

"Presumptuous of you to say that's where things end,"

Wisdom chimed in. "There are a select few things which do not have to change even when the world is turned upside down."

It was then that Anger, the ridiculous and oversized rodent, scuttled forward with Will's bag and dropped it in front of him. Anger also held what looked to be a photograph in his pink, hairy, ugly little hands.

"Give him the knife," Wisdom said.

"Uh, what?" Will thought he must have misheard.

"Give him the knife and he will give you the picture."

Will was reluctant. It was difficult to fully understand the toll that it takes on one's mind to be living for weeks in a nightmare that one can dream in, but never wake up from. It was hard enough on his mind that the world ended and there was no knowledge of how family members were doing or if they made it somewhere safe. It was harder still that he was in unfamiliar territory. It was even more difficult that everywhere was suddenly dangerous with chemicals and radiation. Finally, there was an indescribable horror in each of these scenarios Will kept finding himself in. Every part of him flinched at the very thought of going through a further two states and then Florida. There could be anything down there. Will considered the possibility of a situation, similar to the recently deceased Southern Rangers, that would force him to dispose of whatever humanity he had left in his worn-out body.

Regardless, he felt that he would hesitate less in continuing his journey than he would in trying to end things here and now. That was the simple fact. Will was upset and in distress and rightly so. But he wasn't actually suicidal. He didn't want to die, per se. He just wanted to be rid of the circumstances that caused him grief. He could do that by moving on. Death was always an option later. But if he died now, finding Rachel wasn't an option anymore. He handed over the knife and the creature took it in its weird little worm-fingered hand and gave him the photo with the other hand.

It was Rachel. It was the precise photo of her that Will had been dreading that he forgot. She was gorgeous, as he had always believed, proving that some truths remain immutable, unaltered by circumstance, pressure, or trauma. He realized at that point that he still had something worth living for, even if it was just to bury her if she didn't make it. He had one last promise to fulfill and one last dream to see through.

He picked himself up with reluctance. He feared the road ahead but was relieved that a few minutes of emotion didn't end his life with unfinished business. He felt like he was out of control, however. He felt as though his emotions and wants and needs had been all over the place. He didn't feel focused or sure of himself anymore. He decided that he would make it to Florida regardless and pick up the pieces of himself later. This time he traveled while planning to not stop anywhere.

CHAPTER 28

WILL HAD MADE it to the sign. That same "Welcome to Florida!" sign that he saw in his near-death experience. It was the light of morning. Will realized that in all the drama of the preceding night and the travel through South Carolina and Georgia, he had not slept in nearly two days. The rising sun of the morning punished him for it, making his eyes sting and water in just that way when one's distress is the only thing keeping them upright. He was carried mostly by adrenaline and a certain fatalistic resignation that kept him from blinking until he reminded himself to squeeze his eyelids together. He was going to find her if he had to bust down every door in Daytona Beach. He had suffered too much to continue without doing so.

He felt some feeling of objective success when he passed that sign. He knew he was closing in on the end of his journey. South Carolina wasn't much to talk about. It was a very similar situation to the southern part of North Carolina. Much of it was overgrown. The colors were deep and sickening. Occasionally he would pass by a splash of color where trees and bushes were blooming flowers he had never seen before. Sometimes he would pass a strange creature that he couldn't get a clear picture of. Nothing was going to stop him from pushing forward, however. He had no curiosity left.

He did try to fill his mind with thoughts that weren't so horrible. He analyzed his meeting with Fear, Death, Anger and Wisdom after the Rangers' house blew up. The things they said to him were strange, indeed. Fear had tried to get him to calm down. Death had convinced him of the value of his life. Anger had brought him a picture that made him happy and gave him purpose. Wisdom had been consistent, at least. What could be the reason for the changes? Will didn't know for sure, but the switch in their ideologies might have been related to the circumstances in which they met. Sure, Will was near death on both occasions. But the first time he met them, he wanted to live. The second time he met them, he thought he wanted to die. He couldn't know anything for sure, of course. But this was the only opposite he could find between their two meetings.

He asked himself if that could really be the reason they all made the opposite argument to the ones they had made before. But he considered that it could also be self-preservation on their part. If they were all in his head, then first of all he had some very dangerous psychosis. He wasn't too worried about that now, though. The real question was that if they were all in his head, then they could have simply said what they needed to say to survive. If Will died, then so would their representations in his mind. He wasn't so sure about that one. They seemed very convinced of their own immortality. Plus, he didn't want to believe he hallucinated characters in his brain that took on personalities and acted autonomously. He would rather have them be real to some degree. But that's what someone with a mental illness would say.

He shook himself, veering the car side to side as he did so. He tried to focus. Lack of sleep, lack of nutrients and *murder* were working against his efforts. He had to keep at it quickly. He hoped to get to Florida before his eventual collapse. However, that wasn't the only reason for his non-stop mindset. Throughout the rest of his journey to Florida, Will had this consistent feeling that he was being followed. He originally dismissed it as guilt. He tried his best to forget it, but he couldn't. His eyes were divided between the road and the rear-view mirror. This feeling would persist and worsen through the southern part of Georgia that he had to pass through.

Really, he had no evidence that he was being followed. Throughout the whole night he never noticed headlights in the distance or anything. He didn't even know who would have been following him. But the feeling was so persistent. Finally, before going any further, he decided that if there was someone, he would wait them out for an hour. He didn't want to risk bringing trouble to Rachel's doorstep. So, he pulled over behind some trees, turned off the car and waited. After fifteen minutes, Will was convinced that it was just guilt that was following him. Until it wasn't. A car came through after Will. The only working car Will had seen on the road since the start of his journey. It was a burgundy sedan. But who could be in it? Will got back in the car and gave chase from outside of visual distance.

He didn't see the other car again until he arrived at the outskirts of Daytona Beach. He dreaded seeing that burgundy car again. That meant he would have to deal with whoever was in it. But Will was there, finally. He never truly appreciated just how flat Florida was. He could smell the saltwater from where he stood. The ocean seemed like it could surge at any moment and wipe out the whole state, starting with Daytona Beach on the coast. Daytona Beach was empty, like all the other cities.

It was so quiet that Will could hear the waves on the other side of the city. It was full of things, but empty of people. Pieces of buildings clung onto the sides of the structures, fighting a losing battle against gravity. This place looked like it was definitely hit with a conventional nuclear weapon. Steel wasn't supposed to bubble like that. There were not supposed to be puddles of solidified metal where signs once stood. There were shadows on those walls which only remained standing further away from the city center. In the center, the city was a flattened husk.

For some reason, this gave Will a bit of relief. At least it was *just* a nuclear strike and nothing more. He couldn't believe his experiences. It was odd to feel relief upon seeing the typical aftermath of nuclear destruction, compared to the fresh hell he had witnessed elsewhere. It was especially strange to feel this way about a city he knew his wife was in. The fact that it was just a normal nuclear weapon gave her a chance at survival that wasn't possible in the other states.

He didn't think he could handle it if he came down here and there was another supermarket issue. What if she was one of those shoppers at the store? What if she had been forced to eat people as well? Most groceries would have burned under the intense heat of the conventional nuclear detonation. He also knew she didn't stock any emergency food as she had just arrived at the rental when she called him for the last time...

Stop it! he yelled at himself. He had one job and he needed to stick to it. *Find her.*

It occurred to Will that he didn't know the address of where Rachel would have gone to meet her client. He didn't know the address of the house her company rented for her stay in this city. An address wouldn't do him much good anyway, given that every human sign and symbol was erased in a several-hundred-meter radius of ground zero. There were simply no legible street signs or house numbers. As a matter of fact, there were hardly any distinguishing traits with any of the buildings, save for whatever size Will could assume they used to be. The paint would have burned off and it left only gray and black on every building. There were no identifiers for Will to guide himself by.

He knew that, with a conventional nuclear weapon, Rachel's chances of survival depended entirely on proximity. If she was near the outskirts of the city, she was nearly guaranteed to survive the initial blast. Will didn't think the buildings looked that bad on the way in. So, he thought it was a lower yield bomb. Plus, Daytona Beach wasn't exactly a high-priority target. The radioactive fallout would have been worrisome for a few days. But with adequate shelter, that wouldn't have been an immediate problem for her survival even if it contaminated the water table a little. It would be a problem five years from now, but it wouldn't affect her survival just two weeks after the event.

That was the strange thing, he thought. The world only ended about two weeks ago. The probability of survival on the outskirts of the city was very high for this short a time period. Many would be sick, but many more would be alive. Yet, on his way in, he saw no one. Not a single soul. Furthermore, he didn't see any dust on the ground like he did in Canada. The fallout would have accumulated like ash had this been the same type of conventional weapon. The ground, however, was clear and clean of everything except for the debris around nearby structures.

He walked around for some time trying to think of what could have caused this combination. That was when he realized there were very few cars near the edge of the city and—

"WILL!!" A scream pierced the air from his right, and he turned.

There Rachel was. Thinking about her along this journey was one thing. It was another revelation to see her picture that Anger gave him. But seeing her in person was... something else entirely. It was the difference between setting a goal and achieving it, yes. But more broadly, and Will didn't like to exaggerate anything, it was the difference between suffering and salvation. Seeing her running towards him right now was the very sign of the end of hardship. The idea was such a gooey romantic trope.

If she embraced him in her unique way, kissing him on the cheek with that special touch he longed for, then all past sins and the pain of his journey would fade, overshadowed by the realization that it had all been worth it. It was a nice thing to hope for. But what Will didn't recognize yet was that salvation couldn't come from her. It had to come from him.

She embraced him, nearly knocking over his beleaguered frame. It was the *warmth* that he didn't expect. When he was in New York earlier, he had felt the *heat* of that Inferno. He had felt the sun beating down on him through the windshield of the car on his journey. He had felt the heat of those grenades going off in the Ranger base. But all of that was just heat. Heat was so... cause and effect. It was too logical. It was simply the result of energetic processes giving off energy into the medium around it. But warmth comprises something more.

Even though heat can make one feel warm, it cannot explain warmth. Will and Rachel were in Florida, and it was hot and humid near the coast. He shouldn't be able to feel such a complete difference in warmth when she embraced him. But such warmth was undeniably human. Warmth was a mixture of heat, assurance, security and promise.

They kissed and then he had to ask, "How did you find me? Were you just... in the area?"

That was an odd question for Will to ask his wife who he hadn't seen for two weeks after the end of the world. Surely someone that he had been praying to find alive all this time, the whole reason for his journey in the first place, should be met with more warmth and less suspicion. But Will was suspicious anyway. He just then realized that this could all be some kind of trick. Already, a giant floating fireball had toyed with his memories. They were so realistic that they almost lulled him into a false sense of belonging. He never knew that he could be forced to hallucinate to the degree of being able to physically touch his memories. But he could be. New York proved that. Not to mention his near-death experience with the Rangers and the hallucinations back there. How could he be sure that he had finally made it?

Will had defeated the Inferno only by cleverly questioning its illusions and by remaining skeptical of the familiar images it presented. However painful it might've been to be distrustful of them. He had experienced dreams so convincing he could not tell the difference between them and reality. He had touched the skeleton of a little girl and seemed to be transported back in a time and place before the bombs. He had a near-death experience and had seen these experiences come to life in living hallucinations after he blew up the Ranger compound. Will felt like he was merely a visitor on planet Earth. He felt strange and surreal, like a tourist, even though he never left Earth once in his life.

Will had a reality problem. And for all he knew, reality had a Will problem. So, he accepted her, for now because it was irresistible. But also, because this world had broken his emotional resilience so thoroughly that he almost didn't care anymore if he *was* being fooled. However, he still held on to that resentment of whatever trickster might be parroting the memories of those Will loved. He still held that guard up, expecting to be attacked again either in mind or body. Rachel picked up on this.

"What kind of question is that?" she giggled. "You know, if anything I should be skeptical of you." Her face changed when she said that. Her eyes fluttered as though she was flinching. Or allergic. Or even emotional. It was an odd twitching that took over her composure.

"No. It can't be…" she said, almost under her breath. Her tone was desperate.

She stepped back a few paces. Her face changed yet again to a harder one and her whole posture was more defensive than before. "You don't look very much like Will. You've done a terrible job of recreating him. He's too tall, skinny and slightly uglier than I had remembered." Then she pulled a pistol out from the small of her back and leveled it at his stomach, cool as a cucumber. Like she had been forced to do this before.

Will's eyes widened in shock. He realized now that it was either the case that she was very much real, or that the thing that was showing him her image was a lot more clever than the Inferno of New York. If there was another force, something that was manipulating Will's memories again, it would have to know that Will went through physical changes. It would also have to know that Rachel would react differently to them. Either Rachel was real, or this trickster had mastered the ancient human art of gaslighting. And the "ugly" remark stung, but Will realized he had better play along and try to prove himself or the bullet would sting more.

"I..." he began.

Ironically, he hit the same snag that he hit when the Baroness had asked him about up north. It was simply impossible to tell the truth. It sank in immediately that there was no place to even begin to give a realistic story. He really couldn't account for himself over the last two weeks. Giant metal pipes arising from the ruins of Buffalo and propelling themselves like a giant tumbleweed? A man named James caused Will to go to the one place on the east coast that he wanted to avoid at all costs. A man who turned out to be an alien using Will as evidence in some galactic case against humanity, and then he disappeared without a trace. Seeing ghosts of black soot? The cannibals pretending their way into managing a grocery store? Forget it. She'd shoot him if was too truthful. She would shoot him if she caught him lying as well.

"Well, what have you got? Hmm?" she prompted him.

"It wasn't enough that you had to bring my parents into this. You had to trick me with the image of my husband, too? The only thing that remains is that you haven't faded away now that I've figured you out. So, I assume you have something for me."

"Wait, what?" Will looked at the ground for a moment in disbelief. She was rattling off accusations. But in them there was a truth that Will recognized. Something similar to his situation when the Inferno of New York tried to trick him with family members. "You had a giant fireball here too?" he asked.

Rachel's jaw dropped when he said that. "Oh, now you've just given yourself away. Will could never possibly know about the fireball. It was only in *my* dreams. It never existed. God damn it… I can't believe I have to do this." A tear rushed down her cheek over the thought of harming him. Will was absolutely convinced she was real, now. But he had run out of time for that. She leveled the gun at his head.

"Wait! Wait!" he yelled; eyes closed. "Those dreams stopped several days ago, right?"

"If you're in my head then, yes, you would know that" she said, unconvinced.

"It must have had a broader range than I thought. It was real. It was in New York. I'm the one who killed it."

Rachel roared with an unhealthy laughter at that claim. "Oh, really, humor me then, how?"

Will explained the plan, how he met Jeremiah and the events that took place on the streets and in the subways.

"It's a cool story, but none of it is convincing me that you're real," she said with a tired and impatient twinge in her voice. "It doesn't even sound like Will would do that."

"We've both seen that there's something deeply wrong with this world," Will said. "I had to do something. It posed a threat to you if it expanded any more. What else have you seen here?" He was grasping for straws to get the pressure off himself.

"I'm the one asking the questions," she said bluntly.

Will was more exhausted than he was scared now. The adrenaline finally wore off completely. He hadn't had good sleep in a long time. He sat down on the pavement awaiting his judgment. "Then ask me something that I would only know if I were real. Something you don't know the answer to, but you are sure of what the answer isn't. That's how I did it when I was confronted with my mother in New York. I asked her about an oil company. The Inferno gave me a fake name for one. If I'm just a projection, I'll try to make up an answer that likely doesn't exist in reality." He started swaying involuntarily. His muscles were starting to shut down.

Rachel pondered about this for a long time, or at least it felt that way. She paced back and forth, never really looking at him. Finally, she turned around and said, "You know, it's funny that you said that because that's exactly how I dealt with my parents—" She stopped short when she turned to him and saw that he was unconscious.

CHAPTER 29

RACHEL WOKE HIM up and, while he was delirious, she walked him back to her place. She reasoned that if he was real enough to pass out from exhaustion, then she should give him a chance. It had been a few days since the Inferno's last attempt to influence her. It was unlikely that it did still exist. She took him to a very cozy little basement of a house that had seen better days before the war. Inside were various electronic devices with exposed wiring that made them look makeshift. Will marveled at them for a moment when he regained consciousness when he finally asked about it.

"What is all this stuff?" he asked as she put him in a chair facing a screen.

"How much do you know about the effects of the Inferno?" she countered, beginning the interrogation.

"Well, I know it made me stronger, faster and taller. A little uglier too, apparently," Will said, still sleepy.

"Interesting…" She paused, deep in thought. "You asked before how I found you. Wanna know?"

"That would be a good start," Will said.

"Thanks to a nearby factory that no one was using anymore, I used industrial photoreceptors and a few miles of wiring connected to car batteries that the EMP didn't fry. An interruption between two sensors would be reported here."

Will paused in place, trying to process what he just heard. "Holy shit, I didn't know you were that crafty," he finally said.

"I wasn't. I never was. I never messed with electronics before in my life."

Will looked confused even though the conclusion was obvious. "So, you think that it changed you like it changed me? Affected your brain rather than your body? Made you smarter…"

"At first, I thought I was just going insane. The whole reason for the sensors was to detect real people from fake people. If they were merely figments of my imagination, they wouldn't register on these sensors."

"Wow, that's cool." Will had woken up fully now from his powernap, though he still desperately needed real sleep. He was actually very proud of her ingenuity. He smiled at her, and she smiled back, proud of herself too. She quickly lost the smile as she was still distrustful of the general circumstance.

"Well, don't think so yet. Because it did work for a little while. Then I started to hear it go off today," she said.

"Wait, there were more times it went off?" Will asked, wondering about the person driving the burgundy car.

"There was one time, before you and at the same sensor that you crossed. But I couldn't find anyone there, so I just assumed that the hallucinations would begin again. I was still in the area looking when I found you. I was so sure it was you who set it off. Then we come back here, and I see another register in the computer. When I thought you were a figment of my imagination, I thought this sensor reading was a more profound trick than any I had dealt with before. And when I thought that the Inferno had found your memory in me, despite my best efforts to hide it, I wanted to defy it by killing you... but I couldn't."

"Well, I'm glad you didn't," Will said, earnestly. "I thought you might be some kind of trick on the eyes as well. It's weird how the world changed our thinking so quickly. I mean two weeks..." He approached the table where the sensor readouts would be monitored and displayed on an old screen. He took his kukri and laid it on the table and took it out of its sheath. He thought the thing would maybe like to breathe, which was a stupid thought. He wasn't thinking clearly. Exhaustion was tearing him apart. He leaned over the table of electronics. "Where did you get all this stuff anyway?"

There was a silence, and a feeling. It was a difficult feeling to describe. Something was different in that room. Will closed his eyes to capture it. It was a very mild feeling that washed over him. It was as if the temperature of the room increased suddenly. It was like the air of the room moved more than you would expect from just himself and Rachel standing still. It couldn't be a draft. This was the basement and the air he felt was warmer than it should be. It made the hair stand up on the back of his neck. It was as if someone else had entered from the stairs and swiftly moved in. But that would be crazy.

Then Will heard it. The sound. The collected sound of

his own heartbeat, one person breathing very shakily and another person trying to breathe very quietly. Will was holding his breath, so there had to be another person in the room besides himself and Rachel. But that would be crazy. That would be crazy unless… that false sensor reading earlier in the day was actually true. That the reading did pick up a real person who hid when Rachel went looking because they didn't want to be found. Someone who was waiting for the right time. Waiting for him.

Will looked at the old computer screen for help in finding who was behind him. If there wasn't something wrong, Rachel would have answered his question by now. The screen was on, so reflections were scarce. But he could make out enough detail to know that he was on Rachel's right side. He could see the arms of the man over her, with what looked like a gun pointed at her head. Whoever this was had wanted him to turn around first. If he merely wanted them both dead, he would have done it already as he had them completely surprised. Yet he waited. Will had no idea who would want this. Who would be willing to take her hostage and wait for him to—

"Turn around," the man's voice commanded. Rachel whimpered from behind the hand that was covering her mouth.

Will recognized the voice instantly. It was Greg from the Ranger compound. He was dismissed by the Baroness and then went outside. He must have been out there when the grenades went off and was knocked unconscious instead of killed like the others. He would have overheard Will talking about Daytona Beach. He would have had the skills to track a person and follow them, just as the Rangers knew how to victimize someone. Will had a pretty good guess that

Greg was about to enact vengeance for the destruction of the Ranger base and the killing of the Baroness and needed Will to turn around to watch it happen for his satisfaction. That wasn't going to happen.

"Come on, now, don't be shy," Greg said. Each word dripped and he hung off of them. "You took what I loved from me. Now I'm gonna do it to you. You had to know this would happen, you fucking freak."

Will felt his hands shaking with incompetence, anger and weakness. His body needed rest and was now demanding it. Will begged in his mind to whoever would listen. He begged that he still retained the speed and strength that he had been given in New York. He prayed that this terrible journey hadn't sapped him of the reflexes to do what had to happen next. He pleaded that the exhaustion, the sleep that his body desperately needed, could hold off a few more minutes. Then his hands stabilized. One last flush of anger and adrenaline that his body shouldn't have been able to produce. He didn't let it go to waste.

In one fluid motion, he grabbed the machete in his fingers, twirled around and threw that two and a half pounds of steel at Greg's head in less than a second. It flashed through the air and missed his head, but it did hit the pistol and the hand that was holding it. The machete ended up about two inches deep in the opposing wall with shattered bits of plastic and metal exploding every which way. Will lunged at Greg and threw him up against the wall. Will threw a knee into his guts and a fist across his chin. Then he levered the machete out of the wall and dragged Greg outside to finish him off. Will lorded over the squirming body of this unconscious savage.

Will wanted to kill him. He had killed people for so much less than what Greg just did in this journey of his. This was the classic problem of murder, whether justified or not. Once one does it, it becomes a viable option. It loses its taboo. It becomes another way to solve problems. It is brought to the same table as any cost to benefit measure. It becomes a resource. Will couldn't feel his way back from this. He wanted to, but he hated this man. He hated the presumption by this man that their two situations were equal. That he could simply kill Rachel in front of him for recompense.

The gall of it was staggering. There really was no excuse for it in Will's mind. Perhaps if Greg had loved something better than a group of predatory cannibals with a whore running the show, then maybe they wouldn't have died in a fiery explosion. Perhaps *their* sins wouldn't come back to hurt *them*. These thoughts consumed Will as he stood over Greg. They made so much sense from his perspective. Will's knuckles turned white, grasping the handle of the blade. But he felt a little strange. He realized that his perspective wasn't the only one present.

He turned around and saw Rachel leaning in the doorway. She was watching him with a panicked stare, blissfully unaware of that house of horrors that both he and Greg shared as a memory. He would have to explain it to her at some point, but how? How on Earth could he explain the very particular and specific feeling he got from the room that caused him to kill over twenty people on purpose? How does one explain the feeling? Would he even remember the exact feeling? Or would Rachel think he was a mass murderer with psychotic impulses who was trying to justify it after the fact? Would she still love him if she knew everything he did?

These were the questions that burned the most. Will had never considered this before because he honestly believed at some point in his journey that she would be dead. Or that James was wrong about her survival. He wouldn't have to explain it all. He wouldn't have to be accountable for it with hers being the only opinion in the world he valued. He wouldn't have to explain how, despite being a killer of opportunity, he still allowed Greg to go unchecked. That if it weren't for Greg's ego, both Rachel and he would be dead because of his inability to perform a headcount and realize there was a man missing at that dinner table.

He returned his attention to Greg. He was now unsure of what to do. It was one thing to admit to being a killer and quite another to actually do the deed in front of his wife. He had to keep her safe, yes, but he also couldn't risk losing her love. He would love to ask her opinion, but then, if she approved, it would be blood on her hands too. He wanted to keep that harshness of the world as far away from her mind as possible.

Then the ground gave way across the neighborhood street and Fear the serpent burst through the crust of the Earth and coiled himself a front row seat close to Greg. The neighbor's house to the left of Will suddenly burst into splinters and planks. The debris, panel siding and roof reorganized into the enormous arachnid form of Death. Anger plodded along from the street and Wisdom sat in a bright green lawn chair that Will was sure didn't exist earlier.

He looked back to Rachel, stunned that these beings would make their entrance in plain view of her. But when he turned around, she seemed unaffected. She couldn't see them. She was only looking at him. Wondering what he was going to do. The four figures who made their entrance decided to chime in, with each manifestation speaking to what they represented.

"Kill him. Death must come for all, but for those who seek out revenge, it must come early," Death said. Her voice was serious, terrible and scratchy but Will thought she held a reasonable point.

"Get rid of him," Fear agreed. "If this man has tracked you this far, this effectively, then he will be a threat to your future. You'll feel the need to look over your shoulder. You'll wake up in the middle of the night thinking you heard a sound. You'll feel watched," Fear said. Will couldn't agree more.

Anger, the ugly oversized rodent, merely approached and held up a cardboard sign autographed by the Baroness that read, "I want you, tonight." Somehow this felt like the most effective point. Remembering the absolute psychosis of her and that place was infuriating, and Greg was the very poster boy for everything that was wrong and twisted with it.

Then Will turned to Wisdom, expecting him to make an argument. Wisdom merely stared back at Will and raised his eyebrows, expecting that Will already knew the argument. Will had two choices. He could either kill this man and finally be rid of the threat that he posed or let him live so that his wife didn't have to see him kill. But there was something else, too. There was, since the beginning, this hopeful wish that this was all a bad dream and that he could wake up from it all at any time. The hope that in the morning he would find them both in bed in their apartment in Canada. That none of this murder had to stick to him permanently.

He could tell her all about the dream. About the time

that she pointed a gun at him in post-apocalyptic Florida and they would laugh awkwardly before she sat him down on the edge of their bed. She would plead with him to go and see the psychiatrist again and to tell the doctor it was urgent. She would say that she cared for him and didn't like to see him distressed. He knew how distressing and real those dreams could feel. He would agree to it. What he wouldn't give for that damn doctor and her clinical gaze to prove that it was all in his head.

"Will," Rachel began. He looked back at her and suddenly had an idea of how he could relegate this nightmare to the past, at least for now. She continued, "He's moving again!"

Greg was starting to wake up, and Will was running out of time for deliberation. He knew what had to be done. To put this nightmare of a world behind him, he had to not be a killer in front of his wife. He couldn't tarnish this as well. If she weren't here, maybe this would be different. He would probably kill Greg, then. Perhaps she wouldn't blame Will if he did kill him. In some ways, that would be the hardest thing out of all of it. That the harshness of the world got to her as well. She would understand that he had to do it and that he was capable of this act. This act, which just two weeks ago was a heinous offense both morally and legally. This act, which had now become so necessary and common for his survival, and maybe for hers too.

But he could not rewrite nearly thirty years of their lives on Earth when they thought murder was unthinkable. You could not replace the morals that were upright and pure and necessary for a good life back then with two weeks of chaos. She still expected Will to be a good man. Maybe now that meant Will had to kill Greg to protect himself and Rachel and ensure that Greg could not follow them. But that image in his mind—waking up to something normal and continuing his life with her, while potentially keeping some awful secrets—was too tempting. She loved him for who he was. The fear of this bloody and violent murder changing that love was too much. Would she still want to sleep in the same bed as him after this? Or would she move over to create a safe distance between them? Would she feel safe around him? Or would she feel like she had to watch out for his anger and murderous impulses? The machete was too heavy, and he was too tired to butcher this man. For the first time since the world ended and changed, he had the opportunity for love, sleep and a future.

He turned the blade around in his hand and struck Greg on the temple with the back of the machete. The weight of the blade knocked him out cold and apparently vanished the four members of the audience that were watching just moments ago. Will wouldn't kill him. He should, maybe. But killing a man wasn't like pushing a button. The question wasn't as abstract as whether he should or shouldn't. It was a visceral question, too.

He didn't want her to experience the revelatory shock of watching the flesh split open under the pressure of the blood forcing its way out. He didn't want her to watch him bleed all over the ground. He knew all too well what that felt like from his experience with the Baroness. Whether she was evil or not, both of them were still human. He could only stomach so much. It was a disgusting thing to do and to deal with. However, it was all quiet now. It seemed like all of Florida belonged to Will and Rachel.

"I appreciate that," Rachel said.

"What?" Will asked, playing dumb.

"Not killing him. You could have, I wouldn't have blamed you. Whatever past you two have clearly involved violence at some point. But I'm glad this world hasn't made you too desperate to kill without thinking it through. I'm glad you're still in control of yourself." She smiled with her own pride now placed in him. For once in this whole journey, he felt like he made the right decision.

Those words washed over Will like baptism. Not because it washed away the sins. No, those traumas were going to haunt him for a long time. But this seemed to be the first step in that long journey to healing. No, it didn't wash it away. But it did put things in perspective. Along this terrible journey, the world threatened to overshadow his memory of her. That was why he dreaded the fact that he didn't have a picture of her with him. It wass why he hated the Inferno so much for manipulating her image to suit its purposes. He feared losing clear sight of the reason he was doing all this to begin with.

He feared that if he lost the memory of his better half, he would turn as rotten, rusted, and burned out as the cars abandoned on the road. Or like anything else in this world, really. If he were to lose his ideas of her then he would have succumbed to the apocalypse, whether dead or alive. His memories of the way things used to be were of such importance that they carried him through this world. Now, at the end, he saw how things could still be that way, in time.

"We have to get back to Canada," Will said. "It's the only place I've seen that's... well... habitable. Everywhere else is cursed by something."

"Yes," Rachel agreed. "Soon enough it'll be hurricane season for Florida, and I really don't fancy radioactive salt-water hurricanes washing ashore god-knows-what kind of eldritch horror from the depths." She smiled at him. "I'll get my things and then we can take your car."

Will followed her and asked, "Wait, you never told me how you survived down here. After the loaded greeting you gave me, which you still haven't apologized for, and all these electronics, you know I've gotta ask. What the hell happened to you in Florida?"

She turned to him and gave him the first trusting smile he had seen in two weeks. "Let's focus on getting outta here, babe. Because all of that? That's a story for another day."

Note from the Author

This was my first work of fiction ever, not merely my first book. I sincerely hope you enjoyed reading it as much as I enjoyed writing it. It's an insane story, and I will not pretend that it should be for everyone. It's the insanity of it that made it such a force in my imagination. Madness played a key role in the story thematically, as you could tell. I wanted the world to truly affect the character. I wanted to see what a combination of radiation, malnutrition and sleep deprivation could do to a woefully unprepared person at the end of the world. I wanted to test if human willpower could make it beyond the barrier of madness and if we could still accomplish things beyond the Veil of our understanding. Thank you for joining me in that journey.

My girlfriend was the perfect balance between being excited about the book and critical of things when they didn't make sense. I wouldn't have called myself a creative person before I met her. I was too convinced that being logical and being creative were opposites. That I could only be one or the other. Therefore, I failed at being either. She somehow teased out this creative drive and the confidence by which to do it. I am in her debt for more than just that. Every year that I'm with her, I discover that I am capable of more than I thought.

When I first told my mother that I wanted to be a writer because I had all of these crazy stories in my head that wouldn't go away, I thought she would be reluctant at least. I underestimated her. She was gleeful that I had chosen something that she thought was so fitting. She used words like, "With that mind of yours..." The way that an awesome mother will talk you up like you're the greatest thing on the planet. Thanks for the support, mom.

I would like to take the opportunity to let you in on a little secret. This is not the only book idea I have. A "book idea" to me is fleshed out a bit with a few pages of structural planning on a Word document. This story was one of them. I have thirty-five more.

My next one is a proper spacefaring Sci-Fi that takes place almost fifteen hundred years into the future and during a time when humanity has forgotten their technology, history and galaxy. As the result of a war, dangerous viruses plague all the existing sensors, A.I., and measurement devices. It forces humanity to get creative and reignite the age of exploration in deep space where a sensor anomaly can kill a ship, and explorers don't last long before becoming either dead or mad. The A.I. of all our advanced industry have gone rogue and entire manufacturing planets become conscious after decades of isolation. The human race doesn't even understand who the enemy was in this supposed war, merely that they appear to be gone now. I play on themes like 14th century exploration, the archaeology of the deep past, and the assumptions we make on history. It's a mind-warper and I think you'll enjoy it very much.

Finally, I know that I ended Earth's Veil with the idea that there would in fact be a "story for another day," as Rachel put it. I'm unsure when I'll write that. I want to work on other projects for the time being. I would like some distance from the original story before I embark on a sequel because this one will be from Rachel's perspective. You see, Rachel is a special character in her own right. She is not merely some damsel in distress that must be saved by her even more distressed hero. It may have appeared that way at first because this was a limited narration from Will's perspective.

In reality, multiple things happened to Rachel in Florida. The book will answer many questions, such as...

Why was there no one in Daytona Beach when Will finally arrived?

What is Rachel's relationship to the Inferno of New York?

What happened to the wildlife in Florida?

Why did Rachel fear the potential hurricane season and what it would dredge up from the depths?

A few more questions I'm sure will be answered about the world and its changes. But that is enough of your time taken. I would like to end here with a promise. Bold, I know. My promise to you is to give you the craziest stories I can possibly think of. From the bottom of my heart, I hope you enjoy.

Sincerely,
J.F. Bloomfield

Made in the USA
Middletown, DE
14 September 2024

60945998R00188